Ruff Justice

**Center Point
Large Print**

Also by Laurien Berenson and available from
Center Point Large Print:

Live and Let Growl
Murder at the Puppy Fest

**This Large Print Book carries the
Seal of Approval of N.A.V.H.**

Ruff Justice

LAURIEN
BERENSON

CENTER POINT LARGE PRINT
THORNDIKE, MAINE

This Center Point Large Print edition
is published in the year 2018 by arrangement with
Kensington Publishing Corp.

The text of this Large Print edition is unabridged.
In other aspects, this book may vary
from the original edition.
Printed in the United States of America
on permanent paper.
Set in 16-point Times New Roman type.

ISBN: 978-1-68324-927-6

Library of Congress Cataloging-in-Publication Data

Names: Berenson, Laurien, author.
Title: Ruff justice / Laurien Berenson.
Description: Large print edition. | Thorndike, Maine :
    Center Point Large Print, 2018.
Identifiers: LCCN 2018025050 | ISBN 9781683249276
    (hardcover : alk. paper)
Subjects: LCSH: Travis, Melanie (Fictitious character)--Fiction. |
    Women detectives--Fiction. | Women dog owners—Fiction. |
    Murder—Investigation—Fiction. | Large type books. |
    GSAFD: Mystery fiction.
Classification: LCC PS3552.E6963 R84 2018 | DDC 813/.54—dc23
LC record available at https://lccn.loc.gov/2018025050

For Chase and Charla,
Wishing you all good things to come

Chapter 1

It is a truth universally acknowledged that a Standard Poodle in possession of eleven points toward a championship must be in want of a dog show.

Okay, Jane Austen didn't use those exact words. But if she had been a member of my family she might well have because dog shows are a way of life for us. I met my husband, Sam, at a dog show, and our blended canine crew currently includes five black Standard Poodles and a small, spotted mutt named Bud.

All our Poodles are retired show champions, except for one: Kirkwood's Keep Away, more casually known as Augie. He belongs to my thirteen-year-old son, Davey. A novice dog handler with plenty of other interests to keep him busy, Davey had been working on finishing Augie's championship for nearly two years.

Now we were all in agreement that it was time to finally buckle down and get the job done. Which had brought us to yet another dog show. Like all exhibitors, we were eternal optimists.

Connecticut weather in early April was notoriously fickle. Though the show scene had moved back outdoors for the spring season, the day was chilly enough for everyone to be bundled into warm jackets. Still, after a winter spent at often cramped indoor venues, we were all delighted to be outside in a spacious park. The air might have been unseasonably brisk but at least it wasn't raining. Or snowing.

Twelve large rings had been set up in the center of the big field. They were positioned in two rows of six, with a wide alleyway between them, covered by a green-and-white striped tent. At each end of the competition area was another, smaller tent where exhibitors set up their grooming equipment and completed their preshow ring preparations.

By the time we arrived midmorning, most of the available space under the grooming tent nearest the Poodle ring had already been claimed by the professional handlers who'd been at the show site since dawn. Sam pulled the SUV into the unloading area beside the tent. I got out and had a look around, hoping to find a small spot to wedge our gear in.

The scene beneath the tent was hectic. I saw dozens of wooden crates stacked on top of each other, and rows of rubber-matted grooming tables squashed into narrow aisles. I heard the loud, persistent whine of free-standing blow dryers. Some exhibitors were working on their dogs while others were dashing back and forth to the rings.

To the uninitiated, it might have looked like pandemonium. To me, it looked like home.

Suddenly a familiar head popped up. A hand lifted and waved in the air. "Melanie!" Aunt Peg called. "Over here."

Even in the midst of all that chaos, Margaret Turnbull was hard to overlook. She stood six feet tall and had a direct gaze that missed nothing. Her posture was impeccable, and her demeanor was that of a woman who knew exactly what she wanted and almost always got it.

Over the decades, Aunt Peg's successes in the dog show world had earned her a reputation for excellence and the lasting respect of her peers. Her Cedar Crest Kennel had not only produced a number of the country's best Standard Poodles, it had also provided foundation stock for those discerning breeders who'd followed in her footsteps.

Now nearing seventy, Aunt Peg had scaled back her involvement in breeding and exhibiting to concentrate on her busy career as a multi-group judge. She'd had a litter of Standard Poodle puppies the previous fall—her first in several years. I knew she'd retained the best bitch puppy for herself, but now I was surprised to see Aunt Peg standing in the middle of her own setup. The Poodle, Cedar Crest Coral, was sitting on a grooming table beside her.

It looked as though Aunt Peg would be showing today too. Somehow she'd neglected to mention that.

Aunt Peg had a word with the puppy, then left her sitting on her monogrammed towel. She slipped through the setups between us and came to help unload the SUV.

The four of us worked together with a practiced ease born of repetition. By the time Aunt Peg and I reached the vehicle, Sam already had the hatch open. He'd pulled out the dolly and he and Davey were loading Augie's crate onto it.

In my sometimes crazy world, Sam was my rock. We'd known each other for nearly a decade and been married for half that time. I loved that he was smart and perceptive. I also loved that Sam had sun-bleached blond hair, a killer smile, and a body buff enough to draw second looks from girls half our age.

As I reached around him to grab the wooden tack box, I trailed my fingers across Sam's back. He shifted slightly in my direction and winked.

Davey was threading a noose carefully through Augie's thick neck hair before hopping the big Poodle out of the car. He caught the interaction between his stepfather and me and shook his head. Thirteen was a tough age for kids and parents both.

"What about me?" asked a plaintive voice. "What should I carry?"

Our younger son, Kevin, had turned four in March. He was enrolled in preschool now. As a consequence, he was feeling very grown up.

I looked around for something to hand him and settled upon a small, soft-sided cooler.

"You can take this," I said.

Kev thrust out his lower lip. "I want something big."

Aunt Peg leaned down and examined my choice. "Don't lose that, it's very important. The cooler has Augie's bait in it. Without it, Davey will be in trouble when he goes in the ring."

The thought of his brother in trouble immediately brightened my younger son's face. Kevin had his father's sandy hair and slate-blue eyes. When he smiled it was like looking at a version of Sam in miniature.

"I have Augie's bait," he echoed happily. "Cool."

We moved Aunt Peg's equipment to one side and squeezed our own stuff in next to it. Sam wedged the crate up against a tent pole. Then he and Kev went to move the SUV to the parking lot. I put the tack box within easy reach on top of the crate and stashed the cooler and Kevin's toy bag behind it.

Davey set up the grooming table. When it was ready, he lifted Augie up into place. I saw him cast a glance in Coral's direction and frown. Aunt Peg's pretty puppy had already been brushed out. With her dense black coat and soft, dark eyes, she looked like a perfect, plush doll. When Davey looked her way Coral stood up and wagged her tail.

"What's the matter?" I asked him.

"Aunt Peg is showing."

I understood his consternation. It had been a long time since I'd seen Aunt Peg in a ring with a Poodle on the end of her leash. "Now we'll have two chances to win," I said brightly.

"Now I'll have to beat her too," Davey grumbled.

"You have a dog and I have a bitch," Aunt Peg reminded him. "We won't meet in the classes. And besides, Coral is only six months old. We're just here today for the experience."

I leaned down and whispered to Davey, "You should be happy Aunt Peg has her own entry to concentrate on. That'll give her less time to worry about what you and Augie are doing."

"I heard that," Aunt Peg snapped. The woman has ears like a fox.

Ignoring her, I opened the tack box and took out the tools Davey would need to start preparing Augie for the ring. A fully mature Standard Poodle dog, Augie was wearing the continental clip, one of three trims approved for AKC breed competition. His face and throat were clipped to the skin, and he had a dense coat of long, shaped hair covering the front half of his body. His hindquarter and legs were mostly shaved as well, leaving only rounded rosettes on each of his hips, bracelets on his lower legs, and a large pompon on the end of his tail.

Beginning the grooming session required a pin brush, a slicker brush, a greyhound comb, and a water bottle for misting the coat. I lined up the equipment along the edge of the tabletop.

Davey looped his arms around Augie's legs and gently lowered the Poodle into a prone position. Augie knew what to expect. He relaxed and lay quietly on his left side. Hands moving quickly through the hair, Davey started line brushing the Poodle's mane coat.

"I see the gang's all here," said Terry Denunzio. Sweeping past me with a Japanese Chin tucked beneath each arm, he aimed an air kiss in my direction. *"Finally,"* he added with a smirk.

That last part was a dig at Aunt Peg, who always beat us to shows, then complained vociferously that we were late, even when we had hours to spare. Assistant to top professional handler Crawford Langley, Terry was one of my best buddies. Nearing thirty, he was ten years younger than me and impossibly cute. He was also flamboyantly gay. Terry's antics were the perfect foil for Crawford's calm, dignified manner. The two of them made a great couple.

Terry often entertained himself by taking potshots at people. And since it wasn't unusual for me to be the target of his biting wit, now I couldn't resist having some fun at his expense. Terry's hair color seemed to change with his moods. Or maybe the time of day. But this tint was something I hadn't seen before.

"Red?" I said incredulously. "You've got to be kidding."

"What?" He stashed the two toy dogs in a pair of crates and straightened and twirled for effect. "You don't love it?"

"I don't even like it." I wrinkled my nose. "You look like Howdy Doody."

"That's what I told him." Crawford entered the neighboring setup from the other side. He was carrying another Chin and a fistful of ribbons.

"And I said"—Terry paused and looked around to make sure we were all listening—"who the heck is Howdy Doody?"

Back at her own grooming table, Aunt Peg barked out a laugh. "Good for you, Terry. It's wise to be impervious to insult."

"Who are we insulting now?" Bertie Kennedy came flying into the tent towing a Bearded Collie. Another professional handler, Bertie was married to my younger brother, Frank. The couple had two children: six-year-old Maggie and a son named Josh, who'd been born the previous September.

Crawford had been showing dogs successfully for decades. Bertie's experience comprised only a fraction of that time. But she was talented and worked hard. The fact that she was tall and gorgeous didn't hurt either. As she hopped the

Beardie onto a nearby table, I leaned over to give her a hug. Apparently the setup on our other side belonged to her.

"Terry," I told her. "We're laughing at his hair."

"Hey." She pulled back and gave me a stern look. "I could be offended by that." Bertie's hair was a deep, rich shade of auburn. Terry's was flaming red.

"You tell 'em, doll." Terry plucked a Mini Poodle out of a crate and went to work. "We redheads have to stick together."

"At least until Tuesday or so," I said. "By then he'll probably be blond again."

"Somebody woke up on the wrong side of bed this morning." Terry fluttered his fingers in Aunt Peg's direction. "Competition a little tough for you today?"

"I might ask the same of you," I shot back. Davey was showing one Standard Poodle. Crawford and Terry had three. And as Aunt Peg had pointed out earlier, since the initial classes were divided by sex, it was unlikely that Augie and Coral would meet in the show ring.

"You two quit fussing." Aunt Peg was busy putting up her puppy's topknot. "Coral is a baby. She's just here to learn what dog shows are all about."

"A puppy of yours needing experience?" Sam said. He and Kev had returned from parking the SUV. "That sounds unlikely."

Sam released Kevin's hand and I handed my son the bag of toys. He sat down in the grass, took out a pair of Matchbox cars, and began to zoom them around the table legs.

"I can't believe how much I've missed this," Aunt Peg said with a smile. "It's been entirely too long since I had a Poodle to show. Judging is a wonderful way to give back to the sport, but this . . ." She waved a hand to encompass all the activity under the tent and the other exhibitors around us. "This is what it's really about. The dogs, the grooming, the competition, the camaraderie—"

"The smell of hairspray in the morning?" I teased.

"Laugh if you will, but I'm perfectly serious. Judging is a fruitful occupation and agility is loads of fun. But nothing can compare with the satisfaction you feel, walking into the breed ring with a beautiful, home-bred dog on the end of your leash."

"Here, here," said Crawford.

The rest of us nodded in agreement. Dog shows had an addictive quality and we were all well aware of it. The competition was always interesting, and occasionally even rewarding. But that was only part of the equation. Exhibiting gave breeders the opportunity to form relationships, to compare notes, and to analyze the results of their efforts. We came to the shows for the dogs, but the people were every bit as important.

"Speaking of judging," said Sam. "When are you going to apply for a license, Crawford?"

The handler gave him a sideways look. "Is that your way of saying you think I'm of an age where I ought to be slowing down?"

Sam reddened. I'd rarely seen him at a loss for words, but now he looked as if he wished he'd never asked the question.

I quickly intervened. "What Sam meant, Crawford, is that the judging pool would be enriched by your experience and expertise."

"That's what I thought." The handler cracked a grin. "But the judging pool will have to wait. I'm too busy doing what I do best." He swept a Toy Poodle off a tabletop and exited the tent. Terry picked up two more ring-ready Toys and followed.

"That's my cue," said Bertie. She left with a Duck Toller.

"And mine as well," Aunt Peg announced. "Keep an eye on Coral for me, will you? I'll be back in just a few minutes."

"Where are you going?" I asked.

"I decided that a return to the ring deserved a nice new piece of equipment. I ordered a beaded show leash for Coral from Jasmine Crane. She told me it would be ready for pick up today."

Sam and I exchanged a look. We were both remembering that most of Aunt Peg's old equipment had burned up in a kennel fire the previous summer.

"That sounds perfect," I said. "Jasmine's leashes are beautiful."

Every dog show drew a variety of canine-centric concession booths, offering all manner of dog-related products. I'd seen everything from sheepskin beds and squeaky toys, to canine books and figurines. In vendor's row, there was something for every dog lover to drool over.

Jasmine Crane's specialty was canine art. Working in oils and pastels, she created original paintings and took commissions for pet portraits. Jasmine was a skilled artist, deft at capturing both her subjects' looks and their personalities. When passing by her booth, I'd often admired the merchandise she had on display.

Recently Jasmine had expanded into the growing market for custom-made collars and leashes. Her eye for color and symmetry lent her products a special flair, and her strapworks were quickly becoming as popular as her art.

Like all show Poodles, Coral was table trained. When Aunt Peg left, Coral lay down on the tabletop with her head between her front paws, patiently waiting for Aunt Peg to return.

Davey had finished line-brushing Augie and put on his slender show collar. Now Sam supervised as Davey parted the long hair on the Poodle's head and banded together the numerous ponytails that would support Augie's towering topknot. Davey and Sam were spraying up Augie's coat when Aunt Peg reappeared ten minutes later.

"Let me see." I held out my hand. "I bet it's gorgeous."

"I'd be delighted to show it to you," Aunt Peg replied unhappily, "except I don't have it. Jasmine wasn't in her booth. I even waited a few minutes, hoping she'd return, but she never showed up."

"That's odd," Sam commented. "How does she expect to make sales if she isn't there for her customers?"

"I haven't a clue." Aunt Peg sounded huffy. "And it's very disappointing. I had that leash made specially, so I could start Coral's career off right. Now we'll have to do without."

Davey looked over. "I can lend you a lead, Aunt Peg. I have extras."

"Thank you, but no." She walked over and dug around in her tack box. "I have a leash. It's just not the *right* leash."

Aunt Peg reveled in her dog show superstitions. Heaven forbid you wished her luck before she went in the ring. She would react as though you'd driven a dagger into her heart.

Davey looked at me and shrugged. I returned the gesture.

Aunt Peg sighed. Loudly. "There's nothing to be done for it. We shall simply have to rise above."

My sympathy for her plight was muted. Trust me, if anyone was capable of rising above, it was surely Aunt Peg.

She took out her scissors and applied the final finish to Coral's trim. Over in our setup, Sam and Davey were doing the same to Augie. Crawford and Terry came running back to the tent with their Toy Poodles. They exchanged them for the Standards and quickly got ready to leave again.

Aunt Peg lifted Coral off her grooming table and set her on the ground. Davey followed suit with Augie. In a procession of Poodles, we all headed over to the ring.

Following behind with Kevin, I felt a frisson of excitement in the air. Things were about to get serious. It was time to find out if all the hard work we'd done to ready Augie for the show had been worth it. For Davey's sake, I really hoped today was going to be his day.

Chapter 2

Poodles come in three varieties, divided by size. From the tiniest city apartment to the expanse of a rural ranch, a Poodle can fit in anywhere. Despite their differences in stature, all Poodles share the same whip-smart, eager to please, fun-loving disposition. Plus, they're people dogs. So most are kind enough to hide the fact that they can out-think their owners. There's nothing a Poodle enjoys more than a good joke, especially one at their person's expense.

Though the breed was originally developed to retrieve, the gaiety of the Poodle temperament is uniquely suited to the show ring. Poodles are natural entertainers. In the breed ring, a judge is looking for a sound, typey dog with correct conformation. But Poodles bring something more.

They walk into a dog show ring and make it their own. They play with their handlers. They flirt with the spectators. They charm the socks off the judges. Poodles understand that dog shows are supposed to be fun. And they want everyone else to be having a great time too.

We crossed the short expanse between the handlers' tent and the show ring in the company of more than a dozen other Standard Poodles.

Davey kept Augie close to his side. His right hand was holding the end of the lead, his left was cupped beneath the dog's muzzle. His arm, looped around Augie's mane coat, prevented anyone from stepping too close and jostling the carefully coiffed hair.

By contrast, Aunt Peg was letting Coral play at the end of her leash. The rambunctious puppy briefly dropped her head to sniff at something enticing in the grass, before bounding back up like a gazelle. Her pomponned tail, held high in the air, wagged back and forth with delight.

I watched the boisterous display with surprise. Aunt Peg was a formidable competitor. And this carefree behavior—on the way to the show ring, no less—was very unlike her.

"I guess you really *are* here for the experience," I said.

"Every puppy should have a good time at her first dog show," Aunt Peg replied. "Besides, it's not as if she has any real hair to muss."

Augie's regal topknot towered nearly a foot in the air. Coral's resembled a wispy black bottle brush. The fringe on her ears barely reached the end of the leathers. In her puppy trim—with a blanket of shaped hair covering her entire body—Coral was more cute than imposing. Compared to the other Standard bitches, Coral would look like a baby. Which was exactly what she was.

Aunt Peg reached over and poked Davey in the shoulder. "There's a major today in dogs. I expect you to look sharp. Augie should be very competitive in this company."

Davey nodded but didn't reply. He already knew what was on the line. And unfortunately, pressure from Aunt Peg was nothing new.

In order to attain its championship, a dog needed to earn fifteen points in same-sex competition. The judging began with the classes for unfinished dogs. As she had yet to turn a year old, Coral was entered in the Puppy Bitch class. Augie, a mature dog ready to take on the toughest class competitors, was in Open Dogs.

When the class judging had been completed, each individual class winner returned to the ring to vie for the titles of Winners Dog and Winners Bitch. Those two were the only entrants to receive points. The number of points awarded ranged from one to five, and was determined by the amount of competition beaten.

Two majors—awards of three or more points—were required to complete a dog's championship. Major wins were highly sought after and always difficult to attain. Augie had previously accumulated eleven points toward his championship, including one major. Coral, about to make her show ring debut, obviously had yet to earn even one.

The area near the in-gate of the Standard

Poodle ring was already crowded with handlers and dogs. Inside the ring, the judge was quickly working his way through a small entry of Löwchen. Aunt Peg stopped to talk to someone she knew. Davey paused at the fringes of the activity, eager to keep Augie out of the fray. While Sam remained with him and kept a firm grip on Kev's hand, I slithered between people and Poodles and made my way to the steward's table to pick up our numbered armbands.

As I waited my turn, Terry appeared beside me, intent on the same mission. In Standard Poodles, he and Crawford had a class dog, a class bitch, and a champion "specials dog" who would be competing for Best of Variety.

Terry sidled closer and said out of the side of his mouth, "How is Augie's bite?"

"Fine," I whispered back.

"He's not missing any teeth?"

"No. Why?"

"Mr. Logan is a real stickler for correct dentition."

Some breed standards disqualify dogs for an incorrect bite or missing teeth. The Poodle standard wasn't one of them. But even so, every judge carried his own preferences and idiosyncrasies into the ring with him.

"You can't blame him," Terry said.

That piqued my interest. I turned and stared until he continued.

24

"Mr. Logan once stuck his hand into a Doberman's mouth and cut his finger on the dog's braces. He had to go get stitches."

I reared back in surprise. Missing teeth were a minor infraction compared to *braces*. Artificial enhancements were strictly forbidden.

"You're making that up," I accused.

"No, really." Terry was all innocence. Like butter wouldn't melt in his mouth. That was the problem with Terry's gossip. I never knew how much to believe. "Ask Peg, she'll tell you."

Aunt Peg was all the way on the other side of the ring. As Terry knew perfectly well. I grabbed our numbers from the steward and went back to join my family.

"Mr. Logan hasn't even started judging Standards yet and already you look outraged," Sam said mildly. "What is Terry up to now?"

"Apparently an exhibitor once took a dog into Mr. Logan's ring that was wearing braces on its teeth."

"Oh yeah." Sam didn't even blink. "That's old news."

Even after all the years I'd been involved, when it came to showing dogs, I still sometimes felt like the new kid. Why did everybody always know this stuff but me?

"The judge had to get *stitches*," I said.

Sam still wasn't impressed. "I wouldn't worry about that. I'm sure the cut is healed by now."

"Mom, Puppy Dogs are in the ring," Davey said urgently. "I need my number."

Oh. Right. Time to get back to business.

Davey held out his arm. I ran two rubber bands up the sleeve of his jacket, then slid the cardboard square securely underneath. Inside the ring, Mr. Logan was taking his last look at four Standard puppies before pinning the class. Aunt Peg came around from the other side of the ring to watch the remainder of the dog judging with us. I handed over her armband and she slipped it on.

"Crawford should win that class handily," she remarked. "That's a nice puppy he has. He'll give Augie a run for his money in Winners."

"Augie has to get out of the Open class first," I reminded her.

Aunt Peg waved a hand as if that was a given. I wished I had even half her confidence.

As usual, however, it turned out that Aunt Peg was right.

Crawford's white puppy topped his class easily. And after a prolonged battle, Davey and Augie prevailed over three other dogs in Open. Davey accepted his blue ribbon with a grateful smile. Then he hurried Augie back into position as Crawford brought his puppy back into the ring so the two could be judged against each other for Winners Dog.

Mr. Logan made it look like a close decision.

And it probably was. He left Augie at the head of the line until the very last moment. Then, as the two dogs circled the ring one final time, the judge looked back and pointed to Crawford's puppy for the win.

My heart sank like a stone. Sam was standing beside me. I felt his shoulders slump. The fact that Davey had been so close to nabbing Augie's elusive second major made us both feel even worse.

"Did Davey win?" Kevin asked. He had yet to master the intricacies of the judging system.

"No," I said glumly. "Not this time."

Looking resigned, Davey moved Augie back into line. The dog who'd placed second earlier to Crawford's puppy returned to the ring to be judged for Reserve Winners. This time the decision took only a few seconds. Mr. Logan quickly motioned Augie over to the marker and handed Davey the purple-and-white-striped ribbon.

Davey exited the ring with a frown on his face. He wasn't upset, just disappointed. We all were.

"I really wanted to win that one," he said dejectedly.

"I know you did, sweetie." I looped my arms around his shoulders and pulled him close for a hug. Davey usually objects to PDAs from his parents. This time he didn't even murmur a protest. "But you'll have another chance next

27

week. Augie looks great and he was really showing well for you."

"That puppy of Crawford's is a star in the making," Sam added. "It was just bad luck that you and Augie ran into him today. I'm pretty sure the win finished him, so at least you won't have to worry about him in the future."

"That's pathetic," Davey muttered. "That dog finished as a *puppy,* and I've been showing Augie forever."

"Pathetic, is it?" Aunt Peg inquired. The judge was still busy marking his book, so the Puppy Bitches had yet to be called to the ring. "I thought you wanted to show Augie yourself."

"I do," Davey protested, but Aunt Peg wasn't finished.

"If all that mattered was getting the job done, we could put that dog with a professional handler and have him finished in no time. Would you prefer that?"

"No, of course not."

"That's what I thought," Aunt Peg sniffed. "Now give your nice Poodle a pat and let me go take my turn."

Mr. Logan had returned to the center of his ring. The steward called out the numbers of the two Standard Poodle Puppy Bitches. Aunt Peg went sweeping past us with Coral bouncing at her side.

The fact that Aunt Peg won her small class

didn't come as a surprise. Coral might have been immature and inexperienced, but she was still a very pretty Poodle. But what happened after that was totally unexpected.

The Bred-by-Exhibitor class had only a single entry, but there were five nice bitches in Open. A lovely brown Poodle with a professional handler prevailed, and I assumed she would go on to take the points.

That decision looked like an easy one to me. But apparently not to Mr. Logan.

He motioned Coral forward to the head of the line and turned the contest into a duel between the puppy and the Open Bitch. Judging by the expression on Aunt Peg's face, she hadn't anticipated this turn of events either.

Aunt Peg is a competitor to the core, however. I could see the exact moment she put aside the notion of Coral using the dog show for experience—and got to work beating that other bitch. All at once, she began presenting Coral to the judge as if she was offering the rarest of diamonds for his perusal.

The best handlers are skilled at showcasing a dog's good points and drawing the judge's eye away from its faults. Coral was a bit small. Her tail set could have been higher and she was somewhat lacking in under jaw. However those flaws were more than offset by her lovely face and expression, her well-angulated shoulder, and her solid topline. When the puppy settled down and moved right, she appeared to float over the ground.

And suddenly Aunt Peg was doing everything she could to make sure Coral was settled and showing effectively.

Mr. Logan waffled and wavered for what seemed like an inordinate amount of time. Usually when that happened it meant a judge didn't particularly like either offering. But Mr. Logan had two nice bitches in front of him. He also had two Poodles who couldn't have been more different in age and condition. Under those circumstances, most judges would opt to reward the mature entry. So what was this judge spending so much time thinking about?

"Aunt Peg's going to win," Kevin said. Sam had picked him up so he could see the ring better.

"I think you're right." I sounded shocked. I *was* shocked.

And I wasn't the only one. When the judge pointed to Coral for Winners Bitch, Davey released his breath on a long exhale. "How did Aunt Peg *do* that?" he asked.

Sam shrugged, looking equally bemused. "Magic?"

When it came to Aunt Peg's powers, anything was possible.

After that, the Best of Variety judging proceeded in a more conventional manner.

Crawford's handsome special was awarded BOV over two other champions. His white puppy, now being handled by Terry, was Best of Winners. Coral, the only bitch in the ring, was awarded Best of Opposite Sex.

With an auspicious debut like that, I assumed Aunt Peg would remain at ringside to have Coral's picture taken with the judge. But when the rest of the family went trooping back to the handlers' tent, Aunt Peg and Coral fell in behind us. I started to ask her about a win photo, then saw the expression on her face and thought better of the idea.

Aunt Peg appeared to be seriously disgruntled by the outcome.

Crawford and Terry had stayed to have their winners' pictures taken, but Bertie was standing in her setup when we returned. There was a Sheltie on one of her grooming tables and a Smooth Collie on another, but Bertie was taking a break to consult her program and drink a soda. Her gaze slid over us, one by one.

"I'm guessing it wasn't your best day," she said.

"Augie was Reserve," Davey told her. He put the Poodle back on the tabletop. Augie would now need to have his tight topknot taken down and the hairspray brushed from his coat. "But Coral won."

"Congratulations!" Bertie cried. Then she

looked at Aunt Peg, who was glumly slipping Coral into a crate. The puppy didn't have enough hair to even need brushing out. "Wait. That's good news, isn't it?"

"You would think," I said. "If Augie had won, we'd all be dancing in the aisles."

Well maybe not Davey, who rolled his eyes at that. But hey, he's thirteen, so that's par for the course. The rest of us would have been doing a serious jitterbug.

Bertie watched as Aunt Peg silently pulled the two ribbons out of her pocket and tossed them into her tack box. "Coral was Best Opposite too? That's terrific. Did you get a picture?"

"No." Aunt Peg frowned.

"Why not?"

Instead of replying, Aunt Peg turned to Sam. "Suppose you were judging bitches today. Who would you have put up?"

Sam answered without hesitation. "The brown bitch. She deserved the win."

"Yes, she did," Aunt Peg agreed. "Coral never should have beaten her."

"So what?" I said. "We've all had days when we should have won, but didn't. It's nice to have things go the other way for a change."

"It's not *nice,*" Aunt Peg grumbled. "Walter Logan should have known better. He should have *judged* better. That result never should have happened."

32

"So why did it?" I asked.

"I have no idea. I suppose I'll have to ask him the next time I see him."

Bertie snorted under her breath. We all looked her way.

"What?" asked Aunt Peg.

"You're kidding, right? Your puppy won the points on a day when she shouldn't have and you honestly don't know why?"

"Certainly not," Aunt Peg said sharply. "Please enlighten me."

Sam cleared his throat. Suddenly I realized he also knew what Bertie was thinking. "As Melanie said, we've all been beaten when we shouldn't have been. Sometimes because a judge plays politics and puts up a professional over an owner-handler."

"I certainly don't see how that applies." Aunt Peg looked nonplussed. "*I'm* an owner-handler."

"Oh please," said Bertie. "If you're a normal owner-handler, I'm Winnie the Pooh."

Aunt Peg's eyes narrowed. She was not amused. "Are you saying that my win was due to politics?"

"Think about it," I said. "You're a judge yourself. And you obviously know Walter Logan—"

"I know *everybody* in the dog world," Aunt Peg sputtered.

"Precisely my point," I affirmed.

"And don't forget about the intimidation factor," Bertie added.

"What intimidation factor?" asked Aunt Peg.

Davey laughed out loud. After a few seconds the rest of us—except for Aunt Peg—followed.

"But it shouldn't matter who is showing the dog." Aunt Peg's tone bordered on outrage. "They're supposed to be judging the other end of the lead!"

"That's how it works in your ring," Sam replied mildly. "But not everywhere."

"But . . ." Aunt Peg was sputtering again. "That's not fair."

"Maybe you should hire a professional handler for Coral, Aunt Peg," Davey said innocently.

Okay, that was fresh. But it was also pretty funny.

Sam spun away to hide a grin. Bertie abruptly got busy digging in her tack box. I swallowed a laugh and bent down under the grooming table to see how Kevin was doing.

Aunt Peg drew herself up to her full height. She glared around at us as if we'd suddenly morphed into a bunch of back-stabbing traitors. "You people are all annoying me," she announced. "I'm going to go pick up my new leash. Hopefully by the time I return, you will have realized the error of your ways."

"Fat chance of that," Davey muttered under his breath.

Thankfully I appeared to be the only one who heard him.

Aunt Peg hadn't even been gone five minutes when my cell phone rang. I showed the name on the screen to Sam and Bertie and said, "Do you think she wants to apologize?"

I should have known better.

Aunt Peg was already talking before I even got the phone to my ear. "Melanie, run quickly to the ambulance at the end of the field. It's needed right away at Jasmine's booth."

"Is somebody hurt?" All at once I felt guilty. "It's not you, is it?"

"I'm fine," Aunt Peg snapped. "More or less, anyway. But Jasmine Crane isn't. She appears to be dead."

Chapter 3

No," I said. "That can't be right."

"What can't?" asked Sam. He came and took the phone out of my hand. He listened for a few seconds and then said, "We'll be right there."

Bertie beckoned me into her setup, away from the boys. "What's the matter?"

"You know Jasmine, the art lady who makes the custom leashes?" I whispered.

Bertie nodded.

"Aunt Peg said she's dead."

Bertie's face paled. "How? When?"

"I don't know. That's all she told me." I was still having trouble absorbing the news myself. I turned back to Davey and raised my voice to normal volume. "Sam and I are going to go see about something with Aunt Peg. You're in charge of Kevin."

"But—"

The magnitude of my glare stopped that protest in its tracks.

"Okay," Davey said grudgingly. Not perfect, but I'd take it. I currently had bigger problems to worry about than a mouthy teenager.

Sam headed for the ambulance and the EMTs. I went straight to Jasmine Crane's booth. It was on the edge of the park, located near the end of a long line of concessions. Most of them appeared to be doing a brisk business.

With the sun shining and the first hint of spring in the air, it was a beautiful day for a dog show. Scores of spectators were wandering around the area, checking out the wares. Even as I hurried closer, nothing looked amiss. I knew Aunt Peg almost never got things wrong, but I was desperately hoping she'd been mistaken.

On one side of Jasmine's booth, another vendor was selling dog-related books. On the other, a pet supply company had set out pallets of kibble and stacks of brightly colored, foam-padded beds. Intent on reaching Aunt Peg, I barely spared either business a glance.

As I approached from the front, Jasmine's booth looked much the same as it always had. Like the other concessions, it was covered by a tent. But while the others were open on the sides for easy access, Jasmine's booth was partially enclosed by the portable walls on which she showcased her paintings. A table at the front of the enclosure displayed samples of her collars and leashes, notable for their exotic materials and intricate beading.

On a normal day, Jasmine would have been standing out in front of her booth, talking to browsers and inviting them to step inside for a closer look. Though I didn't know her personally, our paths had crossed on numerous occasions.

The dog show circuit was like a giant traveling circus. The locations changed from week to week, but the same participants showed up repeatedly. After a while, almost everyone started to look familiar.

Now I pictured a woman in her forties, with dark, curly hair and striking green eyes. Jasmine's clothing style was Bohemian chic. She favored peasant tops and colorful, tiered skirts, often accented with oversized jewelry. I assumed that her free spirit, flower child look was probably part preference and part performance, meant to enhance her image as an *artiste*.

The front section of Jasmine's booth was empty. I strode past the table and dodged around a tall, free-standing partition that served as an interior display. Now I could see the rear portion of the enclosed stand. With the sun shining behind her, Aunt Peg was outlined in a narrow doorway. The opening led to the area behind the booths where the vendors parked their trucks and stored their extra stock.

Aunt Peg spun around as I approached. "Finally! Did you bring help?"

"Sam went to get the EMTs. He and the ambulance should be here soon." I skidded to a stop beside her and tried to peer through the doorway.

Aunt Peg yanked me back. "Don't look. Trust me, you'd rather not see that."

"What happened? Are you sure Jasmine is

dead? Did she have a heart attack? I know CPR. Maybe we can help—"

"We can't." Aunt Peg's forceful reply left no room for argument. "Jasmine is beyond our help. Or anyone's for that matter. I've called nine-one-one. The police are on their way."

I fell back in shock. Suddenly I was quite sure that Aunt Peg was right: I didn't want to see what lay on the other side of the doorway.

"The police?" I blew out a breath. Immediately I felt as though I needed more air. "But why . . . ?"

"Jasmine was strangled. And it looks like one of her own leashes was used to do the job."

"Not yours, I hope." The words just popped out. Then I wanted to kick myself.

"No," Aunt Peg said drily. "Though I suspect my hopes of securing that particular item will go unfulfilled." She stopped and shook her head. "What a shame."

Hopefully she was talking about Jasmine's death. And not her missing custom order.

We couldn't see the rest of the showground from where we were, but Aunt Peg and I both heard the sound of running feet. Sam must have arrived with the medics. I stepped around the partition and went out the front of the booth. The ambulance was now parked at the end of the vendors' row. Sam and two EMTs were covering the last bit of distance on foot.

I waved them over to the right place, then moved aside to let them pass. Sam stopped when he saw me. The medics kept going and ducked inside the booth. I figured Aunt Peg could tell them what they needed to know.

Sam looked at me inquiringly. Slowly I shook my head. "It wasn't an accident. Jasmine was strangled. Aunt Peg has called the police."

"How awful." Sam briefly closed his eyes as he processed the news. "And even worse for Peg to have been the one who found her."

Aunt Peg's voice reached us from the back of the booth. "Young man, the police are on their way. I think you'd better wait until they arrive before touching anything." If she received a reply, it wasn't audible.

A moment later Aunt Peg came around the partition and walked outside to join us. "Well, I tried. But those two were determined to go about their business, even if it meant contaminating a crime scene. If I'm so intimidating, how come I couldn't intimidate them?"

"You can't blame them for wanting to do their job," Sam said. "And I'm glad they're here to take charge. Now that Jasmine's death has been reported, I think we should leave the authorities to deal with it."

"Good idea," I replied. Knowing what lay on the other side of those walls, I had no desire to linger.

Sam and I started to walk away. Aunt Peg didn't move. Instead she positioned herself in the entrance to Jasmine's booth, crossed her arms over her chest, and stood like a sentinel poised to deny access to interlopers.

Sam paused. "Peg, are you coming?"

"No, I'll wait here until the police arrive. I'd imagine they'll want to talk to me."

Knowing Aunt Peg, she'd probably have questions for them too.

Back at the grooming tent, Davey had finished taking Augie's hair down and was giving the Standard Poodle a drink. Bertie must have been up at the rings, but in the setup on our other side there was a rare lull in the activity. Crawford was leaning against a stack of crates, looking at something on his phone. Terry was sitting in the grass, playing with Kevin.

Terry saw Sam and me and shot to his feet. "Something's happened," he said.

So help me, there was *more?*

"What now?" I asked.

"I have no idea, but you two look awful. What's wrong?"

Sam gave his head a slight shake to silence us. Then he turned to Davey. "Hey sport, why don't you take your brother over to the rings to watch the Dalmatian judging? You know how Kev loves dogs with spots."

Davey wasn't dumb. He knew something was

41

up. "You guys are going to talk about something you don't want me to hear."

Before I could reply, Terry chimed in. "Yes, we are." His voice dropped to a confidential tone. "But don't worry, I'll tell you all about it later."

I waited until Davey had taken his brother's hand and the two of them had departed before saying, "You will not."

"Of course I won't," Terry agreed. "But it got them moving, didn't it?"

"You lied to my children."

"It's good for them. They should know better than to trust strangers."

"You're not a stranger," Sam pointed out.

"Oh, for Pete's sake." Crawford looked up from his phone. "If I promise to yell at him later, will you quit bickering and tell us what's the matter?"

"Jasmine Crane is dead," I said. "She was strangled with one of her leashes."

For a minute there was only silence. Terry's eyes widened, his mouth opened in surprise. Crawford set down his phone and walked over to stand beside us. The two of them might have been expecting bad news, but I doubted they'd anticipated something of this magnitude.

"Well, there you go," Terry said finally. "Now you have another mystery to solve."

I turned and glared at him.

"What?" He was unrepentant. "I'm only saying

42

what everybody else is thinking. Besides, it's not as if I knew the woman."

"I know her." Crawford stopped and frowned. "I guess I mean . . . I knew her."

"I knew her too," said Sam.

That surprised me. "You did?"

"Sure." He shrugged. "Jasmine has been part of the dog show scene forever. I believe she started as an exhibitor."

"Afghan Hounds," Crawford said.

That made sense. Afghans were gorgeous. They were exactly the kind of dog I would expect an artist to own.

"She never had much success in the show ring," Crawford added. "Jasmine was a hippie-dippy kind of handler, if you know what I mean. The judge would ask her for one thing and she'd do something else entirely. She always had her head in the clouds."

"She must have had an artistic background," said Sam. "Because overnight it seemed like she went from showing dogs to painting them."

"Now I know who you're talking about." Terry looked interested again. "The Leash Lady, right? The one with the art concession?"

I nodded. "Yes, that was Jasmine. I browsed around her booth a few times. She appeared to be a talented artist."

"She was," Sam agreed. "I even thought about commissioning a painting from her once, but it never came together. I can't imagine why anyone would have wanted to harm her though."

"Here comes Aunt Peg." I pointed across the open field. "Maybe she knows something."

We stopped talking and waited for her to draw near. Terry started firing questions as soon as Aunt Peg was within earshot, but it didn't do any good. She was still as baffled by Jasmine Crane's death as we were.

"The police are here," she told us. "They've cordoned off the area and now they're busy doing whatever else needs doing at times like this."

"But you must have talked to them," Terry pressed.

"Of course I talked to them. It wasn't as if I had a choice. After all, I was the one who found Jasmine's body."

I wondered if I was the only one who noticed that Aunt Peg sounded almost pleased to have played a central role in the drama.

"Unfortunately, the two officers weren't interested in telling me anything. They did, however, have plenty of questions. Like what was my relationship with Jasmine? When was the last time I'd seen her before today? What had I been doing poking around in the back of her booth?"

Terry's brow rose. "What *were* you doing nosing around in her booth?"

"If you must know I was looking for my leash. I was disappointed not to be able to show Coral in it this morning, but I was determined to have it for next time. Jasmine had promised it to me today, so I was sure it had to be there somewhere. The officers did not appear to be impressed by my explanation."

"At least they didn't arrest you." I was only half joking.

"No, but they did ask me to stop by the police station on my way back to Greenwich and fill out a statement regarding the day's events. I told them I would be happy to."

"I'm sure the police will talk to the vendors on either side of Jasmine's booth," I said. "Maybe somebody saw something."

Aunt Peg's lips pursed. "If so, you'd think they would have had the decency to say something before I went and stumbled over her body."

She had a point.

Despite the fact that there had been a death on the showground, the competition continued. Crawford and Terry went back to their setup to prepare their dogs for the group judging. Usually the rest of us hung around to cheer them on. Today, our hearts weren't in it.

News of Jasmine's death had to be rocketing around the park. No one would be paying attention to the competition in the rings. Instead people would be chattering and speculating, perhaps even reveling in the shocking news.

I didn't want the boys listening to that. I didn't

want to hear it myself. I hadn't known Jasmine Crane, but nevertheless I felt her loss.

Instead we packed up and went home.

The show had taken place in eastern Connecticut. It was a subdued two-hour drive back to our home in North Stamford. Between Augie's loss and Jasmine's death, the only one in the car who was feeling cheerful was Kevin. And that was because he was mostly oblivious to the day's events.

Stamford is a thriving city on the Connecticut coast in lower Fairfield County. Our house was located in a residential area far from the bustle of downtown. In our small neighborhood, homes had two acre lots, streets were shady and quiet, and children could play outside all day. Colonial in style, our house was set back from the road and surrounded by trees. Its best feature was a spacious backyard, enclosed by a tall cedar fence.

When we finally arrived home, Sam and Davey began to unload the car while Kevin and I went to let the dogs out. Kev and I had the better end of that deal. No matter how bad your day had been, it was impossible to remain dejected in the face of a dog's ecstatic welcome. And the Poodle pack never disappointed.

First to come flying out the door was Tar. Tall and handsome, he was Sam's retired specials dog and our resident goofball. Right behind him were the two younger bitches, Eve and Raven. Always anxious not to be left behind, Bud came scrambling out between their legs. He was a rescue dog of mixed heritage, and a relatively recent addition to the family. Bud was also the dog most likely to be causing mayhem at any given moment.

When the first four had gone dashing by, only one dog remained. Faith, our oldest Standard Poodle, had hung back and waited for the melee to subside. A gift from Aunt Peg eight years earlier, Faith was the first pet I'd ever owned. I could still remember vividly the moment Aunt Peg had placed her in my arms. As I'd held the small, black puppy close, my heart had unfurled like a blossom after a long drought.

Now I let the other dogs race around the yard and went straight to Faith. She was waiting for me. When I crouched down and opened my arms, the Poodle walked into my embrace and we shared a warm hug.

"Did you have a good day?" I asked her.

Faith wagged her tail in reply.

Good. That meant the boys hadn't gotten up to too much mischief while we'd been gone.

Poodles are easy to train and all of ours knew how to behave in the house. But Tar, who was incredibly sweet and well-meaning, was also the only dumb Poodle I'd ever met. And on those rare occasions when he got a new idea, he was apt to get so excited about it that every sensible thought flew right out of his head.

As for Bud, training-wise he was still a work in progress. Tell one of the Poodles to do something, and they leapt to obey. Bud assumed that all commands were open to negotiation. In the nine months he'd been part of our family, he'd definitely managed to keep things interesting.

After the long day at the dog show, we all went to bed early. I was happy to have a chance to put the day's distressing events behind me. Not only that, but I had another busy week coming up.

Sam was a software designer who worked from home, but early Monday morning the rest of us were due at school. Davey took the bus to Hart Middle School where he was a student in eighth grade. Kevin had started preschool at Graceland Nursery School at the beginning of the new semester. He attended sessions five mornings a week.

Faith and I would be up and on our way to Howard Academy, a private school in Greenwich where I worked as a special needs tutor. Situated on the former estate of an early twentieth century robber baron, the K-through-8 academy catered to the needs of a wealthy and sophisticated clientele. School parents shared the conviction that nothing was too good for their children, and they were willing to pay handsomely for the best educational opportunities.

Howard Academy was governed by headmaster Russell Hanover II. Early in my tenure there, the man's stern demeanor and adherence to exacting standards had intimidated me to near silence when I chanced to be in his presence. But over time, I'd come to admire Mr. Hanover for his absolute refusal to compromise in any aspect of student life relating to the children's education or well-being.

A firm belief that the headmaster would choose to do the right thing—coupled with a healthy dose of self-interest—had led me to present Mr. Hanover with an interesting proposition. Midway through my second semester at Howard Academy, I'd asked for permission to bring Faith to school with me.

The classroom where I held my tutoring sessions was a large, bright, airy space dedicated solely to my use. Students who needed my help were often those struggling with Howard Academy's rigorous curriculum. I'd argued that Faith's presence would have a soothing effect on children who'd been sent to remedial classes. I also hoped that the Poodle's innate charm and lively appeal would transform my classroom from a place where students were assigned to one they visited eagerly.

Mr. Hanover had given my plea due consideration and agreed to give Faith a one week trial. To our mutual satisfaction, the big Poodle had fit into HA's educational program seamlessly.

Now, six years later, Faith was the unofficial school mascot and my classroom had become a popular gathering spot. And if I sometimes felt as though I'd been relegated to a supporting role in my own space, that was okay too. Whatever worked was fine by me.

Chapter 4

After Faith and I dropped Kevin at preschool, we hit traffic on the Merritt Parkway, so we were running late. The Howard Academy grounds were extensive and I often took Faith for a walk around the hockey field upon our arrival. Now there wasn't time to do anything but run inside, grab a cup of coffee from the nearly empty teachers' lounge, and hurry to my classroom.

I switched on the lights and cracked open a window. I filled Faith's water dish and took a rawhide bone out of a desk drawer. The Poodle's cedar-stuffed bed was tucked in a corner. She lay down and got settled.

When Kev had started preschool in January, Mr. Hanover had been amenable to adjusting my schedule to match. Now I was working five mornings a week too. I was grateful for the change as it had made family life much easier. But it also meant that from eight-thirty to one p.m. every day, my tutoring sessions were lined up virtually back to back.

My first student of the morning was a sixth-grade girl who was new to my program. Howard Academy teachers were encouraged to play a very active role in the school community. We took turns eating lunch with the students and we officiated over their clubs. We volunteered to chair fund-raisers and helped out with school plays. So although Francesca Della Cimino wasn't a regular student of mine, I wasn't unfamiliar with her.

Francesca's mother was noted opera singer Arianna Della Cimino. Her father was a talented violinist. Francesca was an only child and the family had recently moved to Greenwich from Vienna. According to the buzz I'd heard in the teachers' lounge, Arianna would soon be starring in a production at the Metropolitan Opera House.

Francesca had transferred in at the start of the new semester and for the first few months it had appeared that all was well. She was a bright and lively child who'd had a more cosmopolitan upbringing than many of her classmates. Her knowledge of American history and English literature was behind that of her peers, but she excelled in math and science. So I'd been surprised that the referral to my program had come from Louisa Delgado, who taught middle school math.

Promptly at eight-thirty, the door to my class-room opened. Francesca stood in the doorway, but made no move to enter the room.

She was tall for her age and plump enough to already possess the coveted curves that most of her classmates lacked. From her arched brows to her wide mouth, the girl had strong features that she had yet to grow into. Someday Francesca would be every bit as arresting as her famous mother. Today, however, with her shoulders hunched downward over her books and her gaze trained on the floor, the sixth-grader looked as though she wished she could disappear.

Surely I wasn't *that* scary?

I could hear the rustle and rumble of students hurrying to classes in the hallway behind her, but Francesca seemed oblivious. When she finally lifted her eyes, they skittered around the room. I wondered what she was looking for. I also wondered what had happened to turn the giggling, loquacious girl I remembered from a previous lunch table into the uncertain child I now saw before me.

I rose from my seat beside one of two round tables in the room. "Please come in. And close the door behind you. It's noisy out there, isn't it?"

"Yes." Francesca's voice was barely louder than a whisper. After a brief pause, she took a step forward and pulled the door shut.

I expected her to come and join me at the table. Instead, Francesca looked at the Poodle lying on her bed in the corner. "Your dog is very pretty. Her name is Faith, right?"

Faith cocked an ear, then lifted her head. Her tail began to thump up and down.

"Yes, that's right. She's a Standard Poodle. Would you like to say hello to her?"

Finally, I got a positive response. The question elicited a smile that lit up Francesca's whole face. "May I?"

"Sure. Faith loves attention." I beckoned with my fingers and the Poodle stood up and trotted across the room to my side.

Francesca quickly followed suit. Reaching the table, she dropped her armload of books with a loud thump. Faith winced at the sound and Francesca grimaced.

"I'm sorry!" she cried, addressing the Poodle. "I should have known better. Of course you have sensitive ears. My father does too."

Faith was wonderfully adept at sensing the emotions of my students. Boisterous children, she greeted with equal exuberance. Shy ones, she held back and let them make the first move. Now she nudged her head forward and pushed her nose into Francesca's palm.

"I'm pretty sure that means you're forgiven," I said. "Faith likes to be scratched behind her ears."

Francesca crouched down in front of the Poodle and lifted a hand tentatively. When her fingers brushed the side of Faith's topknot, she smiled with delight. "Her hair is so soft!"

"She just had a bath a couple of days ago."

Francesca smiled. "Does she like that?"

"Not really. But she's used to it. Faith used to be a show dog. And Standard Poodles are shown with a lot of hair, so they get bathed and clipped all the time."

"Can I sit on the floor and talk to her?"

Some kids arrived in my room full of bluster and ego. They were convinced they didn't need my help. Others felt embarrassed by the fact that they'd fallen behind. So before the topics of school work or grades even came up, my first job was to build a rapport with each student. To make them feel comfortable about being tutored and to encourage them to accept the guidance I could provide. More often than not, Faith was an invaluable partner in the process.

"You can sit anywhere you like," I told her. "Faith might even climb into your lap."

Francesca was surprised. "Is that allowed?"

"Only if you want her to. Otherwise, I can tell her to stay where she is. She's pretty big, after all."

The girl's head dipped downward. I couldn't see her face when she said, "I'm pretty big too." Then quickly, as if she was afraid I might change my mind, Francesca sank down to the floor and crossed her legs. When she patted her lap, Faith delicately draped her front end across the girl's knees.

"It looks like you're an old hand at this," I said. "Do you have a dog of your own?"

"No. I wish I did. I've always wanted one, but my father says we move around too much. He says a pet needs stability to feel safe and know where it belongs."

Children need stability too, I thought. I wondered if that was why Francesca was here. It couldn't have been easy for her to have her whole life uprooted in the middle of a school year, moving four thousand miles away to a new country and a new school.

Although, thinking back, I was quite certain that the sixth-grader had appeared happy when she'd first started at Howard Academy. Unless perhaps she'd been putting on an act, attempting to bluff her way through an uncomfortable situation until she found her footing.

I decided to join the pair on the floor. Reaching over to give Faith a pat, I said, "Francesca is a beautiful name."

The girl's eyes darted toward me, then left again. I got the impression she wasn't sure whether she was being complimented or ridiculed.

"Really," I said. "I mean it."

Francesca still didn't look convinced.

Without stopping to think, I opened my mouth and sang out the syllables, letting each one linger in the air. "Fran—chesss—kaaa . . . See how pretty it sounds?"

The last note of my impromptu song had barely

trailed away when I realized what I'd done. My face grew red. My mouth snapped shut. What a total idiot I must have appeared.

"Oh my God," I said. "I just remembered your mother is a professional singer. That was terrible, wasn't it?"

"No, it was nice," Francesca replied kindly, even though we both knew otherwise. "Sometimes my mother sings my name too."

"I bet it doesn't sound like that."

"No, it doesn't."

A child who didn't think twice about telling the truth to a teacher. How refreshing.

I started to laugh. After a moment, Francesca joined in. Faith tipped her head back and stared at the two of us like we were members of an alien species. She didn't appreciate my singing either. Ask me how I know.

"Are we going to conduct this entire session sitting on the floor?" I shifted to get comfortable.

Francesca's fingers were still tangled in Faith's coat. Both appeared to be enjoying the interaction. The girl hesitated, then nodded shyly.

"In that case, you'd better reach up and get your notebooks so we can start looking at your work. Are there any subjects you're particularly concerned about?"

"No." Now that we'd moved on to the reason for our meeting, Francesca was once again speaking so softly I could hardly hear her.

"Mrs. Delgado tells me that you're a star in math."

"Yes." Her gaze dropped. "I like numbers."

"She said you used to be the first one to raise your hand with an answer. And that you liked going to the board to solve equations."

"Sometimes."

I opened her math notebook and had a look at the previous night's homework. Francesca's writing was neat and precise. A page filled with figures was written in a firm, dark hand. At first glance everything looked fine.

"But now maybe you're struggling a little?" I asked.

"I guess."

"Then let's start by going over this week's lesson to see if we can identify the parts that are giving you trouble. Okay?"

"Okay," Francesca agreed.

She reached for her notebook, turned to the previous page, then handed it back to me. Once we began working together the remainder of the forty minute session flew by. It seemed like no time at all before I was walking Francesca to the door and inviting the next pair of students to come in and take a seat.

I was happy to see the sixth-grader leave the room with her head held higher than it had been when she entered. We were just getting started, but I was satisfied with how our initial meeting had progressed. Even better, Faith wasn't the only one who felt as though she'd made a new friend.

Promptly at one o'clock, Faith and I were out the door. I had asked Sam to pick up Kev at preschool because I had another stop I wanted to make on the way home.

There was nothing Aunt Peg enjoyed more than a good puzzle. Her curiosity was legendary. With her wide network of friends and associates, she had just about the best connections in the dog show world. While I'd been at work that morning, I was quite certain Aunt Peg had been busy too.

When we'd left the show ground the previous afternoon, the news of Jasmine Crane's murder was shocking and all too immediate. People had needed time to come to grips with what'd happened. But I knew that overnight the dog show grapevine would have begun to hum. The news would be shared, pondered, and dissected. Now, if anyone was on top of all the latest developments in the story, it would be Aunt Peg.

She lived in back country Greenwich in a charming old farmhouse that had once been the nucleus of a working farm. Only five acres still remained with the house, but that was enough to accommodate the needs of Aunt Peg's beloved Cedar Crest Kennel. When her husband, Max, was alive the two of them had bred a litter every year and cared for as many as a dozen Standard Poodles at a time. Now, however, the demands of her busy judging career meant she was often away from home, and her current Poodle population had dwindled to only a handful.

I'd called ahead, so Aunt Peg was expecting us. The door to her house drew open and her Poodles came streaming down the front steps as I hopped Faith out of the car. Not even two weeks had passed since all these dogs had last seen each other. Even so, each of Aunt Peg's Poodles had to check out Faith and pass approval on her visit.

Like Sam's and my Standard Poodles, every one of Aunt Peg's dogs was black. Not only that, but all our Poodles were interrelated.

Older bitch, Hope, was Faith's litter sister. The two of them greeted each other like long-lost friends. Zeke was Eve's litter brother. Willow was Tar's sister. She was also the dam of Coral, who was leaping and bobbing around the outskirts of the activity.

Slower down the stairs and last to join the party was Aunt Peg's elderly retiree, Beau. Years earlier, his theft had been the catalyst that had introduced me to the dog show world. Beau's muzzle was gray now and his once fluid gait was stiffened by arthritis, but he was still top dog at Aunt Peg's house. When he came over to sniff my pants, I leaned down to ruffle my hands through his ears.

"What a good old boy you are," I crooned.

Beau's tail swished slowly back and forth. He knew that. Aunt Peg told him the same thing all the time.

"Well?" Aunt Peg stood on her porch with her hands on her hips. "Are you coming inside or not?"

"Coming," I replied.

No surprise, the Poodles beat me to it. At a word from Aunt Peg they spun around and went scrambling up the steps, parting only briefly to eddy around her legs as they raced into the house.

I followed, closed the door behind us, and walked straight to the kitchen. Aunt Peg loved sweets and she always had cake from the St. Moritz Bakery on hand. I couldn't wait to see what kind we'd be having today.

"So," I said, "what have you heard?"

I didn't even have to mention Jasmine Crane's name. We both knew why I was there.

"Nothing," Aunt Peg replied flatly as she poured herself a cup of Earl Grey tea. "Not a blessed thing. Even my stop at the police department after the show didn't turn up anything new. They simply took down my statement and told me I was free to go."

A kettle sat on the stove top. I filled it with water and turned on the burner. There was a jar of instant coffee in the cupboard. Beyond that meager concession, coffee drinkers were on their own in Aunt Peg's house.

"That's disappointing," I said.

"I agree. The problem appears to be that although everyone knew who Jasmine was, nobody was close to her. I can't find a single person who thought of her as a friend."

"How very odd."

Friendships sprouted like weeds in the dog show world, and it wasn't hard to see why. People traveled together week after week and worked together in close proximity. They shared common goals and spent their downtime socializing.

Jasmine Crane had been part of the dog show community longer than I had. So the fact that nobody had much to say about her was indeed unusual.

The kettle whistled. I poured the hot water into my mug, added milk, then sat down at the butcher block table. Aunt Peg had her head in the refrigerator. I hoped she was looking for cake.

"There they are," she said.

They?

She brought a bakery box over to the table. I lifted the top and saw scones. Cranberry, unless I missed my guess. They looked perfectly nice. But they weren't cake.

Aunt Peg returned with plates and silverware. After another trip to the refrigerator, she added butter and a jar of clotted cream. Then she took a seat opposite me.

"Don't frown so," she said. "They came from St. Moritz. They're lovely."

Well, sure, I thought mulishly. For *scones*.

"You know I'm supposed to be watching my weight. Scones are less fattening than cake."

"Maybe in their virgin state," I said. "But not by the time you get done adding butter and clotted cream."

"Oh pish. I can't abstain from everything. Besides, they have cranberries in them. That makes them healthy."

Perhaps in an alternative universe. One inhabited solely by six-foot-tall women who made their own rules.

"Dig in," said Aunt Peg. "Otherwise I shall be forced to eat them all by myself."

I reached into the box, took out a scone, and put it on my plate. I had to admit, it did smell wonderful.

I had just broken off a piece and covered it liberally with butter when a chorus of canine voices erupted in ragged harmony. The Poodles had gone on the alert. A moment later, the doorbell rang.

"Oh bother." Aunt Peg frowned. "I wonder who that is? I'm not expecting anyone."

We got up and walked to the front hall where all six Standard Poodles were waiting for us impatiently. "Mind your manners," Aunt Peg told them as she opened the door.

The young woman standing on the porch looked familiar, though I couldn't immediately place her. She had bland features and straight blond hair that was parted in the middle and hung halfway down her back. Her cropped pants were a loud floral print and her T-shirt had a picture of a Borzoi on it.

The woman's hand was raised to ring the doorbell again. Her fingers were long and delicate, and her nails were painted bright blue. Poised in the air between us, her hand appeared to be trembling.

Her name was Abby Burke, I remembered suddenly. She was a young professional handler who specialized in hound breeds. We'd never been introduced but I'd seen her around the shows.

Abby ignored the horde of big, black dogs who spilled through the open doorway and swarmed around her legs. She ignored me too. Instead she immediately zeroed in on Aunt Peg.

"You have to help me," she said.

"Of course. What's wrong?"

"It's Amanda." The words were delivered in a breathless rush. "She's missing."

Chapter 5

Y ou'd better come inside," said Aunt Peg. She took Abby's arm, nudged the Poodles out of the way, and led the girl toward the living room. Now I knew things were serious. Aunt Peg never entertained in her living room. It was too far removed from the food.

It was left to me to count canine noses and shut the front door. By the time I joined them, Abby and Aunt Peg were settled across from one another on a pair of matching love seats. Abby was perched on the edge of the cushion. Her fingers were twisting in her lap.

Faith knew something was wrong. She came and pressed her body against my legs. Considering Aunt Peg's response to Abby's announcement, I was pretty worried myself, but I gave the Poodle a reassuring pat anyway. There was no use in all of us being on edge.

"Who's Amanda?" I asked.

Abby turned to look at me. She seemed surprised to see me standing there. Maybe she was wondering who I was. Then she and Aunt Peg both answered at the same time.

"My twin sister," Abby told me.

"My dog sitter," Aunt Peg said.

Okay, right. *That* Amanda.

The Poodles were getting settled around us on the floor. I perched on the broad arm of a nearby upholstered chair. I knew that Aunt Peg's travel schedule would have been impossible without the assistance of someone whom she could trust implicitly to take great care of the Poodles in her absence. And Amanda fit the bill perfectly.

The young woman was capable, caring, and very well qualified, having been raised in a family as canine-centric as Aunt Peg's. Before their retirement to Pinehurst, both of Amanda's parents had been successful handlers and popular fixtures on the show circuit. Amanda had grown up training puppies, cleaning x-pens, and spending every weekend at the shows.

As Aunt Peg's emergency contact, I'd met Amanda once about a year earlier. Fortunately there had never been a reason for the dog sitter to get in touch with me since. I'd had no idea that Amanda had a twin sister. Nor that her sister was a member of the dog show community.

Not unexpectedly, Aunt Peg wasn't at all surprised by that information. "Tell me what's happened," she said calmly. "Why do you think Amanda is missing? I just talked to her."

Abby nearly bounced out of her seat. "When?"

Aunt Peg thought back. "Just a few days ago. Probably Friday. I'll be judging in Wisconsin next month and I wanted to confirm that she'd be available. Amanda said the dates I needed her would be fine."

"You see?" Abby said urgently. "That's precisely the problem. Amanda wasn't planning on going anywhere. And now she's disappeared."

"What makes you think that?" I asked.

"She and I were supposed to have dinner last night. She didn't show up and she didn't get in touch with me to cancel either."

"That doesn't sound like Amanda." Aunt Peg frowned. "She's always been totally reliable."

"I know. Right?" Abby's gaze flew back and forth between Aunt Peg and me. "Amanda's predictable that way. She's always right where she's supposed to be. Last night I called her to see what was up, but she never called me back. I started to get worried, so I drove over to her apartment to check on her. Amanda's car was sitting in the driveway, but she wasn't there."

"Are you sure?" I asked.

"Yes, I have a key. I let myself in and had a look around. It's a small place, just two rooms over a garage at a lady's house in Weston. The apartment was empty. That doesn't make sense. Where would Amanda have gone without her car?"

"Did you ask the woman who owns the house if she'd seen her?" I asked.

Abby swallowed heavily. "I would have but it wasn't possible."

67

"Why not?" Aunt Peg wanted to know.

"You were at the dog show yesterday, weren't you?"

Aunt Peg and I nodded together.

"It was Jasmine Crane's house. That's where Amanda's been living."

Oh. *Oh wow.* That got my attention in a hurry.

Aunt Peg's too. We shared a startled glance.

First to speak, Aunt Peg merely said, "How did that come about?"

"We've known Jasmine for a while," Abby replied. "Back in the old days, our parents handled some of her dogs. Even then, I already knew that showing dogs was going to be my life. But Amanda, she couldn't wait to get away."

"How come?" I asked.

Abby shrugged. "All the shows we were dragged to when we were kids inspired me. But Amanda had the opposite reaction. They just made her determined to do something else. Anything else. She grabbed the first job she could get, and ended up selling clothes in the mall."

"It's hard to live on that kind of salary in Fairfield County," Aunt Peg mentioned.

"Tell me about it," said Abby. "Jasmine told Amanda she had a couple of rooms over her garage. She'd been using the space as a studio or something but now it was empty. If Amanda wanted to fix the place up, make it habitable, she could have it at a reduced rent. Amanda jumped at the chance."

"How long ago was that?" I asked.

"Last year sometime?" Abby didn't look certain. "She got her boyfriend to help out. The two of them put in a bathroom and added a little kitchen. She's been living there ever since."

"What about the job at the mall?" I asked. "Does she still have it? Did you check with them to see if she showed up this morning?"

"No, that's long gone. Once Amanda moved into the apartment, she and Jasmine got to be friends. Pretty soon, Jasmine convinced Amanda that with her background and skills, she could make more money pet-sitting than she could selling dresses. And it turned out that she was right."

"Back to the boyfriend," Aunt Peg interjected. "What does he have to say for himself?"

"Rick was the first person I called. I figured if anyone would know where Amanda was, it would be him. He told me he hadn't seen her since yesterday afternoon at the dog show. I guess she'd been there helping him."

"You guess?" I said.

"She does that sometimes. Weird, huh? After Amanda was so determined to get away from the whole show scene, Rick Fanelli manages to convince her to come back anyway whenever he decides he needs a free assistant. Thank God I don't have a boyfriend telling me what to do."

"Rick Fanelli," Aunt Peg mused. "That name sounds familiar."

"You've probably seen him around the shows," Abby told her. "Tall, skinny, guy? Decent looking for a geek? Amanda is just besotted. I don't see it myself, but supposedly it's true love."

"What does Rick do?" I asked.

"He's a handler. Kind of." Abby stopped just short of rolling her eyes, but her disdain was perfectly clear. "I think it's something he fell into because he thought it looked like an easy way to make money. Which, of course, it isn't. When his schedule is tight, Amanda goes along to give him a hand."

"So they were together yesterday at the show," I said. "Did Rick know about your plans with Amanda for last night?"

"I guess so. He said he dropped Amanda off at her apartment after the show, then went back to his own place. He hasn't heard from her since."

"Is it unusual for her not to be in touch with him?" Aunt Peg asked.

"Apparently, no. At least not that he would admit to me. Rick just said 'Amanda is her own woman.' Like he was regurgitating some stupid platitude he'd heard on *The View*. It didn't seem to bother him in the slightest that he didn't know where she was."

"But it bothers you," Aunt Peg said gently.

"Of course it does," Abby replied. "Amanda's

not just my sister, she's my twin. I can't imagine her going away somewhere without letting me know. Something has to be wrong."

"When was the last time you saw Amanda?" I asked.

"Last Tuesday. She came over to my place for dinner. We thought it would be warm enough to cook outdoors so we bought hamburgers and set up the grill." Abby smiled at the memory. "Then the sun went down and it turned cold. Like really cold. I was freezing my butt off, flipping burgers with one hand and guzzling wine with the other. Amanda was laughing at me from inside the kitchen. She kept popping out with the wine bottle to refill my glass."

It was nice to see Abby finally start to relax, I thought. "And Amanda seemed fine to you then?"

"Yes, same as ever. If something had been wrong, I know she would have told me."

"And now she's vanished," Aunt Peg said with a frown. "And the woman from whom she rents her apartment has been murdered."

"So it's true then." Abby sounded resigned. "I heard that Jasmine died yesterday. That news was all over the show grounds. But I wasn't sure about the rest of it. I'm sure you know how unreliable dog show gossip can be. Was she really strangled with one of her own leashes?"

"I'm afraid so," said Aunt Peg. "Jasmine's death wasn't an accident. Which tells me that you're right to be concerned about your sister's whereabouts."

"You should talk to the police," I said to Abby.

"I've already done that. I called this morning and talked to a detective in Weston." Abruptly she stood up and began to pace. That was no mean feat considering how many Poodles were lying on the floor around us.

"And?" Aunt Peg prompted.

"I didn't accomplish a thing. The problem is that Amanda's an adult. And that she hasn't even been missing for a day. And that her apartment wasn't trashed or anything. And her car hasn't been stolen. The detective I spoke to told me to calm down."

Abby spun back around to face us. Apparently the detective's advice had had the opposite effect. "You know," she snapped, "like I hadn't thought of that myself."

Several of the dogs in the room lifted their heads as Abby's voice rose. Poodles are naturally empathetic, and the tenor of conversation was beginning to worry them too.

"The detective said maybe the battery on Amanda's phone had run down. And that she might have gone for a walk or something, and doesn't know I'm trying to reach her. Apparently nothing that's happened is reason enough for them to file a missing persons report."

"That can't be right," Aunt Peg said sharply.

"Not under these circumstances. Did you explain about what happened to Jasmine?"

"Of course I did. At least, I tried to. But what little I knew was pretty sketchy. I was busy showing dogs all day, so I didn't even hear about it until after Best in Show. Plus Jasmine died in eastern Connecticut and I was talking to a detective all the way on the other side of the state. So it's like, different jurisdictions or precincts or something. . . ."

Abby threw up her hands in frustration. I could sympathize. There were times I'd felt much the same way when dealing with the police.

I watched her slowly exhale, then draw in a deep breath. Her gaze dropped to the floor as if she'd suddenly become aware of all the Poodles in the room. Legs folding beneath her, Abby crouched down and wound her arms around Willow's neck. The Poodle shifted slightly and curled her body into the embrace.

When in doubt, hug a dog. That's my mantra. It looked as though it was Abby's too.

When she looked up again a minute later, Abby was once more in control of her emotions. She gave Willow one last pat and went back to the love seat. Then she sat down and looked directly at Aunt Peg. "So that's why I'm here. I need your help. You have a reputation. Everybody knows you're good at getting to the bottom of things."

"Perhaps you mean Melanie." Aunt Peg nodded my way.

"Either one of you," Abby said quickly. "Or both of you, I don't care. I just need someone who will believe me when I say that something's wrong. Peg, you *know* Amanda. She's worked for you for more than a year. You know she's not some flakey, flighty girl who would just disappear for no reason."

"Quite right," Aunt Peg agreed. "This kind of behavior certainly seems out of character."

"So then you'll help me find her?" Abby stared hard at the two of us, willing us to give her the response she wanted. *"Please?"*

When I was a child, I'd always wanted a sister. Now I was fortunate to have several women friends who were every bit as close to me as a sibling would have been. If something had happened to one of them, I would have done everything in my power to fix it.

Now, gazing at Abby, I knew how she was feeling. There was no way I could turn her down.

"We'll see what we can do," I said.

I never got to finish my cranberry scone. Indeed, after listening to what Abby'd had to say, I'd forgotten all about it. Before she left, I'd already decided where I was going to start my search for her missing twin: Amanda's apartment. Abby fished her key out of her purse and handed it over.

As I was loading Faith in the Volvo, Aunt Peg came running outside with a small bundle in her hand. She'd wrapped the scone in a napkin for me. Faith and I shared it on the drive to Weston.

I also called Sam and let him know that I was going to be home a little later than expected.

"What's in Weston?" he asked.

"Jasmine Crane's house. But it isn't what you think."

"Oh?" He chuckled softly. Living with me has turned that man into a skeptic.

"There's been a new development," I said. "Aunt Peg's dog sitter has disappeared."

"Her dog sitter." There was a pause as he considered that. "Didn't we meet her once?"

"Yes, it was a while ago though. Her name is Amanda Burke. Her sister is Abby Burke, who shows hounds."

I could have described Abby physically, but we were dog people. Giving Sam her breed affiliation instead worked as a handy short cut. I knew he'd be able to picture her immediately.

"I didn't know those two were related," he said.

"I didn't either. Abby showed up at Aunt Peg's house this afternoon to tell her that Amanda was missing. And—get this—it turns out that Amanda lives over Jasmine Crane's garage."

"That's an interesting coincidence," Sam mused. "How long has Amanda been missing?"

"Since yesterday evening—"

I heard a loud *thunk,* then Kevin's voice broke into the conversation. "Hi, Mom!"

"Hi, sweetie. What happened to your father?"

"I threw him a ball so we could play catch and he dropped the phone. Do you want to talk to Bud?"

"No, I—"

"Does Faith want to talk to Bud? He's right here."

"No, thank you. Put Daddy back on, okay?"

"Sorry about that." Sam was breathing heavily. "I didn't see the baseball coming. And Kev has a better arm than you'd expect on a four-year-old. Unfortunately . . . the ball . . . hit me in the wrong place."

"Oh. That's too bad." Even though I knew it was wrong, I almost laughed anyway.

"Don't you dare laugh," said Sam.

"Of course not. I wouldn't dream of it."

"What do you expect to find at Jasmine's house?"

"Not her house," I corrected. "Just the apartment over her garage. I have a key."

"I guess that's a good thing." Sam didn't sound convinced. Or maybe he was still trying to catch his breath. "Stay out of trouble."

"I'll do my best," I replied.

As if either one of us believed that.

Chapter 6

Faith and I took the Merritt Parkway to Westport, then headed north. Picturesque Weston looked like a Norman Rockwell painting of the quintessential small New England town. The community was mostly residential, with houses well spaced on generous, private lots.

I rolled down the car window as we slowed to look for Jasmine's address. It was a beautiful April day, and spring was in the air. On either side of the road, crocuses were beginning to appear. Tree branches overhead were starting to bud. The warmth of the sun on my face felt wonderful.

Jasmine's ranch-style home was situated on a slight rise at the end of a curving driveway. The house was painted dark red with black shutters. The focal point of the paneled front door was a shiny brass knocker shaped like a fox's head. Twenty feet from the house was a matching, detached two car garage. The second story above it looked barely big enough to house an apartment, but its peaked roof had skylights on either side.

A white Toyota was parked in front of the garage. I assumed that was Amanda's car. But I was surprised to also see another vehicle in Jasmine's driveway. A navy blue minivan had been pulled up next to the house. Its sliding door was sitting open. The sun glinted off an elaborate key chain, dangling from the key in the van's ignition.

"That's odd," I said to Faith. "I wonder who's here?"

She stood up on the seat and took a look. Faith likes meeting new people no matter who they are. Obviously she didn't share my concern.

I'd only planned to have a look around Amanda's apartment. I'd had no intention of going anywhere near Jasmine's house. But the only place to park was behind the minivan, effectively blocking it in place. Not only that, but I didn't want whoever was inside Jasmine's house to think that I was skulking around the property illicitly.

Unless of course that person was doing the same.

"You'd better come with me," I said to Faith. I was thinking that there might be safety in numbers. She was thinking, *Yay, an outing!* So we were both happy to get out of the car together.

Not nearly as trusting as the minivan's owner, I locked the Volvo carefully behind us. As I turned toward the garage, a woman came walking around the corner from the rear of the house.

She was middle-aged and had a wiry build. Her frizzy brown hair was liberally peppered with strands of gray. At first glance, the most notable thing about the woman was the large, quilt-covered bundle she held cradled in her arms. Then she drew nearer, and I saw that the side of her face was swollen and she appeared to have a black eye.

Okay, that trumped the bundle thing.

Gaze trained downward as she made her way across the uneven ground, it took the woman a moment to realize she was no longer alone. Then she stopped so abruptly that the bulky parcel she was carrying shifted in her arms. It slipped from her grasp and started to fall.

Without thinking, I stepped forward to help. Her glare stopped me in my tracks.

"Who are you?" she demanded.

"Melanie Travis." My tone was slightly more civil, but not much. "Who are you?"

"Sadie Foster. I'm a friend of Jasmine's. I don't think I've seen you around here before."

"Maybe not," I agreed. I wasn't about to offer any more information than I had to before I found out why the woman was removing things from Jasmine's home. "What's that you're carrying?"

"None of your business."

Suddenly the heavy bundle shifted again. As Sadie's hands scrambled for purchase, I leapt forward to grab it before it could drop. For a moment, we both held on. Then she reset her grip and I stepped back.

"Thank you," she said grudgingly. "I would have hated for these to hit the ground."

Close up, Sadie's face looked even worse than it had from afar. The delicate skin above her eye was so puffy that the lid was nearly swollen shut. Purple and yellow bruises bloomed along the top of her cheek. The injury looked recent. And painful.

"Are you all right?" I asked.

Sadie blinked, then winced. Even that small movement looked like a mistake. "Yeah, I'm fine. More or less." She walked past me to the minivan and set the quilt-covered items down on the floor just inside the door. "I tripped over a dog."

Faith had started to follow Sadie across the driveway. Now I snapped my fingers and returned her to my side.

Sadie saw the move and smiled ruefully. "A little dog. Not something big and pretty like your Poodle there. I guess anyone who owns a dog like that can't be all bad. Maybe we'd better start over." She walked toward me and extended her hand. "Hi, I'm Sadie Foster."

Her fingers were callused and her grip was firm. I returned her smile and said, "Melanie Travis. I'm pleased to meet you. And this is Faith."

"How do you know Jasmine?" Sadie asked.

"I show Poodles." I would have elaborated but

Sadie was already nodding. She'd immediately made the connection. "I've always thought that Jasmine's artwork was beautiful."

"I guess you know about what happened," Sadie said.

"Yes." There didn't seem to be any point in mentioning how close I'd actually been to the tragic event.

"I've known Jasmine forever," Sadie told me. "Someone called me with the news last night and I could hardly believe it. What a shock right out of the blue. Then my next thought was, *What about Hazel and Toby?* I wondered if anyone was looking out for them."

"Hazel and Toby?" I looked around. I hoped they weren't Jasmine's children.

"Jasmine's two dogs," Sadie said. "Her fur babies, as she calls them. Hazel and Toby are just a couple of pound puppies, but Jasmine couldn't have loved them more if they were Best in Show winners. When she left here yesterday morning, I know it never occurred to her that she wouldn't be back last night to take care of them."

"Is that how you fell?" I asked.

Sadie grimaced. "That was just a stupid thing. It was late and those pups were waiting anxiously for Jasmine to come home, and then I showed up instead. They've known me for years, but they still got all skittish for some reason. I had to chase them all around the house before I could even get my hands on them. I slipped in the kitchen and caught my face on the side of a counter."

"It was kind of you to come and take care of them," I said.

"If I hadn't done it, nobody else was going to. Jasmine doesn't have any family that I know of. I couldn't stand the thought of those two sitting here by themselves all night. I took them home with me and gave them a good meal. They'll be safe with me for a while anyway."

"That was last night," I said. "Why did you come back today?"

"I woke up this morning, looked at Hazel and Toby, and thought, *What about Jasmine's paintings?* They might not be living creatures, but that art was Jasmine's life's work. I couldn't just leave it sitting here in an empty house either."

I gestured toward the bundle in the minivan. "So that's what's wrapped inside the quilt?"

Sadie nodded. "That's just the first load. There'll be several more to follow. This stuff is valuable. Who knows, maybe even more so now that Jasmine is gone. I'm going to box it up and store it somewhere out of harm's way."

It was one thing for Sadie to have rescued Jasmine's dogs, I thought. But taking possession of her artwork was something else entirely. The woman appeared to have made rather a large assumption about what she might be entitled to do.

"I notice you're not using the front door," I said. "How did you get into Jasmine's house?"

Sadie peered up at me with a scowl on her face. "Don't go thinking about anything nefarious now. Everything I'm doing here is on the up-and-up. Jasmine keeps a couple of spare keys on a hook in her garage. Would I know about that if she didn't want me to look after things in her absence? There's one key for her house and one for the garage apartment."

That sounded all right, I thought. *Maybe.*

"That's Amanda Burke's apartment," I said. "She's actually the reason I'm here. Do you know Amanda?"

"I guess I've met her once or twice. She seems like a nice enough kid. But if you've come to see her, you're out of luck. I'm pretty sure she's not home."

We both lifted our gazes to the apartment's windows. Everything was dark and still.

"Amanda's sister is worried about her," I said. "She's been trying to get in touch with her. You wouldn't happen to know where she is, would you?"

"How would I know something like that? I'm not sure I even remembered the girl's name until you reminded me just now. Wherever she went is no business of mine."

"In that case, I'm sorry to have bothered you about it. Faith and I are going to go up and have a look around the apartment."

"Oh yeah?" Sadie tipped her head to one side. I knew she was remembering my earlier query. "How do you think you're going to get in?"

I supposed I deserved that. I pulled Abby's key out of my pocket and showed it to her. "This is Amanda's sister's key. She's the one who sent me here."

"Sent you to do what?"

"Try to figure out where Amanda disappeared to."

"Disappeared." Sadie snorted. "Kids come and go all the time these days. Nothing unusual about that. Mark my words, she'll be back in a day or two, probably wondering what all the fuss was about."

I hoped Sadie was right, but I wasn't nearly as sure as she was.

Together Faith and I headed for the narrow wooden staircase that snaked up the outside of the garage wall. At the foot of the steps, I paused and looked back. Sadie was once again on her way around the back of Jasmine's house. Presumably she was going to pick up another load.

"Do you have permission to take Jasmine's paintings?" I asked.

Sadie stopped and turned. "Think about it. Who would you expect me to get permission from?"

There was that.

"I don't know," I said. "Her family. Maybe her lawyer?"

"Jasmine's never mentioned any family to me, but if her relatives show up wanting to pick through her possessions, I'll bring the stuff back. At least when her art's with me I know it's in a safe place. Which is a lot better than the alternative."

Sadie nodded toward the upstairs apartment. "You think that young girl has gone missing? I'll tell you what's missing. The rest of Jasmine's paintings."

I gazed at her in confusion. "Which paintings are you talking about?"

"The ones she took with her to the dog show. The ones that were on display in her booth. Jasmine's a born saleswoman. She always shows off her best stuff at events. Artwork and leashes both. She couldn't have packed up her own booth last night. So where did all her valuables end up?"

Good question, I thought. And one more thing to look in to when I got a chance.

Unfortunately, my search of Amanda's apartment failed to provide me with any answers.

The only thing Faith and I discovered—obvious as soon as we went inside—was that Amanda Burke was an indifferent housekeeper. Faith

85

didn't seem too perturbed by that and, frankly, neither was I. It wasn't my living space that was covered in a layer of dust and badly in need of vacuuming.

The whole apartment consisted of two small rooms. One was a combination living room/ kitchen. The second was a bedroom, just big enough to hold a double bed and narrow, upright dresser. A tiny bathroom was wedged into a corner.

Amanda's bed was unmade. There was a pillow on the floor and the bed covers had been kicked to the foot of the mattress. A stack of dirty dishes was piled in the sink. I wondered if I was seeing signs that Amanda had left in a hurry, or simply more evidence of negligent housekeeping skills.

The only decoration on any of the walls was a vibrant oil painting of two Foxhound puppies, hanging above a threadbare couch. One tricolor pup was playing with a rubber ball. The second was behind it, pudgy body rearing high in the air, ready to pounce. The style of the lovely portrait looked familiar. I wondered if it was one of Jasmine's. I leaned in and took a closer look, but the canvas wasn't signed.

A table in the middle of the room appeared to function as Amanda's desk. I sifted through the papers that were piled on top of it and found nothing of interest. I peeked beneath several gossip magazines scattered across the couch.

I opened the drawers of her dresser and looked underneath the sink. I even checked inside her medicine cabinet.

My search revealed no cell phone, no computer, no tablet of any kind. Nor did I find a calendar or address book. Surely a woman who ran her own pet-sitting business would have need of both?

But aside from that omission, nothing struck me as out of the ordinary. If Amanda had packed a bag before leaving, I saw no evidence of it. Her closet and dresser were filled with clothes. A toothbrush sat in a glass next to her bathroom sink. A contact lens case and a bottle of solution were within easy reach.

There was milk in the refrigerator and three oranges in a bowl on the counter. A book lay open on Amanda's bedside table. The place looked as though she'd left the previous morning to go to the dog show, with every intention of returning home later that evening.

Amanda hadn't needed her car to get to the show, and it was still sitting downstairs parked in front of the garage. Rick told Abby that he'd dropped Amanda back at home last night. But what if he hadn't?

Suppose Rick and Amanda started the day on good terms, then argued over something that caused them to go their separate ways? That seemed like a possibility until I realized that if Amanda had been stuck and needed a ride home, she could have asked her sister, or even Aunt Peg. She would surely have known that plenty of other exhibitors would be heading back to Fairfield County.

My thoughts cycled back to the missing computer. It seemed unlikely that Amanda would have taken it with her to the dog show. Especially as she planned to be gone for less than a day. Was that more proof that she had returned home after the show and then gone out again? But if that was the case, why hadn't she taken her car?

Wherever Amanda was, she surely would have had her phone with her. So why wasn't she taking her sister's calls? Abby had been trying to reach her for nearly twenty-four hours now. It hardly took any time to recharge a battery—unless Amanda was somewhere she didn't have access to electricity.

"This is ridiculous," I said to Faith. "All I have is questions and not a single answer."

The Standard Poodle was sitting by the door waiting for me to finish looking around. She offered a gentle woof in reply. In her world, questions are easy. Her answer is always yes.

We left the apartment together and I locked the door behind me. We'd been inside for less than half an hour, but the navy blue minivan was gone. Sadie must have finished what she was doing and left.

Rather than asking me to move the Volvo, it

looked as though she'd driven across the lawn to get out. I looked at the ruts she'd left in the soft turf and sighed. It wasn't as though Jasmine would care.

I wished I'd thought to ask Sadie for her contact information when we'd been speaking earlier. On the surface, Jasmine Crane's death had nothing to do with me. I was only trying to figure out why Amanda Burke had disappeared. But I couldn't help but feel that the two events were inextricably intertwined.

Chapter 7

To make up for my extended absence that afternoon, I arrived home with two extra-large pizzas. One had pepperoni and sausage on it, the other was covered with vegetables. By now I'd told myself that the veggie option was healthy so many times that I'd almost begun to believe it.

"Mommy's home!" Kev met me in the hallway as I came in from the garage. Faith ran past him to look for the other Poodles. "I missed you."

A sentiment sure to warm a mother's heart.

My son's next words rose on a wail. "You were supposed to bring my project to school when you picked me up!"

Damn. I'd forgotten all about that.

Kevin's preschool class was building a six-inch-tall chess set on which they were going to learn to play the game. Every student was expected to contribute two pieces. The previous Friday, Kevin and I had constructed a rook and a bishop out of papier-mâché. On Saturday while Sam and Davey had been bathing Augie, we'd painted both pieces a glossy black. They were supposed to have been delivered this afternoon.

"Do I smell pizza?" Sam came into the hall.

Bud was hot on his heels. The little dog had been half-starved when we'd picked him up after he was tossed from a car. Though there was no shortage of food in his life now, Bud was always ready to eat. He probably smelled the pizza too.

I sent Sam a beseeching look. "Please tell me you stepped in and saved the day."

"I saved the day," Sam replied automatically. It was clear he had no idea what I was talking about. "At least I hope I did."

"Kevin's chess pieces. Did you take them to school?"

"Daddy to the rescue," Kevin crowed happily.

I guess that answered my question.

"I saw them sitting on the kitchen counter and figured they were supposed to go somewhere," Sam said. "So I put them in the car. It's probably just dumb luck that they ended up in the right place. What kind of preschool gives kids home-work anyway?"

I shrugged. "The same kind that expects them to learn chess?"

That was life in Fairfield County. We weren't just in the fast lane, we were in the rocket zone. The only reason Kevin wasn't already half fluent in Mandarin was because I'd opted out of a neighborhood learning group when he was three. The other mothers told me that Kevin would blame me later for limiting his prospects in life. *Seriously?*

All I knew was that I wanted to raise smart, respectful, happy children. And that I was tired of being pressured to keep my boys perpetually ahead of the curve. I had a sneaking suspicion that someday that darn curve was going to turn around and bite us all in the butt.

Davey set the table. Sam threw together a salad. As we sat down to eat, four Standard Poodles materialized in the kitchen to join Bud around the table.

Faith and Eve sacked out on the floor. Augie lay beneath Davey's chair. Raven and Bud went to Kevin. Even without looking, I would have been able to guess who was missing.

"Davey, where's Tar?"

"How should I know?" Davey was sliding a piece of pizza out of the box onto his plate. When silence greeted *that* remark, he stopped and glanced up. "Sorry. I'll go look."

"No, you guys start eating. I'll go." I rose from my seat.

"Tar's upstairs in the bathroom," Kevin said, munching happily on a green pepper. "I closed the door."

All heads turned his way.

"Why would you do that?" I asked.

"Tar's all wet."

"All what?" I must have misheard. Already on my way to the stairs, I spun back around.

"Tar had a bath," Kevin informed me.

I looked at Sam. Sam looked back at me. We appeared to be equally baffled.

What was wrong with that picture? I'd been out all afternoon. So there was a good reason why I had no idea what had been going on in my house. Sam, however, was supposed to have been in charge.

"Who gave Tar a bath?" Sam choked out the words. Belatedly he was realizing that he'd missed something important.

"I did!" Kev squealed. "I used bubble bath and everything."

"Bubble bath," I repeated faintly.

"I'd better go see." Sam stood up as well.

It was left to Davey to ask the pertinent question that both Sam and I had overlooked. "Kev, why did you give Tar a bath?"

"Ummm . . ." Something was up. My younger son doesn't have a poker face. And Kevin was clearly considering how much information he wanted to divulge. "Tar might have gotten into my finger paints."

"Oh crap," I said.

Davey started laughing.

Sam was already running for the stairs. I was right behind him.

At least for the adults in the house, dinner was going to be delayed.

There were days when it was almost a relief to get up in the morning and go to work. Howard

Academy was, for the most part, a calm and orderly establishment. Classes ran on schedule. Teachers and students obeyed the rules. I was quite certain that never once in the exalted history of the school had anyone ever been tempted to dip a black Standard Poodle into red and yellow paint.

Sam and I had spent almost all of Monday evening dealing with the aftermath of that adventure. I'd intended to call Amanda's boy-friend, Rick Fanelli, after dinner. Not surprisingly, I never got around to it. I tried him several times on Tuesday afternoon, leaving messages each time. Rick never returned my calls.

On Wednesday after school, I decided to head in a different direction. The catalog from the weekend's dog show listed Mrs. Gwen Kimble of Branford, Connecticut, as show chairman. I could have done an internet search to find out more about Mrs. Kimble, but Google is no replacement for Aunt Peg's treasure trove of knowledge.

Of course Aunt Peg's assistance comes at a price. She doesn't offer up anything until her own curiosity has been satisfied. But unfortunately when I called her as Faith and I were leaving Howard Academy, it hardly took any time at all to summarize what I'd learned at Amanda's apartment.

"That's it?" Aunt Peg made no attempt to hide her disappointment.

"I'm afraid so."

"Then I suppose it's no wonder you didn't bother to get back to me. You didn't accomplish much, did you?"

I had no reply for that. Aunt Peg didn't care. She'd already moved on.

"Put Faith on the phone," she said. "Maybe she noticed something you missed."

How Aunt Peg knew I was in my car, coasting down the HA driveway with Faith on the seat beside me, I had no idea. Though I wouldn't have ruled out the possibility that she and Faith were communicating on some telepathic level known only to dogs. And of course Aunt Peg.

I did not put Faith on the phone. Instead I said, "I want to talk to Gwen Kimble."

"Gwen Kimble?" Aunt Peg sounded pleased that I'd managed to surprise her. "Why do you want to see her?"

"She was show chairman of last week's show."

"And because of that you suspect she knows something about Amanda's disappearance?"

"No, but she might know something about the circumstances surrounding Jasmine's death. You know as well as I do that those two things have to be connected. I want to ask Gwen what she knows about Jasmine, and what went on at the show after we left."

"I'm sure Gwen will have plenty to say," Aunt Peg replied. "It's quite clever of you to think of her. I knew there was a reason why I allow you to be my relative."

The reason was because in her youth she had married my father's brother. But whatever.

"I'm assuming you can tell me something about Gwen? And put me in touch with her?"

"Whippets," Aunt Peg said, as if that was all I needed to know.

"She's a breeder?"

"She used to be. Now she mostly runs the Sedgefield Kennel Club. And of course, their yearly show. I haven't spoken to Gwen in a while," Aunt Peg mused. "But I imagine she'll remember me."

As a member of the dog community, Gwen would have to be entirely scatterbrained not to. Aunt Peg was difficult to ignore. And quite impossible to forget.

"Do you think she'd talk to me?" I asked. "Maybe this afternoon?"

"I can't see why not," Aunt Peg said blithely. "I'll call her and set something up."

While I waited to hear what the plan was going to be, I drove to Stamford and dropped Faith off at home. I figured she'd be more comfortable there than riding all the way to Branford with me.

The decision turned out to be a wise one. Because when I arrived at Gwen's house at the appointed time later that afternoon, it was clear that the woman didn't need any additional dogs coming to visit. There were Whippets every-where.

It's often pointed out that people tend to resemble their dogs. That was definitely true in Gwen Kimble's case. Though she looked to be in her sixties, Gwen was as lithe and slender as a willow. Her short gray hair formed a sleek cap around a face that was creased with laugh lines. Her movements were smooth, refined, and made with total assurance.

As for the multitude of Whippets, several were racing around Gwen's fenced backyard. Others accompanied her to the door to greet me. The remainder were reclining on her living room furniture, draped about like ornamental accessories.

With their lean bodies and distinctive outlines, the elegant hounds managed to convey an impression of grace and power even when they weren't moving. I saw white dogs, fawn colored ones, brindles, and every shade in between. Alert and curious, the Whippets checked me over thoroughly.

Gwen smiled fondly at the assembled group. "Whippets are like potato chips. You can't have just one."

"So I see." I smiled too. "How many do you have?"

"Oh dear me, I have no idea. I gave up counting a long time ago." Gwen waved me toward a plump chair that was surprisingly Whippet free.

"Please sit down. Peg tells me you want to talk about the show."

One of the Whippets slipped down off the couch and came to investigate. First she sniffed my pants delicately. I reached down to let her smell my hand, and her ears flicked forward, then quickly pressed back against her skull.

I must have passed inspection because the Whippet lifted one front paw and placed it lightly on the edge of the seat cushion. A moment later, a sudden graceful leap landed her in my lap.

I laughed and cupped my arms around her body so she wouldn't fall off my legs. I needn't have worried. The Whippet was as steady in the chair as I was.

"That's Coco," Gwen told me. "She thinks every piece of furniture in the house belongs to her. Feel free to put her back on the floor if you'd be more comfortable."

"Oh no, we're fine." Coco's coat was warm and silky smooth beneath my fingers. She sniffed my chin and the front of my sweater, then turned a small circle and lay down across my lap.

Gwen's eyes twinkled as she watched the interaction. We both noticed when a second Whippet rose to her feet. She tipped her lean head in my direction, then extended her slender front legs, and stretched languidly.

"You stay right where you are," Gwen told the lissome hound before turning back to me. "Our breed standard says that Whippets are friendly. It might be an understatement. If you're not careful, you'll end up with a chairful."

"That's fine by me." I stroked the bitch in my lap. "I love dogs."

"Peg tells me you have Standard Poodles?"

"Yes. She and I were both showing under Walter Logan last weekend."

"Did you win?"

"Aunt Peg was Winners Bitch. My son's dog was Reserve."

"A good day then." Abruptly Gwen realized what she'd said and frowned. "Well, not entirely."

"That's why I'm here," I said. "How much did Aunt Peg tell you?"

"Only that a woman who dog-sits for her had disappeared and you were trying to track her down. I confess I have no idea how I might be able to help with that."

"The woman who's missing is Amanda Burke. Her sister, Abby, is a professional handler."

Gwen nodded. "I know Abby. She's handled Whippets for friends of mine. She does a lovely job. I don't believe I've ever met her sister though."

"Apparently Amanda doesn't usually go to shows. But she was there on Sunday helping her boyfriend, Rick Fanelli."

"I'm afraid I still don't know what this has to do with me."

"Amanda lives in a garage apartment in

Weston. The woman who owns the house and rents her that apartment is Jasmine Crane."

"Oh, I see." Gwen closed her eyes briefly. "That was a terrible thing. It cast a pall over the whole event."

To say the very least, I thought.

"I'm not sure if you're aware of this, but Aunt Peg was the one who found her."

"No, I wasn't." Gwen looked dismayed. "That must have been ghastly for her."

"I'm reasonably certain that Amanda's disappearance had something to do with Jasmine's death," I said. "You were there at the show. Do you have any ideas about why someone might have wanted to kill her?"

"Me?" Gwen's expression slid from dismay to shock. "No, of course not. How would I know anything about that?"

Her quick response didn't surprise me. I've heard similar denials numerous times before. But I've also learned that when you poke around a little, you often end up learning something entirely different.

"How well did you know Jasmine?" I asked.

"In her role as vendor and mine as show chairman, we'd had occasion to speak."

The Sedgefield dog show was a sizeable event. Which meant that a large show committee would have been needed to put it all together. So I was quite certain there'd been a committee member in charge of dealing with the needs of individual concessionaires. In the normal way of things, a job like that would have fallen well below Gwen Kimble's pay grade.

"Is that the way it usually works? Did you speak with all the vendors?"

"No." Gwen's chin lifted. I suspected I'd struck a nerve. "It wasn't usual. Not at all. But Jasmine was the type of person who liked to make her own rules."

"How did that affect you?" I leaned forward in my seat. Coco shifted in my lap, then quickly resettled.

"Every year we have a set amount of room we can allot for concessions. Originally spaces were offered on a first-come, first-serve basis. But as you might imagine, that became problematic and now placement is assigned by the show committee. It's much easier if each vendor knows ahead of time precisely where their booth is going to be located."

"How is placement determined?" I asked curiously.

"In most cases, by seniority. Vendors who've been loyal supporters through the years get the choicest spots. Then the larger retailers—those who will pay a higher rent—are also well situated. Vendors with small, boutique-type concessions are always made aware that they may be tucked into a less desirable space."

"Where did Jasmine fit in?"

"If you had asked her that question, she would have said that she deserved to be wherever she wanted." Gwen's lips pursed in annoyance. "Did you know her?"

"No, not really. I'd browsed around her booth a few times, but that was the extent of our interaction."

"Jasmine possessed an exaggerated sense of her own importance. It always seemed to me that she felt her artistic ability ought to entitle her to special privileges. The reason I ended up dealing with her was because none of the other committee members could control her."

"What do you mean?"

"Jasmine was very firm about how she felt she should be treated. She expected everyone to indulge her every whim. And when they didn't, she was apt to throw a fit. Most people gave in to Jasmine's demands because placating her was *always* the easier option."

I ran my hand down the length of Coco's well-muscled body and waited for Gwen to continue. It didn't take long.

"No matter which location Jasmine's booth was assigned, she was bound to be unhappy. Jasmine insisted that her exceptional offerings deserved a preferred position. When we were unable to accommodate her, she would retaliate by extending her boundaries and encroaching into neighboring concessions. It got so that none of our other vendors wanted to be near her."

"That must have been annoying," I said.

"It was. And that wasn't the only problem. Jasmine would always want to renegotiate terms. Everyone else was satisfied with our standard contract, but she demanded a discount. Every year we had to have a long, drawn out discussion about it. It was a huge hassle and a major waste of time."

"Would she get a discount?"

"Not when I was in charge," Gwen said with satisfaction. "This year I told her she could either sign the contract or stay home. It was all the same to me. And of course, she eventually capitulated. Thank God I'll never have to go through that process again."

It sounded as though Jasmine Crane had been a persistent thorn in Gwen's side. I wondered if Jasmine had caused further problems for the show committee during the course of the Sedgefield show. And whether Gwen might have been sent to deal with her.

If Jasmine was as combative as Gwen described her to be, it wasn't hard to imagine that she could have pushed her luck one time too many with somebody. Could that person have been Gwen?

I set Coco carefully aside and rose to my feet. "Thank you for taking the time to talk to me."

"You're welcome." Gwen stood up too. "Abby's

a nice girl. I wish I could be more helpful, but I'm sure you'll locate her sister soon."

As we walked to the door together, I had one last question. "On Sunday when the show was over, what became of Jasmine's things?"

Gwen shook her head, remembering. "By the end of the day, the authorities had been on the grounds for hours. The police put crime scene tape around the booth and they weren't allowing anyone access. I had to go and explain that the park was a public space and we had agreed to vacate the premises by sunset. Thankfully they'd begun to wrap up by then. Since Jasmine was found beside her car, the police took that vehicle with them, along with some other items from inside the booth."

"What about her artwork?"

"For the time being, Alan Crandall has it."

That surprised me. "The man from Creature Comforts?"

Gwen nodded. "That's right. Alan stepped in and did the show committee a huge favor. One we won't forget any time soon. Since Creature Comforts was the biggest concession on the grounds, Alan had a handful of workers with him. He also managed to find some extra room in his truck. He volunteered to dismantle Jasmine's booth, and to store it and its contents in his warehouse until someone figures out what should be done with all of it."

"Who will make that decision?" I asked.

"I don't know. And to be perfectly frank, I don't care. It's none of my business and I couldn't be happier about that. Jasmine was one problem after another when she was alive. I'm just glad I don't have to worry about her anymore."

Chapter 8

That weekend there were back-to-back dog shows at the Eastern States Exposition Center, in southern Massachusetts. The indoor venue was the perfect setting for a show. Rings were large and well matted and there was plenty of space for grooming. Along with easy set up and parking, the Big E also had great ventilation and lighting. Events at that location always drew a big entry.

This time Davey and Augie would have two shots at capturing a major. We were all hopeful that they would finally be able to make it happen.

While the rest of my family was working on that, I had plans of my own. I had no idea why Rick Fanelli had been dodging my phone calls, but he wouldn't be able to avoid me so easily when I showed up in person at his setup. I also intended to interview the vendors who'd been on either side of Jasmine's booth the previous weekend.

During the week, I had spoken with Abby twice. She'd been contacting her sister's friends and acquaintances, trying unsuccessfully to come up with a lead of her own. Abby had also gotten back in touch with the police, who were no more helpful this time than they'd been on the previous occasion. With no evidence of foul play, the authorities weren't concerned that a grown woman hadn't been in touch with her sister for a few days. I could feel Abby seething with frustration through the phone connection.

So here we all were, once again back at a dog show. Returning to the scene of the crime, so to speak. It didn't matter that this show was in a different location, or even a different state. Most of the same participants would be in attendance. With luck, I would be able to learn something useful by the end of the weekend.

In the grooming area, exhibitors often grouped themselves together by breed. Half the fun of showing dogs was having the opportunity to hang out with friends and fellow breeders before and after the competition. And on a losing day—of which there were many—that might be the best part of the event. So it was no surprise that we once again found our setup squished between those belonging to Crawford and Bertie.

"You might have left us a little more room," I grumbled to Terry as I struggled to shove Augie's crate between a pillar and a free-standing blow dryer.

Spraying up a Toy Poodle on a nearby table, he spun around in place. Terry's hair was still bright red, and today he was wearing earrings to match. On anyone else, the combination would have been jarring. Somehow Terry made it work.

"Oh please. It's not as if you need the space. You people only have one dog to get ready for the ring. I could do that standing on my head."

Sadly, he was probably right. Terry was a genius when it came to hair. When he wasn't busy scissoring Poodles, he cut and styled mine. For some reason Terry seemed to believe that gave him permission to comment on other aspects of my life that he found amusing. Like my wardrobe.

Today I was dressed for comfort in a long-sleeved T-shirt and khakis. Terry looked like he was ready for Fashion Week. It was a wonder we were even able to be friends.

"Go ahead," Davey told him with a grin. "I'd like to see that."

"I'll just bet you would," Terry shot right back. He flicked his hand at the assorted Poodles sitting out on tabletops in his setup. "But as you can see, I'm much too busy to give you a demonstration."

"My assistant, busy?" Crawford came striding toward us from the direction of the rings. He was carrying a Bichon Frise. "That's a novelty. Chop, chop. Toy Poodles in twenty minutes. Is the Eskie ready?"

"Of course." Terry swept the dog in question up off a table.

In a maneuver they'd performed a thousand times, Terry and Crawford deftly exchanged one white, fluffy dog for the other. Then the handler quickly left the setup again. Terry popped the Bichon inside a crate and went back to work on his Toy.

Sam set up the grooming table. Augie hopped on top of it and lay down. Davey opened up the tack box and got out his combs and brushes. Kev sat down in a folding chair with a Richard Scarry book I'd packed in his bag.

Busy on the other side of her setup, Bertie waited until things had calmed down before beckoning me over. She wasn't showing nearly as many dogs as Crawford, but with no assistant to help out, I knew she would be running around like crazy all day.

Bertie was one of the first friends I'd made in the dog show world. Having grown up without sisters of my own, I'd been surprised by how quickly we'd become close. And when—in a thoroughly unexpected twist of fate—Bertie had fallen in love with my younger brother, Frank, we'd become sisters for real. I had no idea how I'd gotten so lucky.

"You'll never guess where Peg is," she said.

Good question. I stood up on my toes, lifted my head above the crowd of exhibitors, and took a long look around. I knew that Aunt Peg wasn't showing Coral today. Even so, I was sure she would have arrived before we did. Usually she pounced on us the moment we appeared.

I didn't see Aunt Peg anywhere. That was odd.

Then I dropped my gaze and looked around Bertie's setup. In addition to the usual profusion of canine paraphernalia, I also saw a portable baby seat and a quilted diaper bag.

"Wait a minute," I said. "Did you bring Josh with you?"

After Bertie and Frank's son had been born the previous September, Bertie had taken several months off from the show ring. But by the beginning of the new year, she'd been ready and eager to return to handling. Her client roster had rebounded quickly. Once she was working full time again, Bertie had hired an au pair named Daisy to help out.

"Yup. Frank has Maggie, and Josh and Daisy came with me. It was Daisy's idea. That girl loves dogs. She'd come to every single dog show if I let her."

"I can understand that," I said. We all could. "But it still doesn't explain where Aunt Peg is."

"The three of them are over at the rings. Daisy convinced Peg to take her on a tour of the show. Along with expert breed commentary, of course."

That was unexpected.

"And Aunt Peg agreed to that?"

Bertie looked up. "Sure. Why not? Peg loves lecturing people about dogs. And Daisy is eminently teachable. The two of them are perfect for each other."

"Yes, but . . . what about Josh?"

Bertie grinned. "He doesn't even talk yet. There's no point in trying to teach him the finer points of showmanship."

I poked her in the shoulder. "That's not what I meant and you know it. Aunt Peg . . . and babies . . . and never the twain shall meet? She adores puppies, but human babies make her itch. When Kevin was little I could barely get her to sit in the same room with him."

"Maybe Peg has mellowed in her old age," said Sam. The setups were close enough that everyone could contribute to the conversation.

"Or maybe she likes my child better than yours." Bertie poked me right back. Except that she was holding a knitting needle in her hand and that hurt.

Rubbing my arm, I stepped back out of range.

"Poor Melanie," Terry crooned. "Did you just discover that you're not the favorite?"

"Oh pish," I said, borrowing Aunt Peg's favorite phrase. "That's old news."

"What's old news?" asked Aunt Peg.

Suddenly she and Daisy were back. To my amazement, Aunt Peg was holding Josh. She had the chubby baby cradled under her arm the same way she would have carried a small dog, but Josh didn't seem to mind. When he saw Bertie his face lit up. He raised both arms and extended them in her direction.

"I'll take him," said Daisy. In her late teens,

she was petite and slightly pudgy. A thick fringe of light brown hair was tucked behind her ears. The side of her nose was pierced and she had a small butterfly tattoo on her wrist.

Daisy whisked the baby out of Aunt Peg's arms and reached for the cooler that was sitting on top of a crate. "It's almost time for his bottle anyway."

Aunt Peg looked around at the rest of us. "Clearly I interrupted something. Did someone have news to share?"

For a moment there was only silence. No one cared to admit what we'd been talking about. Then, thankfully, Terry piped up.

"I know something new," he announced.

Nobody was surprised by that. Terry had the biggest ears in town. So he always had the best gossip.

"There was a robbery last weekend."

All eyes turned his way. That *was* new. Terry looked suitably gratified by our response.

"Who was robbed?" asked Aunt Peg.

"Marvin Stanberg. You know, the terrier judge?"

We all nodded.

"He was judging last Sunday at Sedgefield, and his house in Trumbull was broken into while he was away at the show."

"That's terrible," Bertie said.

"The thieves took his coin collection, some electronics, and a piece of pre-Colombian art."

"That sounds like quite a haul," said Sam.

"Apparently the police told him that the robbery looked like the work of professionals. The thieves knew just what they wanted and only took the really valuable stuff."

"That's scary." I blew out a breath. "I assume no one was home at the time?"

"No. Luckily Marv's wife, Selma, was at the show with him," Terry replied. "They'd left a couple of dogs loose in the house—"

"Rottweilers?" Aunt Peg asked hopefully.

"Norfolk Terriers."

Oh. Not the best watchdogs then. Norfolks would have been more likely to lick an intruder than to bite one.

"The Norfolks were unharmed?"

Trust Aunt Peg to think of that.

"Not only unharmed, but apparently quite happy about the whole experience. The thieves had planned ahead and brought marrow bones to give them."

Sam frowned. "Crooks are getting smarter all the time."

"Hearing about something like that makes me think I ought to try to convince Crawford to put in an alarm system," Terry said.

"I *have* an alarm system," Aunt Peg replied stoutly. "It's five big, black dogs with sharp teeth."

As if a Standard Poodle would have been any

more help in that circumstance than a Norfolk. Poodles loved everybody. A thief wouldn't even need marrow bones to make friends with them.

"I'd imagine the Stanbergs might have thought much the same thing," said Sam.

While Aunt Peg and Terry continued to discuss the break-in and Sam and Davey got Augie ready for the ring, I went off in search of Rick Fanelli. I didn't have much of a description. *Tall, skinny, and decent looking for a geek* didn't exactly narrow things down. But Bertie said she thought Rick might show Setters or Spaniels, and using that information I'd found his name in the catalog with an English Cocker.

Judging for that breed was about to start in ring eight. I got there just as the two Puppy Dogs were called into the ring. There were five entries in the Open class, one of which was listed as being handled by Rick Fanelli. Most of the Open dogs were already grouped around the in-gate, their handlers wearing identifying armbands.

Rick wasn't among them. I hoped his English Cocker wasn't absent.

The judged pinned his puppies, and the steward called the Open class into the ring. As I watched the four file through the gate, there was a commotion in the crowd behind me. A man with a dog was pushing his way through the assembled spectators.

Tall and geeky. It fit. I'd found Rick Fanelli.

Rick grabbed an armband from the steward and slapped it on his upper arm. Then he dropped his blue roan Cocker on the corner of the mat near the gate. The judge didn't look happy to have been kept waiting. He took a cursory look at Rick's dog, then moved to the head of the line and sent the class around the ring.

I didn't know much about English Cockers. But no one could go to as many shows with Aunt Peg as I had without absorbing at least some of her freely disseminated wisdom. Soundness, balance, and showmanship were valuable attributes across all dog breeds. So, like most of the other spectators standing ringside, I began to evaluate the class along with the judge.

Rick's Cocker wasn't the worst dog in the class, but in my view it wasn't the best either. Nor was Rick's indifferent handling doing his entry any favors. Rick knew the judging routine. He followed the judge's instructions. But there was no dazzle to his presentation. Clearly missing was that special sparkle that tells the judge, *"Look at my dog. He's your winner!"*

The best you could say about Rick's performance in the ring was that it was competent. But no one who paid a professional handler to present their dog was looking for competence. The whole point was to get expertise.

I wasn't surprised when Rick's dog placed third out of the four in the class. Rick didn't look surprised either. He accepted the yellow ribbon from the judge, left the ring, and went striding away. I followed after him.

Rick's setup was on the other side of the building. It consisted of only one grooming table and three or four crates. Business didn't appear to be going too well for Amanda's boyfriend.

Rick dumped the Engie on the tabletop as he went by. He shrugged out of his sports coat and hung it on a hanger dangling from the edge of his tack box. Then he snatched up his judging schedule and looked at it with a frown.

About that time, Rick became aware that I was standing there watching him. He tucked the schedule back in the tack box and said, "Can I help you?"

"I hope so. My name is Melanie Travis. I'd like to ask you a couple of questions if you have a minute."

"Melanie Travis," he repeated. "That name sounds familiar."

I should hope so, I thought.

"I left a couple of messages on your phone this week."

"Oh. Right," he said flatly. "You're Amanda's friend."

"Not exactly. But I am looking for her."

Rick picked up the Cocker and tucked it into a crate. Then he sat on the edge of the table, crossed his arms over his chest, and said, "Why is that?"

"Amanda hasn't been seen or heard from since she was at the show last Sunday. Her sister is worried about her."

"Abby would be." Rick looked annoyed. "She's a piece of work."

"What do you mean?"

"She and Amanda are twins. You know that, right?"

I nodded.

"Abby seems to think that gives her some kind of magical, woo-woo connection to her sister. As well as the right to comment on every decision Amanda makes. It drives Amanda a little crazy, you know?"

I'm a big believer in catching more flies with honey, so I went with it. "I can see that," I said encouragingly.

"Abby is convinced that the two of them ought to be partners in her handling business. She thinks Amanda's wasting her time and her talent dog-sitting. She's always on her case about it."

"What do you think?"

Rick shrugged. "I think Amanda has her own life to live. She ought to do whatever she wants. She likes taking care of other people's dogs. She enjoys going to different houses, looking around at things, and seeing how other people live. Plus Abby's career is twenty-four/seven. Amanda's

117

dog-sitting jobs don't tie her down like that. She likes having the freedom to come and go as she pleases."

That was interesting. I leaned against a nearby stack of wooden crates. "Are you saying it's not unusual for Amanda to disappear for a few days?"

"When you say 'disappear' like that, it makes it sound ominous." Rick grimaced. "Like Amanda is missing or something."

"So she isn't missing?" I hadn't expected to hear that. "Has she been in touch with you?"

"No, but that doesn't mean anything. Amanda and I are both adults. We're mature enough to give each other space when we need it."

I wondered if there was any particular reason why they might be feeling the need for space right now. But I left that for later and said, instead, "You know that Amanda is living above Jasmine Crane's garage, right?"

"Sure." Rick shrugged again. The gesture seemed to be a habitual expression of his feelings. "What about it?"

"I'm sure you're also aware that Jasmine was killed last weekend."

"I never liked that woman." Rick's tone was dismissive. As if his feelings rendered the circumstances of Jasmine's violent death no big deal.

"How did Amanda feel about her?"

"She and Jasmine were friends. They'd known each other a long time. It could be Amanda was upset that she died."

You think?

Rick pushed himself away from the table and stood. "I'd imagine that's probably why I haven't heard from her. Amanda might have wanted some time alone to deal with it."

"It's been almost a week," I pointed out.

"I guess she'll come back when she's ready."

My hands clenched at my sides. Rick Fanelli was a supercilious jerk. I wanted to throttle him. Not that it would do any good.

Instead I said, "My number is in your phone. Will you let me know if you hear from her?"

"Sure." Rick flapped a hand in the air to send me on my way. "If I remember."

It was hardly a promise. But it was probably as much as I was going to get.

Chapter 9

Back at the setup things were moving right along. Augie's topknot was in and he'd already been sprayed up. Under Sam's watchful eye, Davey was now scissoring the final finish to his trim.

Scissoring is an art. It requires an artistic eye, a steady hand, and plenty of patience. When it's done correctly, a Poodle's coat will look as smooth as glass. Davey was still learning but his scissoring technique was already better than mine. One day, if he stayed with it, he might even surpass Sam.

Crawford had won the variety in Minis, then been passed over entirely in Toys. I hoped that didn't mean it would be his turn again in Standards. But with a major on the line, Crawford was only one of half a dozen professional handlers Davey was going to have to beat today to get the points.

Augie was a handsome dog and a deserving champion. He was mature and ready to win. But the Standard Poodle ring was always highly competitive. Even if Augie showed his heart out, it would still take a brave judge to put up a thirteen-year-old boy in such strong company.

Our judge was Mr. Bill Beauman from

Tennessee. I was quite certain we'd never shown to him before. As we made our way over to the ring, I asked Aunt Peg what she knew about him.

"He likes a quality Poodle. And he knows one when he sees one. Augie should be just his cup of tea."

That sounded promising.

"But he also has no patience for games, or politics, or handlers who don't know what they're doing. So Davey had better be on his toes."

Aunt Peg moved on ahead of me and went to stand beside Augie as the first two Standard Dog classes were judged. Taking Davey's comb from his armband, she smoothed down the black Poodle's already smooth ears. Davey ignored her fussing and focused on the ring.

My son had his game face on today. When the steward called Augie's class, he was ready.

There were nine Standard Poodles in the Open class, enough to fill one side of the large ring. Davey and Augie were right in the middle. As the group got themselves lined up and settled in, Terry—who had his hand cupped around the muzzle of Crawford's Puppy Bitch—came over to watch with us.

"Where did you disappear to earlier?" he asked.

"You are so nosy." Even as I spoke to Terry, my eyes remained fastened on the activity in the ring. "Maybe it's none of your business."

"I like the sound of that. Do tell."

121

"I went to talk to Rick Fanelli."

Terry's eyebrows rose. "Why would you want to do that?"

I gave him a quick look out of the corner of my eye. "I needed information."

"I can't imagine why you'd need anything from him." Terry shook his head. "Rick Fanelli's an idiot."

"He's an idiot with a missing girlfriend."

"Amanda Burke?"

Of course he would know about that. I nodded.

Terry snorted under his breath. "If I was Rick's girlfriend, I'd be missing too."

"Shhh!" Aunt Peg nudged me hard enough to nearly push me off my feet. "Pay attention. The judging is about to start."

Augie looked just the way I wanted him to on the first go-round. He was alert and happy, and moving beautifully. As Mr. Beauman perused the group gaiting around the ring, his gaze lingered on our entry for several extra seconds.

That was a good sign. In the show ring, a judge had only a brief amount of time to devote to evaluating each dog. First impressions counted for a lot.

Augie wasn't the only Standard Poodle in the class who caught Mr. Beauman's eye. Crawford's dog was similarly favored—as were three others, all with professional handlers. Still, Davey and Augie were doing everything right. Now all they had to do was keep it up. I had my fingers crossed so tightly that my hands began to cramp.

One by one, the judge performed his individual examinations. As he glanced back and forth between the dogs in front of him and those he'd already judged, we could see Mr. Beauman beginning to sort things out in his mind. The class was large enough that he decided to make a cut. Starting at the front of the line, he pulled out five finalists in the order in which they'd been standing. He then dismissed the remaining four dogs from the ring.

Crawford's black Standard was now at the head of the new line. A handsome brown was second. Augie was still in the middle. There was a nice white dog behind him and another black at the end.

"That's a good looking group of dogs," I said under my breath.

Sam, who was holding Kevin, nodded silently.

"Augie belongs at the head of the line," Aunt Peg muttered. "Let's hope Davey can get him there."

The judge motioned with his hands to send the new group around the ring again. He wanted to see his top contenders moving side by side. The handlers straightened and stepped away from their stacked dogs. They unspooled the leashes they'd held crumpled in their hands.

With their exotic trims and playful personalities, Standard Poodles always drew a crowd of spectators at dog shows. And as Mr. Beauman narrowed down this tough class, the tension at ringside was palpable. We weren't the only ones who were rooting for a favorite to pull off a big win.

Crawford, ever the gentleman, glanced back to make sure everyone else was ready. Then he tapped his Poodle smartly under the chin to lift his head, and took off at a fast trot. His dog glided over the matted floor beside him.

With fewer dogs in the ring, there was now room for the big Poodles to stride out freely. When Augie made his pass in front of the judge, he looked every inch the winner. He had extension, he had drive, and best of all he was having fun. His tail was not only up in the air, it was wagging back and forth.

This time Mr. Beauman's gaze didn't just linger, it followed Augie down the entire long side of the ring. Mentally I congratulated Davey on a job well done, then turned to say something to Sam.

That was when everything fell apart. It happened so fast that I almost missed it. But when Aunt Peg and Terry suddenly gasped in unison, my eyes shot back to the ring.

The white dog behind Davey and Augie was handled by a young professional named Joe Pond. Joe had obviously scoped out the other dogs in the class and decided where his chief competition lay. When he and his Poodle rounded the final corner and the judge's gaze turned back to the remaining entry, Joe suddenly accelerated as the line of dogs in front of him was stopping.

Davey was looking where he was going. As he slowed Augie to a walk, Joe's Poodle rushed up behind him. Moving much too fast, the dog crashed into Augie's hindquarter. Augie yelped in pain and surprise. He went scooting sideways across the mat.

Caught unaware by the sudden move, Davey nearly got yanked off his feet. He and Augie scrambled quickly to right themselves, but the damage had already been done. Augie's tail dropped between his legs. His head whipped from side to side in confusion. His body pretzeled as he tried to spin around and face the unexpected threat behind him.

"Oops," said Joe. Abruptly he yanked his Poodle back. "Sorry about that. He got away from me."

Davey didn't spare the other handler a glance. He was too busy trying to get Augie to settle and regain his composure. As they went back into line, Augie still hadn't lifted his tail. It was clear the Poodle didn't trust the other dog not to run up on him again.

The Poodle breed is known for its wonderful temperament. A show ring adage illustrates the importance of displaying that joyous disposition to the judge: "No tail, no Poodle." If Davey wanted to win, it was vital that he get Augie back in the game. And he needed to do it fast.

From ringside, we were powerless to help. All we could do was watch as Davey quickly examined his options. With Augie already tense, he decided not to ask the Poodle to hold a stack. Instead Davey yanked a furry toy out of his pocket. He squeaked the mouse in front of Augie's nose, tempting him to grab it, asking him to play.

Augie pricked his ears. His tail lifted slightly. But he was still clearly uneasy. It wasn't good enough.

Davey aimed a glare in Joe's direction. Joe just shrugged.

Beside me, Sam stiffened. He was just as upset as I was. There was no way that the incident had been an accident.

Davey shoved the toy back in his pocket and set his knee against Augie's chest. Gently he nudged the Poodle away. Davey was inviting Augie to bounce back. Or to bounce in any direction.

It didn't happen. Instead Augie stood at the end of the leash and gazed at him uncertainly. Mr. Beauman was already at the head of the line. He was working his way toward Augie as he took one final look at each of the competitors.

Staring into the ring, Aunt Peg had her hands

fisted together beneath her chin. "Come *on*," she whispered urgently. "The judge is coming. Get him back. *Get him back.*"

Davey quickly slipped Augie into place. Now he had no choice but to stack the Poodle. If Augie wasn't going to lift his own tail, Davey would have to do it for him. And try to make the stance look entirely natural.

Mr. Beauman paused in front of Augie. Then he glanced back and forth between him and Joe Pond's white dog. It was clear that he'd missed the interaction between the two.

After a minute, the judge lifted his hand and pointed to Augie. He instructed Davey to go to the head of the line. Joe's dog was called out second. Crawford's dog was third.

Davey cupped his hand around Augie's muzzle, offering extra support as he led him forward. Augie trotted at his side like a dog being led to his execution. This was his last chance to recover. It was now or never.

Mr. Beauman sent the group around the ring one last time. He'd arranged the Standard Poodles in the order he wanted them, but the judging wasn't over. Augie still had to show Mr. Beauman that he deserved the win. Joe Pond, looking entirely innocent of anything nefarious, purposely held his dog back and allowed Augie plenty of room.

But that didn't help. It was already too late.

On the last go-round, Augie looked tentative

127

and Joe's dog was showing beautifully. The judge watched the two Standard Poodles for almost the entire circuit of the ring. Then finally—with a gesture that looked almost regretful—he pointed to the white dog for first place and Augie for second.

Abruptly I exhaled the breath I'd been holding. Aunt Peg issued a long, unhappy sigh. Sam just frowned. Even Kevin looked upset.

I couldn't believe Davey and Augie had once again been *right there,* only to have victory snatched away at the last moment.

The Winners Dog class was over in minutes. Mr. Beauman quickly awarded Joe Pond's dog the points. Then Davey and Augie went Reserve to another major.

The previous weekend, Davey had exited the ring looking dejected by his loss. This time he was angry.

"Did you see what happened in there?" he demanded.

"Yes, we did," Sam told him. "And we'll talk about it in a few minutes. But first, I want you to take Kevin and hand Augie to me."

To Davey's surprise, he found Augie's leash being whipped out of his grasp. A moment later his younger brother's hand was placed in his. Sam spun Augie around and trotted the big Poodle away from the crowds standing by the rings. The rest of us followed.

When he'd reached an open area, Sam crouched down in front of Augie. He whispered something in the dog's ear. Then he scratched under his chin. Then he reached around and tickled his belly. After a few seconds, Augie's tail gave a low wag.

Sam stood up and took something out of his pocket. He must have been carrying back-up bait. He fed the Poodle a small chunk of dried liver. Then he took a second piece and dangled it in front of Augie's nose.

"Come on," Sam invited. "Take it."

Augie knew he wasn't allowed to jump up and grab something from Sam's hand. But that liver looked pretty enticing. Especially since Sam kept dropping his hand down and showing it to him. Eyes following the morsel, Augie's feet began to dance in place.

When Sam tossed the piece of liver in the air, the Poodle's head lifted. A moment later, his tail came up too. Augie crouched low on his haunches and gave a low woof.

Sam flicked the liver toward him in a high arc. Augie caught the treat on the fly. Sam tossed another chunk. Augie jumped up and caught that one too.

Then Sam reached around and smacked Augie lightly on the hindquarter. The Poodle spun in place trying to catch him. Now it was a game and Augie wanted to play. All four feet left the ground at the same time as he bounced in the air. The Poodle got another piece of liver for that trick.

"Ready to go?" Sam chucked Augie under the chin. "Ready now? Come on, let's go!"

The two of them took off at a brisk trot down the length of the wide corridor between rings. Augie was gaiting on a loose leash with his head up and his feet flying. His tail was high in the air over his back. Finally the Poodle was having fun again.

At the end of the corridor, Sam stopped and turned. The two of them came trotting back. Sam went straight to Davey. He handed back Augie's leash. Jubilant, maybe even too excited, the Poodle jumped up and planted his front feet on Davey's shoulders. Grinning, Davey gave his dog a hug.

"And that," Aunt Peg said with satisfaction, "is how it's done."

"I know you couldn't do that while you were in the ring being judged," Sam said to Davey. "But out here it's important for Augie to end the day on a good note. Because when we come back to show again tomorrow, you want him to remember what a great time he had. Not something stupid that went wrong before that."

"It wasn't fair." Davey was still angry as he gently dropped Augie to the ground. "Joe Pond did that on purpose."

"Yes, he did," Aunt Peg agreed. "He was afraid Augie was going to beat his dog, and he was probably right."

Davey rounded on her. "Don't tell me you're defending him."

"No indeed," Aunt Peg replied calmly. "What Joe did was reprehensible. You can ruin a dog for life that way. But you bear a small measure of responsibility too. You shouldn't have let it happen."

That was a little harsh, I thought. So did Davey.

"Me?" he cried. "How was it my fault?"

"When you're in the ring you have to be paying attention to everything. You need to be watching not just your dog and the judge, but others around you too. All sorts of things can go wrong unexpectedly. You have to learn to be ready for them."

Aunt Peg reached down and gave Davey's shoulder a reassuring pat. "But other than that," she said, "well done. You and Augie made a great team today." She straightened and glanced toward the Poodle ring. "I see that the Standard judging is just about over. I believe Mr. Pond is about to discover that all sorts of things can go wrong unexpectedly for him too."

Aunt Peg left us and went to wait near the gate as Mr. Beauman handed out his final ribbons. Joe Pond's dog had gone Best of Winners. He was smiling as he exited the ring.

Then he saw Aunt Peg standing there waiting for him.

The two of them moved out of the way of traffic and had a little chat. We couldn't hear what was being said, but it did not appear that things were going well for Mr. Pond.

Two minutes later, Aunt Peg was back. We all looked at her expectantly.

"Joe Pond will not be bothering you again," she said to Davey. "Nor anyone else for that matter."

"What did you say to him?" I asked.

"I told him that I'd seen his maneuver in the ring and was thoroughly disgusted by his unsportsmanlike behavior. I advised him that it wouldn't be in his best interest to show a dog under me anytime soon."

Aunt Peg paused and grinned wolfishly. "Or under any of my friends."

I grinned at that too. Sam smothered a laugh. Even Davey began to look more cheerful.

Right about now, Joe Pond had to be realizing the magnitude of his mistake. Because Aunt Peg knew just about everybody in the dog world. And she had *lots* of friends.

Chapter 10

While Sam and Davey were busy taking Augie's coat apart, Kevin and I went to take a tour of the concessions. I was pleased to see that just about all the vendors who'd been at the Sedgefield show were also present this weekend. Aside from Aunt Peg, who had stumbled over Jasmine Crane's body, nobody had had a better view of what had transpired that afternoon than the owners of the neighboring booths. I was sure the police would have already questioned them, but I was eager to hear what they had to say too.

Having behaved himself beautifully all morning, Kevin was excited by the offer of an adventure. He'd been to enough dog shows that the idea of watching his brother—or anyone else for that matter—groom a big, hairy dog had long since lost its allure. But from his point of view, the concession stands offered a cornucopia of potential treats.

Oh, who was I kidding? Even for an adult, the possibilities were endlessly fascinating. And tempting.

In addition to the vendors who sold the more practical dog-oriented products, I also saw a booth offering canine ceramics and figurines, another with hand-crafted dog biscuits, and yet another selling silk screen T-shirts and accessories. At a glance, the only booth that appeared to be missing from the usual selection was Jasmine Crane's.

I began our passage around the perimeter of the building at a food vendor, where I stopped to buy Kevin a corn dog. When I went to hand it to him, he stared at me in horror.

"No." Kev shook his head firmly. "I don't want that."

"Why not?"

"It's a *corn dog*."

I stared at him, perplexed. "I know."

Kev jutted out his lower lip and crossed his arms over his chest. "I'm not eating a dog."

"Oh, honey, I'm sorry." I crouched down in front of him. "I should have explained. It's not a real dog."

"It's not?"

"No, of course not." I gathered him into my arms for a quick hug. "It's a hot dog. You know, like we put on the grill at home?"

Kevin didn't look convinced. "Then why is it yellow?"

"Because there's a batter on the outside instead of a roll."

"What's in the batter?"

That boy was just like Aunt Peg. He lived to ask questions.

"Cornmeal. It tastes good. Look." I held the

corn up, took a bite and chewed conspicuously. "Mmm, yummy."

"Good," said Kevin. "Then you eat it."

So I did. What choice did I have when I'd been out-argued by my own child? By the time we got to the first booth at the end of the long row of concessions, I had polished off the corn dog and wiped my fingers on a napkin. I was ready to get down to business.

Nettie's Needlepoint Nook offered a huge selection of products combining dogs and needlework. The possibilities included everything from canine-themed patterns, to do-it-yourself projects, to finished tapestries and throw pillows. Nearly every breed of dog appeared to be represented on something that was available for purchase.

Crafts were not my thing and I'd never visited Nettie's booth before. As we entered, Kevin paused in front of a display of embroidered pillows. On top of the pile was a throw pillow featuring three adorable King Charles Spaniels. It was so cute, even I had to take a second look.

"Can I help you?" The woman approaching us was about my age. She had bright blue eyes, plump cheeks, and a welcoming smile. "That's one of my favorite pillows. I keep thinking it would look wonderful on my own couch."

"Did you make it?"

"No." She leaned closer and whispered, "It's

actually a mass-produced item I buy from a supplier. But it's needlepoint, and it's lovely. And they're so popular, I can barely keep them in stock."

"You must be Nettie," I said. "I'm Melanie Travis."

"Pleased to meet you. What kind of project are you looking for?"

"Actually I don't do needlework myself. I was hoping I could ask you a few questions?"

"Sure. Fire away. Are you looking to sign up for a class? I might be able to recommend someone in your area."

I released Kevin's hand and he wandered over to have a look at a needlepoint footstool. In the open booth, it was easy to keep an eye on him.

Satisfied that nothing in the vicinity was breakable, I turned back to Nettie. "No, it's about what happened last week. At the Sedgefield dog show."

"Last week . . . ?" Nettie looked puzzled. Then suddenly she realized what I was referring to. "Oh."

"Your booth was near Jasmine Crane's, wasn't it?"

"In the general area, I guess. We weren't neighbors if that's what you're asking."

"I'm wondering if you noticed anything unusual that afternoon."

Nettie tipped her head to one side. "Apparently

136

a woman died not fifty feet away from where I was doing business. That was pretty damn unusual."

Yes, it was. *My bad.*

"Did you know Jasmine?" I asked.

"Only in passing. We'd see each other at shows and Jasmine always seemed friendly enough. But mostly we just waved and got on with our business." Nettie gave me a curious look. "What's this about, anyway? Do you know how Jasmine died? Because the police asked lots of questions, but no one would tell us anything. What have you heard?"

"I know that her death wasn't an accident," I said quietly.

Nettie didn't look surprised. I guessed that was common knowledge.

"Is it true that when they found her she was wearing a dog collar around her neck?" she asked.

I swallowed wrong and nearly choked. A leash wasn't very different from a collar. But still, it seemed prudent to quash that rumor.

"No, that's not true," I said firmly.

Nettie leaned in toward me. "I heard that Jasmine whispered dying words that pointed toward her killer. But nobody seems to know what she said."

That had to be another wild rumor. Surely if there had been dying words—especially useful ones—Aunt Peg would have thought to mention it.

"No," I said again. "There were no last words. Jasmine was already dead when she was found."

"Oh. That's too bad." Nettie looked disappointed. She'd clearly been hoping I could provide some salacious gossip for her to pass along.

"What else are people saying?" I asked.

She shrugged and glanced around her booth, probably hoping to see other customers. Now that my information had been found wanting, I was no longer interesting.

"Oh, you know," Nettie said. "The usual."

The usual? Was there such a thing? The very idea was horrifying to contemplate.

"Like what?"

"Mostly, the rest of us who have concessions are wondering about our own safety. If something like that could happen to Jasmine right in the middle of a busy afternoon, how do we know that one of us couldn't be next?"

"So you don't think that Jasmine was targeted specifically?"

"I don't know what to think," Nettie replied. "And mostly I don't want to think about it at all."

I found Kevin playing in a bin of brightly colored yarns. I took his hand, and he and I headed down the row. We spoke briefly with a man selling dog beds who said he had nothing to say and didn't want to be involved. The woman in the T-shirt booth was doing a brisk business. She was too busy to stop and talk.

The next booth we came to was Alan Crandall's concession. Creature Comforts was a staple of the New England show scene. Unlike the boutique vendors who specialized in a single canine-related product, Creature Comforts sold almost everything a dog show exhibitor could possibly need.

Leash break on the way to the ring? Creature Comforts to the rescue. Forgot your slicker brush at home? Grab a new one at Creature Comforts. Dog threw up on the cushion in his crate? Replace it with a stock item from Creature Comforts. It wasn't surprising that Alan Crandall had been the one to step in and lend a hand when the Sedgefield show committee had been in a jam.

As usual the Creature Comforts booth was crowded with shoppers. A team of salespeople was busy making sure that no one ever had to wait for service. I was directed to the rear of the booth, where Alan Crandall was standing behind a table, ringing up customers' purchases.

There was a line of people wanting to check out, so I figured Kev and I should probably come back another time. But Alan saw us waiting for him and passed the cash drawer over to an assistant. Though he and I had never formally met, I'd done plenty of business at his booth over the years. I probably looked just as familiar to Alan Crandall as he did to me.

"Tell me what you need," he said. He was tall and thin and leaned down when he spoke to me, as if he was afraid his words would go right over my head otherwise. Behind tortoiseshell frame glasses, he had kindly brown eyes.

We introduced ourselves and shook hands.

"I need answers," I told him with a smile. "Do you have any?"

"I might. It depends on the questions."

"I'm trying to find out what happened to Jasmine Crane."

Alan reared back. He hadn't expected that. "Why?"

"It's a bit of a long story."

"Well, in that case, I'll cut to the chase," Alan replied. "I don't know."

"Gwen Kimble told me that you ended up with Jasmine's things after the show?"

"That's right. The show committee was in a bind. We had the space and the manpower to help out, so we did. That's all there was to it." He paused, then added, "Everything Jasmine took to last week's show is in our warehouse. If you're interested, I'd be happy to have someone take it off my hands."

"Sorry, I'm afraid I can't help you with that." I shrugged apologetically. "Did you know Jasmine well?"

"No, not really. What little relationship we had was based on proximity and common goals. We were cordial with one another, but not particularly friendly."

"Did she have any enemies that you're aware of?"

Alan frowned. "I wouldn't know anything about that. It seemed to me that Jasmine could be a bit prickly at times. She always thought the next guy was getting perks that she wasn't. But something that might have made someone want to strangle her? That goes way beyond my purview."

While we'd been speaking, the checkout line had doubled in size. Alan's assistant was casting anxious glances in our direction. It was time to let him get back to work.

"Thank you for talking to me," I said.

"No problem. Something like that happening here . . . at a dog show . . . it hurts all of us. I hope you find the answers you're looking for."

"I do too," I replied.

Kevin and I had time for one last stop, so we ducked into a bookseller's booth next door. Kev immediately grabbed a picture book with an image of an Old English Sheepdog on the cover. Since it looked like we'd be making a purchase, I sat him down on a nearby bench where he could thumb through the pictures while I had a word with the man in charge.

The concession was mostly empty of people. Apparently books weren't as big a draw as T-shirts and corn dogs. Toward the back of the booth, a portly man with bushy sideburns was bending down to pull books out of a carton. The banner above the booth read MANNING BOOKS, LELAND MANNING, PROPRIETOR so I took a shot.

"Excuse me, are you Leland Manning?"

"That's me." He straightened and turned to face me. "How can I help you?"

"I've been talking to vendors who were at last week's dog show in Sedgefield."

Leland stared and said nothing. His eyes narrowed fractionally.

"You were there, weren't you?" I already knew the answer to that. I'd passed Manning Books on my way to Jasmine's booth. It was right next door.

"Yes, I was there. Quite a mess that day turned into. Not good for business at all. I assume you want to talk about Jasmine Crane. Are you a reporter?"

"No, I'm trying to locate a friend of Jasmine's who disappeared around the same time."

"Who would that be?"

"Amanda Burke."

Leland shook his head. "Don't know her. Sorry. Can't help you."

"Do you have any thoughts about what happened to Jasmine?"

"Just one," said Leland. "Good riddance."

He went back to unloading books. I guess he thought our conversation was finished. But after hearing that answer, I was just getting started. Leland's back was now facing me. I walked around to the other side of the box.

"I take it you and she weren't friends?"

"Nope," Leland muttered. "Not anymore."

"Were you once?"

"I thought so." He dropped a stack of books on a nearby table. "I was mistaken."

"It sounds like there's a story there," I said.

"Did you know Jasmine?"

"Not really. I just looked around her booth a few times, that's all."

"Jasmine was an interesting woman. She had a way about her that was very appealing. She could be funny when she was in the mood. And flirty sometimes too." Leland frowned as though the memory wasn't a happy one.

"She used to come and hang around my booth when business was slow," he continued. "Asked me all about my books. Jasmine was especially interested in the rare editions. She said she'd heard that people collected valuable books and she wanted me to tell her how that worked."

"I didn't realize you had collectible books here," I said, surprised.

"Not many, but I have a few. Just the dog stories, of course. You'd be surprised what

143

people might ask for at a dog show. So I like to be prepared, you know?"

"Of course." I nodded. "That makes sense."

"I showed Jasmine some of the special books I keep locked in a case. She seemed sincerely interested in learning about rare books. We had a wonderful conversation about our favorite authors."

"It sounds as though you got to know her pretty well."

"Maybe," Leland allowed. "But apparently I didn't know her well enough. One night when I went to pack up my booth, I realized that my first edition of *The Call of the Wild* was gone from the case. I'd noticed Jasmine hanging around earlier in the day, but I didn't think anything about it. But once I saw that book was missing, I knew exactly who'd taken it."

"Did you confront her about it?" I asked.

"Of course. That was a signed first edition. It was worth five hundred dollars. I couldn't afford that kind of loss. I asked her if she'd borrowed it while I wasn't looking. I purposely gave her a way to return the book without any recriminations being made."

"And did she?"

"Hell, no," Leland snapped. "Jasmine looked me right in the eye and denied everything. Said she was sorry for my loss but that she'd had nothing to do with it."

"Maybe she was telling the truth," I said.

Leland shook his head. He didn't want to hear it. "It would've had to be a huge coincidence if she was. Jasmine and I had looked at the book together just the week before. She said she was a big fan of Jack London and asked how much a first edition like that was worth. After I told her, I could see her eying it. I could tell that book was something she wanted."

"You said you keep your rare books under lock and key. How did Jasmine gain access to it?"

"That was my fault," Leland grumbled. "More fool, me. Jasmine, she was an attractive woman. I guess maybe I was a little flattered by her attention. I kept the key to the display case in a drawer underneath."

I lifted a brow. "That doesn't sound very secure."

"It's never been a problem before. Not until Jasmine Crane watched me open and shut that case a few times, and saw how easy it would be to help herself to something that didn't belong to her."

"I can understand why you're upset," I said. "But you didn't see Jasmine take the book. Maybe someone else figured out your security system."

"No," Leland replied stubbornly. "It was Jasmine. That woman played me and I fell for it. She was always short on money. Always looking for ways to put a little extra cash in the coffers."

That was the first I'd heard of that.

"Jasmine called herself an entrepreneur. She had her fingers in a lot of different pies. I just wish I'd cottoned on to who she really was before I let her greedy hands on my business."

Chapter 11

I paid for Kevin's picture book, then he and I headed back to the setup. Sam and Davey were waiting for us. While we'd been gone, Augie's coat had been brushed out. His topknot had been taken down and rewrapped. It was time to head home.

Early the next morning, we started the process all over again. We'd left most of our gear in the grooming area overnight, so everyone was back in the same place. Today, however, two things had changed.

The first was that Aunt Peg was showing too. She'd arrived at the show site ahead of us and squeezed her things in between our setup and Bertie's. The second was that today Davey would be showing Augie to a different judge. Lillian Abernathy had given Augie points once before in lesser company. I could only hope she would remember him and like what she saw today.

Aunt Peg seemed to think it could happen. So did Terry. Aunt Peg was too superstitious to say anything. Not Terry. As usual, he couldn't keep his mouth shut.

"Today's your day," he called over to Davey from the neighboring setup as the two of them brushed out Standard Poodles. "Just make sure you give Mrs. Abernathy a good look at that dog's head. She's a sucker for a pretty face."

"Excuse me," Crawford said to his assistant. "I don't think we need to be giving the competition any pointers." Then he looked at Davey and winked. "That dog is going to be tough enough to beat already, without you helping him."

"Do you really think so?" Davey was usually calm in the lead-up to the competition. Today he sounded anxious. The episode in the ring the day before had shaken his confidence. "I just hope we don't end up anywhere near Joe Pond and his dog."

The same thought had crossed my mind. But before I could answer, Terry snorted out a laugh.

"You won't," he said.

Even Crawford permitted himself a small smile.

"No?" Aunt Peg had been perusing her catalog. She looked up inquiringly.

"Joe Pond appears to have scratched his Poodle entry for the rest of the weekend," Bertie spoke up from our other side.

"Is that so?" said Sam.

"Not just his Standards," Terry informed us. "His Minis and Toys are out too. It seems he decided there was somewhere else he would rather be today."

Aunt Peg looked surprised. "The man must be a complete ninny. I didn't mean to scare him that badly." She turned to Crawford. "Please tell me his withdrawal didn't break the majors in Standards."

"No, both majors are still intact," he replied. "And I'm planning to give young Davey a run for his money."

"You can have the one in bitches," Davey told him. He was looking much more cheerful than he had five minutes earlier. "As long as you leave the major in dogs for me."

"Not so fast," said Aunt Peg. "What about Coral?"

"You got your piece last weekend," Terry replied. "And then had the nerve to complain about it. It would serve you right if you didn't even get out of the Puppy class."

"Harrumph," said Aunt Peg.

Terry was right and we all knew it.

There was still more than an hour before the start of the Standard Poodle judging. Everyone, except for me, had a dog in front of them on a grooming table. Everyone else had work to do. I decided to make myself useful by checking out the concessions again. Kevin was happy playing with Josh and Daisy, so I set off on my own.

A woman selling fragrant funnel cakes was too busy to stop and talk to me. The man in the canine photography booth waved me on my way before I'd even finished speaking. The vendor after that was Spenser Pet Supplies.

Over the years, I'd visited Lana Spenser's booth more times than I could count. I'd also made numerous purchases.

Since much of Lana's merchandise was similar to products offered by Creature Comforts, she and Alan Crandall were in direct competition for the same small pool of customers. Lana had made an effort to set her business apart by offering a selection of quirky and unusual items along with her pet supplies. In addition, Lana had the uncanny ability to remember every one of her customers' names and their favorite breed of dog—an attribute that made her popular in the dog show community.

"Good morning, Melanie," Lana sang out cheerfully as I entered the booth. She was dressed in skinny jeans and a colorful sweater. Her dark blond hair fell down her back in a long braid. "Do you need to find something in a hurry or should I let you look around in peace?"

"Peace?" I smiled. "What's that?"

"Oh right. We're at a dog show." She laughed. "I was hoping it was too early in the day for people to be frantic yet."

"If you have a minute," I said, "I'd like to ask you a few questions."

Lana nodded. "Jasmine Crane, right?"

"How did you know that?"

"The police talked to all of us last week. It

150

occurred to me that you might not be far behind."

I guessed my reputation preceded me.

"I'll start by saving you some time," said Lana. "I don't know a darn thing about what happened. My booth was at the other end of the row from Jasmine's and I didn't see anything, or hear anything, until all the excitement was just about over. Which was really annoying, because I hate being the last to know stuff."

"How did you find out?"

"A customer told me. Then the police came by. Then later I saw Alan Crandall loading up Jasmine's things in his truck."

"The show committee had to get everything out of the park by the end of the day," I said. "They needed someone to deal with Jasmine's booth and Alan volunteered to help out."

"Oh, really?" Lana muttered. She didn't sound convinced.

"That's what Gwen Kimble told me. What did you think?"

She shrugged. "Jasmine and Alan . . . those two were thick as thieves. Actually I wouldn't be surprised if, in a week or two, we saw Creature Comforts offering some of Jasmine's artwork for sale."

"He can't do that," I told her. "The art doesn't belong to him. He's just storing it until Jasmine's beneficiaries come to claim it."

"In that case, I hope somebody took inventory

before everything disappeared into the back of his truck."

"You don't like Alan Crandall very much, do you?"

Lana's chin lifted. "No, I don't. And neither would you if you were in my shoes. My store is tiny compared to his. Minuscule. And yet it still bothers him that he doesn't have the pet supply monopoly on the dog show circuit. I guess no one ever told him that a little competition is supposed to be a good thing. Sometimes I feel like I'm a fly and he's a big, fat fly swatter."

"Surely things can't be that bad," I said with a laugh.

Lana smiled reluctantly. "You're right, they're not. Don't pay any attention to me. I shouldn't complain when I'm doing fine."

"I'm glad to hear that." I made a silent vow to shift more of my business in Lana's direction. "Just one last thing. You always seem to know everybody on the showground. I'm wondering if you've run across a woman named Amanda Burke."

"Abby's sister?" Lana sounded surprised. "Sure, I know her. In fact, I know her pretty well. She dog-sits for me sometimes."

"Have you spoken to her recently?"

Lana thought back. "No, probably not for a couple of months. The last time I went out of town was to a trade show in early February. Why?"

"Amanda seems to be missing. She disappeared last Sunday after the show. Abby's pretty worried. She asked me to look for Amanda, but so far I haven't had much luck."

"Missing?" Lana frowned. "I hope nothing's happened to her. Have you talked to Tamryn Klein?"

I searched my memory but the name wasn't familiar. "No, I haven't. Who is she?"

"She and Amanda are in the dog-sitting business together. A couple of times Amanda mentioned that if she ever wasn't available when I needed her, she could get Tamryn to fill in."

I knew that Abby had spoken to her sister's friends. But even if she'd already talked to Tamryn, I figured it wouldn't hurt to cover some of the same ground twice. Tamryn might tell me something that she wouldn't admit to Amanda's twin.

"Do you know how I can get in touch with her?" I asked.

"No, sorry. I never actually used her services myself. And I always figured I could book her through Amanda if I needed to."

"Thanks anyway," I said. "I'll figure out a way to track her down."

I started to turn away but Lana reached out a hand and stopped me. "I'd appreciate it if you let me know what you find out."

"About what happened to Jasmine?"

"No, I couldn't care less about that woman. But now you have me worried about Amanda too. Let me know when she turns up, okay?"

"I will," I promised.

I'd spent so much time at the concessions that the Standards were almost ready to head over to the ring when I returned to the setup.

"You cut that close," Aunt Peg informed me as she hopped Coral down from her table. The puppy stood in place and shook out her coat. Bitches wouldn't be judged until after dogs, but Aunt Peg would want to watch Davey's class from ringside. "I was afraid you might miss the whole thing."

"No way," I told Davey. Augie was already on the ground. I gave my son a quick hug for luck. "Got your comb? Got your armband? Got bait?"

Davey lifted his arm to indicate that his number was already in place. A greyhound comb was hooked along the top of the cardboard square. His jacket pocket bulged with bait. And best of all, Augie looked absolutely gorgeous. We were good to go.

Dog show competition isn't for the faint of heart. There are just too many days when things don't turn out the way you want them to. Sometimes the problems are beyond your control. The weather might be awful, or the ring too small to show off your dog properly. Sometimes the conditions are just right, and your dog has a bad day anyway. Or the judge plays politics. Or he judges the dogs fairly but simply prefers a different kind of Poodle than the one you've brought him.

Over the extended period of time that Davey had been trying to finish Augie's championship, it seemed as though the two of them had found a thousand different ways to lose. That one, narrow path that led to the coveted purple ribbon and the points that came with it had proven elusive many more times than not.

Which was why when things finally went right—when Davey and Augie did all the same things they'd done numerous times before, but on *this* day everything fell into place—I could hardly believe that his turn had come at last.

The Puppy Dog class went by in a flash. Almost before I knew it, Davey was leading Augie into the ring at the head of a long line of Standard Poodle Open Dogs. With so much at stake, I would have been quaking in my boots in his place. Not Davey. He looked like he had everything under control.

Augie walked straight into a stacked position and held it. His head and tail were high, his gaze fastened firmly on the judge. Neither Davey nor the big Poodle even glanced back. Clearly they'd both put the previous day's misadventure behind them.

When Mrs. Abernathy made her first pass down the line, Davey cupped his hands around Augie's head, gently lifting back his ears to allow the judge an unobstructed view of his handsome face. Mrs. Abernathy took a long look and permitted herself a small smile before she moved on.

Thank you, Terry, I thought gratefully.

Augie led the way the first time the Standard dogs were sent around the ring. He was first to be pulled when Mrs. Abernathy made her cut. And he was still at the head of the line when she pointed to her class winner.

Kevin gave a small shriek. He clapped his hands with glee.

"Not yet." Gently I covered his small hands with my own. "Davey still has to win the next class."

But Davey was on a roll and he knew it. With a big smile, he accepted the blue ribbon from the judge, flashed Kev a jaunty thumbs-up from inside the ring, then walked Augie back into place at the head of the mat.

A silver Puppy Dog came back in through the gate. His handler set up that previous class winner behind Augie. The judge stepped back to the middle of the ring and stared at her two contenders.

When Mrs. Abernathy quickly sent the pair of Standard Poodles around the ring, I was holding my breath. Not Sam; he was grinning. He already

156

knew what I hadn't yet realized. The judge's decision had already been made. Augie was so clearly the best that Mrs. Abernathy simply didn't need to see anything more.

With no further ado, she motioned Davey and Augie to the Winners marker at the side of the ring. Sam gave a loud whoop. Aunt Peg and Kevin started to clap. I just stood and stared. Several seconds passed before I was able to process what had happened right in front of me.

Then there was only one thing I could do. "Way to go, Davey!" I yelled.

Trust me, in polite dog show circles that is *not* done. I didn't care one bit.

Davey laughed, then averted his eyes. He was probably trying to pretend he wasn't related to me.

The judge ignored all the commotion outside her ring and handed Davey the purple ribbon. With it came Augie's all-important second major. Now he had fourteen points toward his championship.

Even though Augie wasn't my dog, I suddenly felt as though a huge weight had been lifted from my shoulders. Davey and Augie just needed one more point. Surely that wouldn't be too hard to accomplish.

Coral's Puppy Bitch class was next. Aunt Peg high-fived with Davey as they crossed paths near the in-gate. Davey was beaming with pride and satisfaction. Augie was prancing at his side. The Poodle knew that he had done well too.

We paused our celebration just long enough to watch Coral place second in a class of four. Then while the Open Bitches were being judged, Sam and Davey made minor repairs to Augie's coat. He would be needed back in the ring to compete for Best of Variety.

A nice white bitch won the Open class and was awarded Winners Bitch. Crawford and another professional handler took their Standard specials into the ring. The Winners Bitch lined up behind them. Davey and Augie followed.

While Mrs. Abernathy judged the two champions, Davey took out a squeaky toy and played catch with Augie at the end of the mat. Having already won the important prize, the pair could now relax and have fun.

Crawford's champion won the Variety. The Winners Bitch was Best of Opposite Sex. Augie was awarded Best of Winners. When the class was over, we remained at ringside to have a win picture taken with the judge.

It was a wonderful day. We took our time and savored every minute.

Chapter 12

W hen we got back at the setup, we were all in high spirits.

Crawford had won the variety in Minis and Standards and had put points on both of his Toys. Bertie had won the breed with her Bearded Collie and scored a Sheltie puppy's first point with its happy owner standing ringside. And of course there was Augie's excellent major win.

In fact, the only one in the vicinity who hadn't won something was Aunt Peg. After the way she'd behaved the week before, we all figured she deserved that.

"It won't be long now," Davey whispered in Augie's ear as he jumped the Poodle up on his table. "Then off comes that coat." He mimed the movement of a clipper. "Zip, zip, zip!"

"I heard that," Aunt Peg announced. "Don't you dare go jinxing that dog. He still needs one more win."

"Just a little one," I said.

"Sometimes the little ones are the toughest to get."

Now she was just being contrary. So I changed the subject. "Do you know a woman named Tamryn Klein?"

Aunt Peg turned the name over in her mind. "I don't believe so. Should I?"

"I thought you might have met her through Amanda Burke. Lana Spenser told me that she and Amanda were in the dog-sitting business together. When Amanda was overbooked, Tamryn filled in for her. I was hoping you'd know how to get in touch with her."

"No." Aunt Peg frowned. She hated not having a handy answer to every question. "I have no idea."

"I do," Daisy spoke up from Bertie's setup.

We all turned and looked at her.

"You do?" I asked.

"Sure. Tamryn lives in Norwalk. She and I went to school together. I think she's still living with her parents. And is pretty desperate to move out. Last I heard, she was picking up odd jobs from Jasmine Crane. You know, that lady who . . ." Daisy glanced down at Kev and Josh. Her voice trailed away uncertainly.

"Yes, we know about Jasmine," I told her. "What kind of work was Tamryn doing for her?"

Daisy shrugged. "I hear stuff about Tamryn sometimes, but it's not like we're friends. She's a year or two older than me. Plus, she's not . . ." She paused, as if debating whether or not to continue.

"Not what?" Bertie prodded.

"Tamryn's not a very nice person. Like, you

probably shouldn't leave her in charge of your pets while you're out of town or anything."

"You don't have to worry about that," I said. "I only want to ask her a few questions. Do you happen to have her phone number?"

Daisy looked relieved. "No, but I can give you her parents' address. Does that help?"

"That would be great," I said. "Thank you."

When I finished tucking that information away, I decided to take one last walk down the row of concessions while Sam and Davey were working on Augie. The proprietors of the first three booths I visited didn't have much to say. But at my fourth stop, I hit pay dirt.

Mary and Edgar Daltry were an elderly couple from Brooklyn who sold canine-themed jewelry. Their extensive selection of necklaces, bracelets, and rings showcased the charms of virtually every AKC breed. Some of the pieces were costume jewelry, affordable for most budgets. But others were made of gold and platinum and set with real gemstones.

As soon as I mentioned Jasmine Crane's name, Mary Daltry scowled. "That woman," she spat.

"What about her?"

"I don't want to wish ill on anybody. But *her?*" She made the word sound like a curse. "What happened to her—she had it coming."

That got my attention in a hurry.

"It sounds like you must have known Jasmine pretty well."

"Me? No. Jasmine wasn't interested in me. Edgar was the one she set her sights on." Mary nodded toward the other side of the booth where her husband was showing rings to a customer. Then she drew me behind the back wall of the booth where we could talk in private. "Jasmine Crane was a piece of work. That woman knew all about how to wind men around her little finger. She was full of brilliant ideas, except that the only one they ever worked out for was her."

"Like what?" I asked curiously.

"You know what Jasmine looked like, right?"

I nodded.

"She had that whole sultry, sexy thing going on. Men thought she was exotic, and she used that to her advantage."

This story was beginning to sound familiar. I wondered if the Daltrys had also had something of value disappear from their booth while they weren't looking.

"Jasmine used to come around at the shows and sweet talk my Edgar. She convinced him to let her 'model' some of our better pieces while she was selling artwork at her booth. She told Edgar that when customers commented on how pretty she looked, she would send them over here to look at our jewelry. Edgar thought it was a terrific idea. He was sure that having her help us like that would be great for business."

I was pretty sure I knew the answer. But I had to ask anyway. "And was it?"

"It was good for Jasmine, all right. But not so much for Edgar and me."

"How come?"

"The first month or so, not much happened. Jasmine would stop by and pick out a brooch or a necklace that matched her outfit. She liked the flashy stuff. And I'm no dummy. I made sure to steer her toward the pieces made of silver and colored stones. Later, Jasmine would come flitting back. She'd smile and coo and ask Edgar if he liked all the customers she'd sent."

Mary stopped and frowned. "Thing is, if there were any extra shoppers coming our way, I never noticed them. But Edgar seemed happy and I figured what's the harm? Little did I know."

I could see inside the booth from where we were standing. Edgar had finished waiting on his customer. Now he appeared to be looking around for Mary. He was probably wondering where she'd gone.

Mary must have seen him too because she beckoned me closer and lowered her voice. "Jasmine Crane was a tease and a flirt. She used her feminine wiles to get things she wouldn't have been able to afford otherwise. Edgar's usually a pretty smart cookie, but he couldn't see through her act. More's the pity."

"What did she do?" I asked. I was really hoping that Mary would get to the point of her story before her husband came and interrupted us.

"One morning when Jasmine came around, I wasn't here. She got Edgar to let her try on a diamond brooch. Not cubic zirconia, the real stuff. Edgar told me that it looked so pretty on her, he didn't have the heart to tell her that the piece wasn't supposed to come out of the showcase."

"Men." I just sighed.

Mary nodded unhappily.

"Of course when I got back, I noticed right away that the brooch wasn't where it was supposed to be. I was livid when Edgar told me what he'd done. But he just told me to calm down, that it would be back in our hands soon enough."

"But it wasn't, was it?"

"Not even close. Edgar and I never saw that diamond brooch again. Later that afternoon, Jasmine comes by looking all teary-like. She says the clasp was loose, and it must have come open at some point during the day. She doesn't have the brooch and she doesn't know where it is."

"That's terrible," I said.

"What it is, is outright thievery," Mary snapped. "Especially since I knew darn well that the clasp had been fine that morning, before Jasmine got hold of it."

"Did she offer to pay for your missing jewelry?"

"You gotta be kidding me." She looked at me like she thought I was crazy. "Jasmine just mumbled something about how she was sure we must be well insured, and she was sorry for the inconvenience. I'll tell you what. Only an idiot would believe a story like that. I wanted to march right over to Jasmine's booth and tear that place apart, looking for what was mine."

"I take it you didn't actually do that," I said with a half smile.

"No. But only because Edgar wouldn't let me. Speaking of idiots." Mary grimaced. "*He* forgave her. He told her it wasn't her fault, that he should have checked the clasp himself before letting her put it on."

"It sounds as though you're still angry," I said.

"You got that right," Mary shot right back. "Unless of course you're asking me if I was mad enough to go and strangle Jasmine with one of her own leashes."

"Were you?"

The question made her laugh. Mary had wispy white hair and barely came up to my chin. "Maybe I would have if I coulda figured out how to reach up that high."

Point taken.

"Now Edgar, that damn fool is another story." Mary slipped me a wink. "You ever hear he's come to grief, you'd better come around and check back with me."

"I'll do that," I agreed. "You're not the first person I've spoken with who had a problem with Jasmine. It doesn't seem as though she had many friends in the dog show community."

Mary nodded. She wasn't surprised. "Jasmine was the kind of person you liked a whole lot better before you got to know her. You want my advice?"

"Sure."

"You want to figure out who killed that woman, look for someone who knew what she was really like. Because in that crowd, I bet she had enemies all over the place."

I spent the walk back to the setup pondering what Mary had told me. But once there, I put her caustic words out of my mind. The mood there was still jubilant, and deservedly so. Augie had finally won his second major. Today was a day for celebration.

I cupped Augie's muzzle in my palm and kissed him on the nose. "What a superior Poodle you are. You were such a good boy."

"What about me?" Davey complained good naturedly. "I did all the work."

So I hugged Davey. Then I hugged Bertie. I gave Sam a big kiss and Kevin a little one.

Never one to miss a festive occasion, Terry grabbed me, spun me around, and kissed my nose. To Crawford's utter bemusement, I bussed him on the lips. Aunt Peg watched my exuberant display with her eyes narrowed and her hands propped on her hips.

I didn't even try to kiss her.

"Apparently it's a good thing your son doesn't win majors more often," she said drily.

I was tempted to stick out my tongue, but at the last minute I remembered I was too mature for behavior like that. So instead I gave Aunt Peg a big smile.

"Just for ten minutes, let me be happy in peace," I told her.

"Amen to that," said Terry.

Monday morning, it was time to go back to work.

Faith was much more enthusiastic about that than I was. Having remained home for most of the weekend, she was delighted to run outside and jump in the car. Faith didn't even care where I was going as long as she was coming too. That Poodle was pretty good at keeping a schedule, however. She probably knew it was the start of a new week.

Our first student of the day was Francesca Della Cimino. She and I were scheduled to spend forty-five minutes together on Monday, Wednesday, and Friday mornings. This would be the fourth session I'd had with the sixth-grader.

So far, I was still baffled. Francesca was undeniably smart. And though the Howard Academy curriculum was tougher than most, I was quite sure it shouldn't have been beyond her abilities. Which left me wondering why a girl who had started the semester with such promise, was now inexplicably falling behind in her classes.

I'd checked in with Louisa Delgado and two of Francesca's other teachers and discovered that they were equally mystified. "Gain her trust and figure it out," Louisa told me. "You're good at that."

For Francesca's sake, I hoped Louisa was right.

Francesca began the session the same way as always. She walked in the room and went straight to Faith. The big Poodle jumped up out of her bed and met Francesca halfway across the floor. The two of them did a happy dance around the room.

If the sixth-grader had had a tail, it would have been wagging too, I thought. She was so lively and unguarded in her interactions with Faith. Why did the walls come back up as soon as she had to talk to me?

Francesca dropped her backpack on the table and unzipped an outer pocket. "I brought Faith a peanut butter biscuit. You told me that was her favorite kind. Is it all right if I give it to her?"

"I'm sure Faith would love that," I said with a

smile. "But thank you for being polite and asking first."

"My mother says no matter how logical things appear to you, you should never assume that other people feel the same way," Francesca told me.

"Your mother sounds like a wise woman."

"She is," she replied seriously. "At least that's what my father says."

I took a seat at the table. Francesca would follow when she was ready. There was no hurry.

"Was your mother good in school?" I asked.

The girl brushed aside her hair and looked up at me. "Do you want the true answer or do you want me to tell you what her official bio says?"

What a question, I thought. What a world this child lived in.

"Since you know the truth, that's what I'd rather hear."

"Mother didn't love going to school, but she was good at her classes. Just like she's good at everything she does. She makes it all look easy." It sounded as though Francesca sighed as she left Faith and joined me at the table.

"You must take after your mother then. School is easy for you too. At least it used to be."

Francesca shrugged. She unzipped the top of her backpack and took out her English book. "This is what you wanted to work on today, right? My essay for English lit?"

"Sure, but we can get to that in a minute. First let's talk about your classes."

Francesca's gaze slipped away. "What about them?"

"Which one is your favorite?"

She considered briefly, then shook her head. "I guess I don't have one."

"Really? Are you sure? There must be a subject that you enjoy more than the others."

"No, I don't think so."

"All right. Then who's your favorite teacher?"

Francesca shrugged again. This was like pulling teeth.

"There's nobody?"

She stared at me mutinously. "If I *have* to give you a name, I'll pick Mr. Babic."

"Mr. Babic," I repeated. The name wasn't familiar. I ran through the roster of HA teachers in my mind. Nope, still nothing. "I don't think I know him. What does he teach?"

"Mr. Babic taught mathematics," Francesca blurted. "At my old school in Vienna. That was a better school than this one. I want to go back there."

Her face crumpled. The girl looked like she was trying not to cry. She turned away from me and began digging in her backpack. I heard a loud sniffle.

There was a box of tissues on my desk. I got up and brought it over. Francesca ignored it. And me.

I waited a minute, then said gently, "I'm sorry you're not happy here. And I can understand how you might be homesick. But your parents are working in New York now. I don't think it's possible for you to go back to Vienna."

"Nobody asked me if I wanted to move here," Francesca complained. "Nobody cares what I think about anything."

"I'm sure that's not true. But performing at the Met is a wonderful opportunity for your mother. And I know your parents thought you would like being in school at Howard Academy."

Francesca spun around to face me. Her arms were crossed tightly over her chest. "Well, I don't."

"Is there anything I can do to help?"

"No," she mumbled.

"I know this is a big adjustment for you. Howard Academy is a very different environment than the one you were used to. It can take time to figure out where you fit in."

"That's just it," Francesca said. "I don't want to fit in. I don't even like anybody here."

"That's too bad. There are lots of great kids who go to this school. Maybe if you gave them a chance—"

Francesca pushed her essay toward me, across the table. "You're supposed to be helping me with my paper. Can we do that now?"

I paused, hoping for a bright idea. Nothing

171

happened, darn it. "Yes, we can get to work. If that's what you want."

"It is."

So I helped her with her essay. When our session was finished, Francesca couldn't get out of my room fast enough. I'm a teacher. I'm supposed to have the answers. But in Francesca's case, I kept coming up blank. Something was going on with that girl. I wished I knew what it was.

Chapter 13

Aunt Peg called as Faith and I were leaving Howard Academy. I don't know if she monitors my schedule or if she has a tracking device on my car. I probably don't even want to know.

The purpose of the call was to invite me to her house for cake. Not scones, mind you. *Cake.* Aunt Peg suggested that I arrive *tout de suite.* As if the offer of cake wouldn't have been enough to ensure that.

Our conversation was unusually brief. Something had to be up, but Aunt Peg wouldn't tell me what it was. She likes to remain a woman of mystery.

Sam had dropped Kev off at preschool that morning, so it was my turn to pick him up. But I was already in Greenwich where Aunt Peg lived, and Graceland was in Stamford. By the time I swung by the school and came back, that whole toot sweet thing would be right out the window.

Curiosity won out over family obligation. I called Sam and he agreed to fill in for me. There's a reason Bertie calls Sam "the long-suffering husband" but mostly I try not to think too much about that.

When Faith and I arrived at Aunt Peg's house,

Abby Burke's car was parked in the driveway. So that was one puzzle solved. I hoped that Abby had something interesting to tell us and hadn't just stopped by for cake too.

We got out of the car together. Faith led the way up the steps to the front porch. Had it really only been a week since the three of us had met here previously? I wondered. It felt like much longer. And yet I hadn't learned nearly enough in the meantime.

"It's about time you got here," Aunt Peg said when she opened the door and her Poodles came swarming out. "We almost started without you."

Barely more than ten minutes had passed since she'd called. But Aunt Peg didn't believe in speed limits. She also possessed an uncanny ability to talk her way out of tickets. Mere mortals like me were not so fortunate, so yes, I had crawled the length of North Street.

"Don't just stand there." She deftly shooed both me and the dogs inside the house. "Hurry up and come along."

Aunt Peg veered toward her living room. Faith and I followed behind. Abby was on a love seat, clutching her phone. There wasn't a piece of cake in sight.

"I hope you have good news for us," I said.

"I do," Abby replied happily. "I've heard from Amanda. She's okay."

174

"Excellent." I sat down opposite her. "Where is she?"

"She didn't say."

That wasn't the answer I'd been hoping for. "Did you ask?"

"We didn't actually talk. She sent a text."

"A text," I echoed. My voice sounded hollow. Anyone could have sent a text from Amanda's phone. Apparently that hadn't occurred to Abby. "What did it say?"

"Here." Abby handed over the device. "You can read it for yourself."

Aunt Peg and I both leaned in to look at the message. It wasn't much. Hi, Babes, sorry 2 B out of touch. Im ok. Just needed some vacay time. Talk soon.

I looked up. "Babes?"

"Amanda and I always call each other that." Abby smiled fondly. "That's how I knew the text was from her."

"Does anyone else know about that name?"

"Well, family of course. And maybe a few friends. And I guess Rick might have heard us use it."

I saw the moment the realization hit her. Abby's smile faded. The identity of the person who'd sent the message wasn't as definite as she'd assumed.

"Did you text her back?" Aunt Peg asked.

"Of course. Right away. But there was no reply. So then I called, but Amanda didn't pick up."

"Assuming your sister did send that text," I said, "do you have any idea why she might have suddenly felt the need for vacay time?"

"I've been wracking my brain, trying to figure that out." Abby sounded frustrated. "The only thing I can think of is Rick."

Funny the way his name kept popping up.

"What about him?" I asked.

"He and Amanda have been together for a long time, but lately they haven't been getting along very well. Amanda and I have had a couple of heart-to-heart talks about whether or not he's the right guy for her. She's been thinking about breaking up with him."

"Why would that make her want to disappear?" asked Aunt Peg—the woman who'd never shirked a confrontation in her life.

"You don't know Rick. He can be difficult."

"Difficult how?" I prompted.

"He's the kind of guy who thinks he's always right. Like his opinions are the only ones that matter. Lately Amanda had been feeling like he was always criticizing her, finding fault with everything she did. I don't know why Amanda wants to put up with his domineering crap. She deserves better, you know?"

Aunt Peg and I both nodded.

"And it didn't help that lately Rick had developed this weird fascination with Amanda's landlady."

"Landlady?" That got my attention. "You mean Jasmine Crane."

"That's right."

"Explain," said Aunt Peg.

"I guess Rick ran into Jasmine a few times when he was visiting Amanda. That was how the two of them got to know each other. Amanda didn't think anything about it at first. But then suddenly it seemed like Rick was always talking about Jasmine. He'd ask Amanda about her artwork and stuff." Abby looked annoyed on her twin's behalf. "I don't know if I would say that Amanda was jealous exactly, but I know she didn't like it."

"Amanda wasn't the only one who felt that way when Jasmine was around," I said. "I keep hearing about her talent for flirting with men, making them feel important, and then getting them to do what she wanted."

"Rick didn't need anybody to make him feel important," Abby said with a grim smile. "According to Amanda, he also wanted to know all about the jobs Jasmine was getting for her. Like every little detail. Even stuff Amanda thought was none of his business. Lately things had gotten pretty intense between them. Amanda didn't come right out and say it, but I think she was a little bit afraid of him."

"Another excellent reason for giving him the boot," Aunt Peg said firmly.

"What kind of jobs was Jasmine getting Amanda?" I asked.

"Oh, you know. The pet-sitting stuff. Back when Amanda was getting started, before she'd made connections of her own, Jasmine was a real help to her. Even now, Jasmine was still drumming up work for her sometimes. Amanda took some of the jobs and another girl did the rest."

I straightened in my seat. "Would that be Tamryn Klein?"

"Yes, I think so. At least the name sounds familiar. I've never met her though."

"That's the girl Daisy knew," Aunt Peg remembered. "The one you were talking about yesterday."

I nodded, then turned back to Abby. "So when you got in touch with Amanda's friends last week, you didn't talk to Tamryn?"

"No. Truthfully, she never crossed my mind. And even if she had, I wouldn't have known how to get in touch with her."

"That's all right, I'll take care of it," I said. "Thanks to Daisy, I know how to find Tamryn. And I was planning to talk to her anyway."

Abby nodded. She gazed back and forth between Aunt Peg and me. When I'd arrived, she'd been smiling. Now her expression was guarded.

"When I came to tell Peg that I'd heard from

Amanda, I was feeling so relieved to know that she was all right," she told us. "But now I don't know what to think."

"Only good thoughts," I said. "And keep trying to get in touch with your sister. Maybe that text did come from her. It could mean she's getting ready to open the lines of communication."

"I hope so." Abby tucked the phone in her purse and stood. Zeke, who'd been lying beside her, got up as well. Absently Abby's hand drifted downward. Her fingers scratched the top of the Poodle's head. Once a dog person, always a dog person.

"Let us know if you hear anything else," I said.

"Of course I will. And thank you for your help."

Aunt Peg walked Abby to the door. A minute later she was back.

"Well?" she asked. "What do you make of that?"

"I'm not sure," I said. "I think we should discuss it over cake. I'm pretty sure you promised there was going to be some."

"No, I believe I *offered*. It's not the same thing at all."

I walked past her and headed for the kitchen. Faith was immediately at my side. The rest of the Poodles fell into line behind us. "I hope you didn't lure me here under false pretenses."

"Perish the thought. Of course I have cake."

179

"Before I met you," I said over my shoulder, "I never ate cake. I preferred pie."

"Clearly there was something wrong with your upbringing."

There'd been plenty of things wrong with my upbringing. But I had no desire to enumerate them now. Instead I poured us two tall glasses of milk while Aunt Peg dished out the cake. The slices she cut were so big they almost didn't fit on the plates.

Not that I was complaining. I'd lucked out. It was St. Moritz mocha cake. I was salivating just thinking about it.

In exchange for transporting my taste buds to heaven, Aunt Peg wanted information. That seemed like a fair exchange to me.

"I know you were busy at the shows," she said when we were seated across from each other at the kitchen table. "Indeed, we barely saw you back at the setup. Tell me what you found out."

I had my priorities in order. Eat first, talk second. I cut a large wedge of cake with my fork, put it in my mouth, and let it melt on my tongue.

After I swallowed, I said, "Before—when Jasmine was alive—I thought of her as a popular member of the dog show community. But now, talking to the people who worked alongside her, I'm getting a totally different impression. She didn't have many friends among her fellow vendors."

Quickly I summed up everything I'd learned. Aunt Peg polished off most of her cake while I was talking. I hoped she was planning to go back for seconds. Because then I wouldn't feel like a glutton when I did.

"And it wasn't just the other vendors," I said at the end. "Gwen Kimble didn't have anything good to say about her either."

"I suppose that's to be expected," Aunt Peg mused.

I stared at her across the table. "What do you mean?"

And why was I just hearing that now?

"Gossip has it that Gwen and Jasmine engaged in a bit of a squabble recently."

"Something to do with concession space at the Sedgefield show?" I guessed. "Gwen told me that Jasmine was difficult to work with."

"No, not that. It was a different matter entirely. As you know, Jasmine took commissions for pet portraits. She sold artwork she'd created in her booth at the shows, but the portraits were a lucrative sideline for her."

I nodded. "So I've heard. Sam said he'd even thought about hiring her to do a portrait once."

"Well, Gwen not only thought about it, she did commission a painting. She had an elderly Whippet bitch whom she absolutely adored. She wanted Jasmine to preserve the old girl's likeness while there was still time. Gwen had pictures of

181

Lotus, but she requested that Jasmine meet her in person too. Gwen hoped the portrait would capture the Whippet's personality as well as her beauty."

"Did it?" I asked.

"Supposedly it wasn't even close. According to the grapevine, Gwen refused to take possession of the painting and she refused to pay for it."

I was happy to let Aunt Peg do the talking while I ate cake. I even slipped Faith a nibble when no one else was looking. She's a fan of the St. Moritz Bakery too.

"Jasmine wasn't having any of that," Aunt Peg continued. "She told Gwen that she'd adhered to the conditions of their contract, and Gwen needed to do the same. Otherwise Jasmine threatened to sue."

"That seems a little extreme," I said. "Wouldn't it have been easier to just make a few changes to the painting?"

"Frankly, I have no idea if anyone even considered that. By that time, the two of them were so mad at each other that no one was looking to compromise. Jasmine insisted that the portrait was perfect as is. And Gwen called Jasmine a talentless hack who wouldn't know what real art looked like if it jumped up and sat on her easel."

Aunt Peg paused for a sip of milk, then added, "So they both hired lawyers and they'll be hashing out their differences in court."

"Except they won't," I pointed out. "Not

now. Gwen appears to have won her case by default. That seems rather convenient, under the circumstances."

Aunt Peg slid a second piece of cake onto her plate. "It does, doesn't it?"

"Gwen and I discussed Jasmine Crane at length last week." I tried not to sound annoyed. I probably didn't succeed. "Why do you suppose she didn't tell me any of this?"

"I should think the answer to that is obvious, Melanie. You didn't ask the right questions."

Later that evening, I put in a call to the Klein residence in Norwalk. Tamryn's father picked up. I gave my name and told him I was interested in talking to his daughter about a possible dog-sitting job. He passed the phone to Tamryn, who said she'd be delighted to meet with me. We made an appointment at a Starbucks in New Canaan for the following afternoon.

"It's at three o'clock," I told Sam as we were feeding the dogs. "There'll be plenty of time for me to pick Kev up at school, then drop him and Faith off here before I go."

The Poodles were spread out around the kitchen, waiting politely for their dinner to be served. Bud was jumping up and down like a pogo stick, woofing excitedly under his breath. Yet again it occurred to me that his previous owners had a lot to answer for.

"Tamryn . . ." Sam repeated the name thoughtfully. "That's the girl that Daisy used to know?"

"Yes. She works with Amanda Burke. I'm hoping she might be able to give me a lead on where Amanda went."

"Are you sure that's a good idea?"

I looked at him in surprise. As always, I'd kept Sam apprised of what I'd been doing—for the most part anyway. This was the first time he'd voiced a concern. "Why not?"

"Maybe it's time for you to think about the fact that Amanda is an adult, and by all accounts a capable and independent woman. There was no indication of foul play, and the text Abby received appears to confirm that. So Amanda must have had a good reason for leaving. And if she doesn't want to be found, perhaps that should be her prerogative."

I considered what Sam had said while I added chopped meat to the soaked kibble and stirred the mix together. Together we set the bowls down in a long row on the kitchen floor.

"Abby is worried about Amanda," I said finally.

"And yet . . . when Amanda felt the need to get away, she didn't turn to her sister for help."

That was a good point. And one I hadn't previously considered. But still . . . I couldn't stop searching for Abby's twin now.

"I think Amanda is hiding because she knows

something about Jasmine's death," I blurted.

"Is that so?" Sam smiled faintly. All right, so maybe I hadn't told him *everything*. "Now that we're clear on your motive, is it all right if I advise you to be careful?"

"Of course," I said. "I'm always careful."

I was half afraid he'd call me a liar. Sam kissed me instead.

That worked for both of us.

Chapter 14

The New Canaan Starbucks was on the busy corner of Park and Elm Streets, just across from the train station. The interior of the small coffee shop was crowded, but the afternoon was warm enough to sit outside in the park-like area in front of the building.

Having already used up all my extra calories on cake, I ordered a plain dark roast coffee, added a little milk, and carried it out to a table beneath a tree. Though the branches above me were still mostly bare, the scent of spring was in the air. I took off my jacket and draped it over the back of my chair. I'd arrived a little early for our appointment, but I was happy to enjoy the warm spring sunshine while I waited.

Promptly at three o'clock, a girl I assumed was Tamryn Klein came striding around the corner. She looked hardly older than a teenager and was so skinny that I wondered if her bones rattled when she walked. Dressed in jeans, Doc Martens, and a leather jacket, Tamryn had black hair cut in a spiky bob and numerous piercings in each ear. She skipped up the wide stairs and was about to enter the building when she saw me sitting by myself and headed my way instead.

"Are you Melanie Travis?"

"Yes, I am. You must be Tamryn." I stood up and we shook hands.

"Let me just get something to drink," she said. "I'll be right back."

She returned five minutes later with an espresso. Tamryn pulled out a chair and straddled it. "Golden Retriever," she said.

"Excuse me?"

"I'm great at guessing people's dogs. You look like a Golden Retriever. Am I right?"

I started to correct her, then thought better of it. "Before I answer that, tell me what a Golden Retriever person looks like."

She tipped her head to one side and studied me. "Cute, friendly, soft. A little fluffy around the edges."

I sputtered out a laugh. I had definitely been eating too much cake.

"Nope, not even close," I said. Considering how far off the mark Tamryn's first guess had been, it seemed prudent not to let her try again. "I have Standard Poodles."

"Okay. Right. I can see that now. I bet you have the silver ones, don't you?"

"All black," I replied.

"That's great then. I'm terrific with big, scary dogs. In fact, you might say they're my specialty."

I sat back in my seat. This interview wasn't

going at all the way I'd expected it to. "You think Poodles are scary?"

"Nah, not really. I'm just repeating what I've heard."

"From whom?" I asked curiously.

"You know." Tamryn waved a hand in the air. "Word on the street."

It was a stretch to imagine that there might be a street where people were talking about scary Poodles. But whatever.

"So how did you get my name?" she asked.

"Amanda Burke dog sits frequently for my aunt."

"Oh yeah? That's cool. Amanda's great."

"She is," I agreed. "She does a terrific job. In fact I was trying to get in touch with her when someone gave me your name."

Tamryn gulped down a shot of espresso. "I do a great job too."

"I'm sure you do. But I was surprised that Amanda didn't return my calls. Do you know where she is?"

"Nope. Sorry. I haven't seen her in a while."

"I was told that the two of you are pretty good friends."

"Really?" Tamryn's gaze narrowed. "Who told you that?"

I thought fast and said, "Jasmine Crane."

"Oh." Abruptly her shoulders slumped. The girl looked stricken. "That was a horrible thing."

188

"I'm sorry," I said. "Were you and Jasmine close?"

"We just worked together some, that's all."

"I know that Jasmine was getting pet-sitting jobs for Amanda. Did she do the same for you?"

Tamryn gave me an odd look. "Yeah, that's right. I've been trying to move out of my folks' place. Jasmine knew I needed some extra cash. She said she might be able to help out."

"That was kind of her."

"I guess. But that's what Jasmine was like. She always liked to have a hand in everything that was going on."

I could smell the heady aroma of my coffee, sitting neglected in front of me. I picked it up and took a sip. "Jasmine was a talented artist too. Did you ever see any of her paintings?"

"I guess. Maybe a couple of times." Tamryn didn't sound terribly impressed. "Jasmine had this friend, Sadie. Mostly I saw them when she was there. Sadie always seemed to be moving that art stuff around. She'd ask if I could help her load or unload her van. What did she think I was, a pack mule?"

"She probably just figured that you were young and strong," I said. "Why were Sadie and Jasmine moving the paintings—did they say?"

"Something about all that art being too valuable to store in one place. So they divided it up between their two houses for safekeeping. I thought that sounded crazy, but what did I care about two old ladies and all that junk as long as they didn't make me cart it around for them?"

Hmmph, I thought. *Old ladies indeed.*

"So." Tamryn changed the subject. "How many dogs do you have?"

"Six," I replied.

She was impressed. Either that or she was calculating how much she could charge to take care of that many dogs.

"All Poodles?"

"Five Standards and one small mixed breed."

"And everybody gets along?"

"Yes, they all coexist quite happily." Not that they had a choice. I was alpha dog in my house.

"Any meds or special needs?"

I shook my head.

"Fenced yard or do they need to be walked?"

"Fenced," I told her.

"That's great. It makes things easier. How often do you anticipate needing me to dog sit for you?"

Good question.

"It varies." That answer ought to be vague enough. "But I wanted to get someone lined up so I'd be ready when the time came. I was planning to talk to Amanda, but as I said earlier I couldn't seem to locate her."

I paused in case Tamryn wanted to comment. She didn't. She just tipped back her glass and polished off her espresso. I was running out of time.

"I was wondering if you'd ever met Amanda's boyfriend, Rick?" I said.

"I guess I might have run across him a time or two," Tamryn replied.

"What did you think of him?"

"He's not my type, but he seemed okay."

"Rick was friends with Jasmine too, wasn't he?"

"Friends?" Tamryn pushed back her chair. She was ready to go. "That's not what I would have called it."

"Really? That's interesting."

Tamryn shrugged like she didn't agree. "Those two had some kind of business deal going on. I don't know what it was about, and I didn't want to know. Once I overheard Rick go all Incredible Hulk on Jasmine. He said she'd better do what he wanted or she'd be sorry. After that I didn't want any part of whatever they were getting up to."

She jumped out of her seat. I quickly followed suit. It sounded as though Amanda wasn't the only one who might have been afraid of Rick.

"After you heard Jasmine had been killed, did you tell the police about what you'd heard?"

"What? Are you kidding me?" Tamryn skirted around the table and lobbed her empty cup in a trash bin. "First of all, I don't even know any police. And second, it was none of my business."

"Now with Jasmine gone, I guess you'll have to find your own dog-sitting jobs," I said.

191

Tamryn gave me another odd look. As if there was a subtext to our conversation that I didn't understand. I wished I knew what I was missing.

She fished a card out of her jacket pocket and handed it over. "Don't call my parents' house again, okay? You can reach me at the number on here."

"Thanks," I said. "I'll be in touch."

I watched her walk away, then went and tossed my own cup in the trash. I was sure that Tamryn knew more about Amanda's disappearance than she was telling me. But each time I'd brought up Amanda's name, Tamryn had shut me down.

Damn, I thought. *I must be losing my touch.*

Thursday morning I was standing at the stove, frying bacon. Usually our weekday breakfasts consisted of something like cereal and a banana. Pour, peel, eat, and go kind of meals. But I was feeling a little guilty about how many of the parenting chores I'd placed in Sam's lap.

All right, a lot guilty.

And since I'd gotten in touch with Sadie Foster the night before and set up a meeting for this afternoon, things weren't about to improve anytime soon. Hence the bacon. And the waffles.

"It smells good in here." Davey was the first one through the kitchen door. He threw his backpack on the counter and went to the refrigerator to pour himself a glass of orange juice. "What's the occasion?"

"No occasion," I said, turning the bacon to crisp the other side. "Can't I just spoil my family once in a while?"

"Well . . . sure." Davey cracked a grin. "But you never do."

I waggled the cooking fork in his direction. "Watch that mouth."

Unfortunately my impromptu move splattered a few drops of bacon grease on the floor. Bud made a dive for my feet. Tar was right behind him. Within seconds, I was surrounded by scrambling canines.

"I didn't even dribble that much," I said, looking down at them. "And it's gone now. Go away."

Faith, who had too much dignity to join in the action, was sitting and watching from the other side of the room. We'd been a team for a long time. She knew perfectly well that I'd slip her a piece of bacon when no one else was looking.

"What's gone now?" Sam asked. His hair was wet from the shower, and the rugby shirt he'd just pulled on was still rumpled around his torso. He looked way better than bacon and waffles.

"Bacon grease," Davey informed him.

Sam's eyes widened slightly. "That's a good thing, right?"

Kevin came flying into the room behind him.

Kev's overalls were correctly fastened and his shoes were on his feet. The correct feet. It was almost a miracle.

"Hey, squirt." Davey held up his own glass. "Want some orange juice?"

"No." He shook his head firmly. "Apple juice."

Davey turned to me. "Do we have apple juice?"

"Refrigerator door, bottom right," I told him.

Sam walked over to stand beside me. "What's with the bacon?"

"Mom's spoiling us," Davey said with a smirk.

"Since when?" asked Sam.

I turned and gazed around the room. "Anyone who's fresh doesn't get bacon. Or waffles. Kevin and I will have more for ourselves."

"Not me," Kev announced. "Don't like bacon."

I propped my hands on my hips. "When did that happen?"

My younger son shook his head. He didn't know.

Everybody liked bacon, didn't they? How could I possibly have the only child who didn't? So much for making breakfast an occasion. I was beginning to think I should have just slept late.

"There's a catch," said Sam. He knew me all too well. "What is it?"

"Umm . . . I won't be here this afternoon. I have an appointment."

He raised a brow. "Hairdresser? Acupuncture? Podiatrist?"

"None of the above. I'm going to see Sadie Foster. We're meeting in Weston."

"Oh well, then. That clears things right up." Sam turned and mouthed to Davey, *Who's Sadie Foster?*

Davey shrugged in reply.

"Sarcasm doesn't become you," I said.

"As long as it doesn't cost us bacon," Davey replied, "we're okay with that."

Just once, you'd think I'd be able to get in the last word in my own house. Since that didn't seem to be happening, I shut up and served breakfast. It was excellent, if I do say so myself.

To my surprise, Sadie Foster had wanted to meet at Jasmine Crane's house. That seemed like an odd location to me, but I wasn't given a choice. Right from the start of our phone conversation it had been clear that Sadie was calling the shots. She told me she was a busy person, and that if I wanted to impose on her limited time, I could meet her at Jasmine's at two-thirty.

"And don't be late," she said before disconnecting. "I won't wait for you."

Bearing that in mind, I showed up ten minutes early. Sadie's blue minivan was already parked in the driveway. She opened the front door to the house as I was getting out of the Volvo. Apparently we wouldn't be skulking around the backyard during this visit.

"How come you didn't bring the big Poodle with you?" she asked as I approached. "I liked *her*."

I'd left Faith at home because after a long morning at school, I thought she could use a break. But Sadie's comment was a pointed reminder that it was the Poodle who'd broken the ice between us the last time we'd met. Maybe I should have rethought that idea.

"I didn't want to impose," I said.

Sadie flapped a hand in the air. "You're here, aren't you?"

Her face was less swollen than it had been ten days earlier. But the area around her eye was still discolored with bruising. Trying not to stare, I wondered how Sadie was doing with Jasmine's dogs, Hazel and Toby.

Before I could ask, she spun around and went into the house. I paused on the front step and peered inside. The interior of the small, one-story home was only dimly lit. Someone, perhaps Sadie, had drawn all the curtains. Jasmine hadn't even been gone two weeks, but the house already had a vacant, abandoned air.

"Well?" She stood in the small hallway. "What are you waiting for?"

"Are we, um . . . allowed to be in here?"

"I told you—Jasmine and I were friends." Sadie sounded exasperated. "It turns out I was right, and she didn't have any family. In her will, she made me executor of her estate. Jasmine left just about everything she had to a couple of charities. I'm in charge of liquidating her assets. Mostly what that means is that I'm getting this house ready to sell. So *yes,* we're allowed to be in here. Are you coming or not?"

I was.

Sadie closed the door behind me. Then she walked around the house, giving me a quick tour of the rooms. Maybe she was practicing for when the house went on the market. Or maybe she wanted me to see that she was very much at home in Jasmine's space.

"Living room, dining room, two bedrooms over here," she said.

We paused and poked our heads in each.

"Just one bathroom. Most buyers will probably want at least two, but there's nothing I can do about that. The kitchen is this way. There's a little sunroom behind it. We'll sit and you can tell me what you're doing here."

As Sadie strode toward the kitchen in the back of the house, my footsteps slowed. I paused for another look around the hallway.

To my surprise, I'd seen very little artwork on the walls. There was a framed poster in one of the bedrooms and a single watercolor in the living room. I knew that Sadie had removed a number of Jasmine's paintings from the house. Even so, I'd have expected to see evidence of where they'd been hanging.

"Ye gods, you're slow." Sadie stood in the doorway of the sunroom with her hands on her hips. "I don't have all day, you know. It's not like I didn't already have my own life to take care of, before Jasmine put me in charge of all this."

The sunroom was tiny, really just a porch with glass enclosed walls. Two wicker chairs sat across from each other with a small, square table in between. Sadie and I bumped knees as we sat down. It was that close.

"You're off to a good start getting things organized," I said.

"I wish," Sadie grumbled. "I've barely had time to do a thing around here yet. This place is pretty much as Jasmine left it."

"You've already removed her paintings though."

"Yeah, I got a jump on that." She stared at me across the small space. "You were here that day. Did you ever find that girl you were looking for?"

"No, not yet," I admitted. "Though I talked to a friend of hers yesterday who said she knew you."

"Oh? Who's that?"

"Tamryn Klein."

Sadie frowned.

"Short black hair, pierced ears? Jasmine was getting her dog-sitting jobs?"

"You don't have to describe her," Sadie snorted. "I know who Tamryn is—a kid who was always hanging around for no good reason.

She said she was looking for work. Anyway that was the excuse she gave for being here."

"Tamryn told me that she helped you move Jasmine's paintings. She seemed to think you might have been taking things from her." Okay, last part was a little spin of my own. But I was curious to see how Sadie would respond.

It didn't take long. Sadie shot to her feet. Her knees knocked into the table between us. It wobbled and nearly fell.

"What kind of a crazy story is that?" she demanded. "I never took a single thing that I wasn't entitled to. Why would you listen to what some punk kid has to say? You want to hear the truth?"

"Sure," I said.

"Tamryn was moving paintings around all right, but she wasn't doing it for me. She's the one who was stealing from Jasmine. I had to keep an eye on everything whenever Tamryn was around. You never knew what that girl would get her sticky fingers on next."

"You're saying that Tamryn stole some of Jasmine's paintings?"

"That's right." Sadie nodded firmly. "Mostly small stuff. Older pieces she probably thought wouldn't be missed. But Jasmine knew right away they were gone. I told her she should keep an eye out on eBay and Craigslist. Maybe we could catch Tamryn in the act."

"And did you?"

"No. But it didn't matter. Jasmine knew who was responsible. She confronted Tamryn and the two of them had a huge fight about it. I thought they might come to blows, it was that bad."

"It sounds like Jasmine had a temper," I said.

"Not all the time. Only when it was justified."

"I heard she had a fight with Amanda's boyfriend, too. A guy named Rick Fanelli?"

"I wouldn't know anything about that." Sadie suddenly looked nervous.

She hadn't retaken her seat. Instead she was fidgeting on her feet. I stood up as well, and stepped back to put a little distance between us. It didn't help. Sadie was looking like she wished she was anywhere but with me.

"Rick and Jasmine were doing business together, weren't they?" I asked.

"Where'd you get that idea?"

"It's just something I was told."

"Like I said before, you don't want to pay attention to everything you hear."

Sadie walked out of the sunroom. She crossed the kitchen, heading toward the front of the house. I didn't have much choice but to follow. When we reached the door, Sadie opened it and waited pointedly for me to walk through.

I stopped outside on the step. "Jasmine was your friend. I hope you'd want to help me find out what happened to her."

"I do. That's why I told you everything I could." She closed the door sharply between us.

I often do my best thinking when I'm in the car. And a couple of things were niggling at me— like tiny sparks blinking in the back of my brain, begging me to pay attention. On the way home, I realized what they were.

Sadie said that Jasmine's house was just the way she'd left it. But Jasmine was a talented and prolific artist. So why hadn't I seen any art supplies lying around? Had Sadie removed those too? And if so, why?

Not only that, but Sadie had clearly become uncomfortable when I'd asked her about Rick Fanelli. Now I replayed Sadie's parting words in my mind. She'd said she told me everything she could. Not everything she *knew*. Had I found yet another person who was afraid of Amanda's boyfriend?

Chapter 15

Friday morning, Chester Bronson, my eight-thirty student, arrived with a plate of cookies he'd baked the night before. That automatically elevated him to my favorite student of the day. Chester was a proponent of fusion cuisine. He'd made chai-spiced sugar cookies with white chocolate and dried cranberries. The combination didn't sound like it should work, but they were delicious.

Chester was a bright kid. If he'd paid half as much attention to his schoolwork as he did to his experimental recipes, there would have been no need for our tutoring sessions. I'd already sent home two notes praising his culinary aptitude. But with a father who worked on Wall Street and a mother who was a member of the state senate, Chester was being pointed toward the Ivy League rather than the Culinary Institute of America.

So while he pleaded his case at home, Chester and I worked together at school to keep his grades up. Our sessions were always a blast, and I was happy to serve as his gastronomic guinea pig whenever inspiration struck.

As Chester went out the door at nine-fifteen, Francesca came in. Faith immediately stood up, anticipating an effusive greeting and a biscuit. She wasn't disappointed in either regard.

I waited until they were finished, then walked over and gave Francesca a quick hug. Earlier in my career, I used to greet all my students that way. But times had changed, and now an excessive show of affection was frowned upon. In other words, I was supposed to keep my hands to myself.

I loved my job, so for the most part, I did. But there was something about this girl that brought out my maternal instincts. Every time I saw her, I wanted to gather her into my arms and hold on tight.

"Look." I gestured toward the plate Chester had left sitting on our worktable. "I have cookies."

Francesca's eyes lit up. She started to reach for one, then hesitated. Slowly she withdrew her hand. "No, thank you."

"It's okay. Chester brought them." I pulled out a chair and sat. "He made them himself. He's a very talented cook."

"I know he is." The girl eyed the cookies wistfully. "But I better not. I already had breakfast this morning."

"I had breakfast too," I told her. I picked up a cookie—my third, but who was counting—and nibbled around the edges. "But these are too good to pass up."

"You should be careful," Francesca said. "If you eat too much, you'll get fat."

"You're right about that." I felt a twinge of guilt. Surely there was no way she could know about my recent cake binge? "But thanks to my kids and my dogs, I get plenty of exercise. So far, that seems to be keeping things in check."

"Maybe that's my problem," Francesca mused. "I should sign up for an exercise class."

"What problem?"

She glared at me balefully. "I'm fat."

"No, you're not."

She was pleasantly plump, with rounded cheeks and some curves on her still-immature body. But she was also twelve years old. Those few extra pounds were nothing that the next growth spurt wouldn't take care of.

Francesca's mouth thinned. "I look like a blimp."

"You do *not*," I said firmly. "Why would you even say such a thing?"

"I see what girls look like on TV and social media. That's how I'm supposed to look. And I don't."

"Girls on TV are built like twigs. That's not natural. It's not healthy. Most of them starve themselves to be that skinny. Nobody looks like that in real life."

"Brittany and Taylor do." Francesca named two other sixth-graders. Girls whose mothers looked like supermodels and who were being raised to fit the same mold. "And Alicia does, too."

I reached across the table and covered her hand with my own. "Francesca, sweetie, listen to me. Just because a couple of girls in your class are super thin doesn't mean that you have to be."

"That's not what they say."

"Oh?" Abruptly my best teacher's voice asserted itself. "What exactly do those girls say?"

"That I'm fat. That I look like Porky Pig. Or the balloons in the Thanksgiving Day parade. Or the marshmallow man in *Ghostbusters*."

I stared at her in horror as the words came tumbling out.

"Taylor says I need to lose twenty pounds. And Alicia told me that I was too fat for my uniform. She said I should get my mom to buy me a bigger size. But I can't do that. Because if I ask her to, she'll want to know why. And my mom looks just like me. . . ." The words sounded like a long wail. "So I can't tell her *that*."

Oh my. *Oh damn*. Deliberately I kept the anger that was pulsing through me out of my tone. "Your mother looks perfect, Francesca. And so do you."

She shook her head. "Everyone in my family loves to eat. Even my father, and he hardly weighs anything. Nobody ever told me I was fat before. Nobody cared about it until now. I tried eating less. Even a lot less. But it isn't working. I only lost two pounds."

"Francesca, stop. Look at me." I waited until

we were eye to eye. "I want you to listen very carefully to what I'm going to say. Can you do that?"

Silently, she nodded.

"First of all, you are *not* fat."

"But—"

"No," I said firmly. "I don't care what Taylor, and Brittany, and Alicia are telling you. They're *wrong*. And their view of the world is seriously out of whack."

"But then why do they say those things?"

I wished I had a good answer for her.

"Sometimes girls can just be mean for no reason. It makes them feel superior to gang up on someone like that. They get satisfaction from making you feel bad about yourself."

"But why me?" Francesca asked plaintively.

I wanted to say it was because those girls were idiots, but I stopped before the words came out of my mouth. "Maybe it's because you're new here. Or because you react to the things they say. I'm so sorry, Francesca. I wish I could offer you a good explanation, but there isn't one."

"It's not fair," she said in a small voice.

"No, it isn't. What they're doing is horrible. And I'm going to put a stop to it."

Francesca's head lifted. "How?"

"First I'm going to talk to Mr. Hanover—"

"No," she cried. "Please don't tell anyone. If you do, everyone will know I said something.

And that will only make things worse. It's bad enough that they don't like me now."

"Listen to me," I said. "I promise you that whatever steps I take will not make things worse. Howard Academy is not the kind of school that will tolerate behavior like that. And now that I know what's going on, we can make it stop. And as for those girls not liking you, I don't see any reason why you should even care about that."

Francesca looked surprised.

"Do you like them?" I asked.

"Well . . . no. Not really. I thought I did at first. But not now."

"Just because you're at a new school doesn't mean that you have to be friends with everyone you meet here," I told her. "But what everyone *does* have to do is treat each other with respect. And kindness."

"I tried to do that," Francesca replied. "I just wanted them to like me."

"I know you did, because you're a nice person. And those girls took advantage of that. What they're doing is their fault, not yours."

"But they're right," Francesca mumbled. "I *don't* look anything like them. Or the girls I see on TV."

My heart ached for her. It had to be insanely difficult to be a young girl growing up in a world that exposed her to so many frivolous and destructive influences.

"No," I said gently. "You look like your mother. And what a wonderful thing that is. Your mother is one of the most famous sopranos in the world. Her appearances sell out shows at the Metropolitan Opera House. People swoon when they hear her sing. Who wouldn't want to look like her?"

Francesca smiled reluctantly. "Nobody swoons," she said.

"They should," I told her. "I would."

I lifted my arm and pressed the back of my hand to my forehead dramatically. Then I pretended to go limp in my chair. My performance was so stirring that Faith got up and came over to see what was wrong. Well, either that or she came to laugh at me.

Because that's what Francesca was doing. She was giggling uncontrollably. "You're not very good at that."

"That's why I get to be a teacher instead of having to swan around a stage. And then I'm lucky enough to get to meet great kids like you."

Francesca blinked. She thought for a few seconds. "I *am* a great kid," she said.

"Well, finally we agree on something." I held up my hand and we high-fived. "Now let's get down to work, okay?"

Francesca nodded. She reached for her notebook.

"As for the other thing, I'm going to fix it. I promise."

Howard Academy had a strict code of ethics and an equally strict code of behavior. As soon as I could get in to see Mr. Hanover, I intended to invoke both. I knew that our illustrious headmaster would be just as outraged on Francesca's behalf as I was.

I'd seen Mr. Hanover on the warpath before. It was a fearsome sight. I couldn't help smiling at the idea of seeing his wrath directed at somebody else for a change.

Even though Augie had just been clipped, bathed, blown dry, and scissored for the dog shows in Massachusetts, the entire process had to be repeated for Saturday's upcoming show in Dutchess County. Midweek his hindquarter, legs, and the base of his tail had been shaved to the skin. The following day, his face and feet were clipped and his nails were shortened with a grinder. On Friday afternoon, Augie's coat would be bathed and meticulously blown dry. Yet again.

As soon as Davey got home from school, he and Sam went to work. The process would take about three hours to complete. When they were halfway through, Kev and I started making spaghetti sauce for dinner. My own cooking skills were sadly no better than competent, but I was determined that both my sons would grow up knowing their way around a kitchen.

Of course, the job would have proceeded more

smoothly without Kevin's help. But what he lacked in proficiency, my son more than made up for with enthusiasm. By the time he finished chopping up the tomatoes with a suitably dull knife, the counter and sink were both awash in red juice.

I was standing at the stove, browning some ground beef and sausage when Kev hopped down from his step stool and announced that the tomatoes were ready. I turned around and had a look.

The first thing I noticed—aside from the fact that Kevin's T-shirt, his hands, and his hair were all stained and sticky—was that Tar was licking his lips. His nose also had a suspiciously red cast.

"Kev, honey," I said. "What's Tar eating?"

My son grinned. "S'ghetti sauce. He likes it!"

Right. Tar liked everything. He would eat a chocolate bar, a spool of thread, or a stuffed animal if you didn't keep an eye on him. The dog had no sense of preservation.

"How many tomatoes did you give him?" I asked pleasantly.

"Just one." Kev looked sorry about that. Then he brightened. "I gave one to Bud too."

"Bud?" I glanced around the room. I didn't see the spotted dog anywhere. "Where is Bud?"

"He took his tomato in the living room."

Seriously? How had I not seen this happening? My back had only been turned for a minute.

"The living room," I repeated faintly. I turned off the burner and moved the frying pan to the back of the stove top.

"He's probably behind the couch," Kevin informed me. "That's where he takes all his best things."

"Hey," Sam called from the small grooming room near the kitchen. He had to raise his voice to be heard above the whine of the blow dryer. "I see red all over the hallway. Is somebody bleeding out there?"

"No blood," I called back. "Just a runaway tomato. Don't worry, I'm on it."

"Just checking," said Sam. I couldn't see him around the corner, but I was pretty sure he was shaking his head.

The next day's show was back outdoors. Fortunately no April showers had been forecast and it was a beautiful day. This time there wasn't a separate grooming tent for handlers. Instead there were two rows of back-to-back rings, with a wide tent running along the outside of each row. In a smaller space, the layout was more compact. It also enabled exhibitors to groom beside the ring they'd be showing in, a convenience we all appreciated.

The majority of Bertie's entries were herding dogs. She'd set up under the other tent. And Aunt Peg wasn't showing her puppy, so when we arrived we unloaded our equipment beside Crawford and Terry's setup.

"Long time, no see." Terry blew me a kiss as we put everything in place. He was brushing out a Coton de Tulear. Crawford was in a nearby ring showing an Affenpinscher, so Terry stopped to chat. "Did you find that girl you were looking for?"

"Not exactly," I told him.

He waggled his auburn brows. "Which means what? You sort of found her? You found half of her? What?"

"Eww," said Davey. "That's gross. You can't find half of somebody. Or at least you really wouldn't want to."

"I didn't find her at all," I admitted. "But Amanda texted her sister and told her she was all right." It didn't sound like much, so I added, "So that was good."

"All right but . . . still missing?" Terry's brows were working overtime.

"Umm, yes."

"So how is that an improvement?"

"Because it means she isn't dead," Aunt Peg said briskly. "Like her landlady and former employer."

I shot Aunt Peg a look. "Do you mind? There are children present."

"Oh pish." She glanced Kevin's way. He was sitting inside Augie's big crate, unpacking his bag of toys. "He's not paying the slightest bit of attention to us."

"And I'm not a child," Davey said.

"You're not an adult either," I told him.

Davey smirked. "There's stuff on the internet way scarier than what you guys talk about."

"I hope you're not looking at it."

"Who me?" You wouldn't think that a thirteen-year-old boy could pull off a look of utter innocence, but Davey managed it.

The illusion that he might be telling the truth lasted only a few seconds. That was how long it took Terry to burst out laughing.

"Remind me to check the parental controls on your computer when we get home," Sam said to Davey.

"I will," he replied.

When pigs fly, I thought.

Augie was lying down on his tabletop. The grooming tools were out of the tack box and ready to be used. Aunt Peg went over to the ring to watch the Poodle judge evaluate some of his earlier breeds. Everyone else was making themselves useful. It was time for me to do the same.

The last time I'd spoken to Rick Fanelli he'd dismissed my concerns about Amanda's whereabouts. Now another week had passed and his girlfriend had yet to reappear. It was time for us to have another conversation, hopefully one that was more productive.

The sporting breeds were being judged in the rings on the opposite side, which meant that Rick would have his setup in the other tent. This show was quite a bit smaller than the one the previous weekend. Now that I knew what Rick looked like, I was sure I wouldn't have much trouble finding him.

As I approached the far tent, I spotted Rick in one of the rings with an English Springer Spaniel. His liver-and-white bitch was at the end of a long line of Springers and the judge was looking at the first entrant. I could see that I'd have time to wait before he'd be free.

I strolled over to the ring's slatted barrier to watch the class. I hadn't been dazzled by Rick's handling skills the previous week, and that first impression was confirmed by what I saw today. He went through the motions of showing his bitch, but his presentation lacked commitment.

A good handler should be proud of the dog he's brought to show to the judge. But Rick never conveyed that emotion. Or any emotion at all. Considering his apparent lack of interest in the proceedings, he might as well have been offering the judge a plate of string beans.

I sighed and waited for the class to finish. Springer Spaniels are awesome dogs. They're friendly, stylish, and playful. And generally, I could watch dogs run around a show ring all day.

But Rick Fanelli was even managing to bore me. That was pretty pathetic.

Chapter 16

I stepped away from the ring while I waited for Rick's class to end and found myself standing near two women who were engaged in a lively conversation. Both were wearing skirts and flat-soled shoes. One had a number on her upper arm. The other was holding a black-and-white Springer dog on a leash. They were obviously exhibitors.

Terry must be a bad influence on me because I found myself listening in shamelessly. Maybe I'd get the inside scoop about which Springer Spaniels to watch.

"Raina told me she was terrified by the whole experience," the woman with the dog was saying. "She felt as though she'd been violated."

"I can just imagine," her friend replied. "Having strangers in your house, pawing through your things . . . it must have been horrible."

What? That sounded even more interesting than I'd expected.

"It's been almost two months and Raina hasn't been back at a dog show since. She barely even leaves her house anymore because she's afraid of what she might find when she gets back," the first woman was saying. "The thieves went straight for the vintage jewelry she'd inherited from her mother. They got things that were irreplaceable, including a ruby ring that had been in her family for three generations."

"Nothing is irreplaceable except Raina's life," the other woman replied firmly. "Thank goodness she wasn't there when the thieves broke in. Who knows what might have happened?"

The exhibitor reached down and gave her Springer a pat. "That's one good thing anyway. The thieves didn't harm Raina's dogs. Imagine, there were four Chessies loose in the house and they still had the nerve to break in. Raina said she always felt safe surrounded by her dogs, but these thieves knew what they were doing. They brought marrow bones with them."

Marrow bones? That sounded familiar. Abruptly I remembered why. Terry had been telling a story the previous week about a house that had been broken into. Those robbers had used the same ploy to distract the owners' dogs.

"I have six Flat-Coated Retrievers in my house," one of the women was saying. "They raise a hell of a racket whenever anyone comes up the driveway. But this makes me think twice about my own security."

"I know what you mean. Raina thought she was safe too. Until suddenly she wasn't." The second woman shook her head. "It's scary to think that something like that can happen in the middle of the day. Raina wasn't going to be gone for long, so she didn't have the dog sitter there. Her house was empty except for the dogs she thought were guarding it."

The part about the marrow bones had gotten my attention. But now that the women were talking about pet sitters too, I didn't want to miss a single word. Casually, I edged closer.

A sudden burst of applause drew our gazes back to the ring. The judge had pinned his class. Rick and his liver-and-white bitch were standing beside the fourth place marker.

"Springers are almost done," one woman said, turning away. "We're in next. I'd better go get my dog."

"Wait!" I said, before they could leave.

Both women looked at me in surprise.

"I couldn't help but overhear what you were talking about."

"Yes?" said the woman holding the Springer. "What about it?"

"You said your friend Raina used a dog sitter. Do you happen to know the person's name?"

The two women exchanged a look. They were probably thinking I was crazy. I couldn't blame them.

"Please," I said. "It might be important."

"To whom?"

One woman was already walking away. The other looked ready to follow. I wasn't getting anywhere on my own. It was time to pull out my bag of magic beans.

"To Margaret Turnbull," I said.

The remaining exhibitor looked me up and down. "You're not Margaret Turnbull."

"No. She's my aunt."

"Why would the name of Raina's dog sitter be important to her?"

"Because Aunt Peg's dog sitter is missing."

"Is that so?" she said archly.

"Yes."

Her friend stopped again. "Susan, we don't have time for this. Just give her the name, okay?"

"I might if I had a clue what it was." She started to leave too. "I suppose you could call Raina and ask."

"Raina who?" I called after her.

"Raina Gentry. She has Chessies. Don't tell her I sent you."

"Thank you!"

Neither woman responded. I didn't care. I'd already gotten what I needed.

As soon as Rick Fanelli got his fourth place ribbon, he left the ring and went back to his setup. I gave him a couple of minutes to get settled, and then followed. His Springer Spaniel was already back in her crate, and Rick had pulled a can of Red Bull out of a small cooler by the time I reached him.

He looked at me but didn't say a word. Instead he popped the top of the Red Bull, tipped back his head, and took a very long swallow. He nearly drained the tall can. Eventually Rick pulled the drink away from his lips and plunked it down on top of a crate.

"So," he said, "did you find her?"

Startled by the abrupt question, I said, "Amanda?"

"Of course, Amanda. How many people are you looking for?"

"Just one."

"Then I guess we're on the same page."

"No, I didn't find her," I said. "But Abby got a text from her. Amanda said she was fine."

"I could have told you that. In fact I'm pretty sure I did."

"You also told me you thought Amanda went away because she was upset about Jasmine Crane's death."

"So?"

"Abby doesn't think that's what happened."

Rick shrugged out of his sports coat. He hung it on a hanger that was looped through the back of his tack box. Then he reached up and loosened his tie. It was seventy degrees out, but he was sweating pretty hard. The few laps of the ring he'd done in the class shouldn't have caused him to overheat that much.

"Here's the thing," he said after he'd picked up

the energy drink and taken another swallow. "I don't really care what Abby thinks."

"Is Amanda afraid of you?" I asked.

"Hell, no. Why would you say something like that?"

"Because it's what I've heard," I said mildly.

"From Abby? Listen, I told you before. You can't pay any attention to what that girl says. She's loco."

"How about Jasmine? Was she loco too?"

Oddly, the question made Rick smile. Then he sobered and shook his head. "She wasn't entirely normal, that's for sure."

"I heard that the two of you were doing business together. What kind of business was that?"

Rick moved quickly. One second there was a bank of crates between us, and the next there wasn't. All at once he was standing much too close. I took a step back and found myself pressed up against a grooming table. Now I couldn't move away.

There were people at setups all around us. They were talking, grooming their dogs, getting ready to go in the ring. But suddenly everyone else seemed very far away. It felt as though the world had narrowed to just Rick and me.

"Lady, it sounds like you heard a lot of things." His voice edged toward a snarl. "Things that have nothing to do with you. Let me give you a tip. Don't go sticking your nose into stuff that doesn't concern you. Somebody might come along and cut it off."

As his hand lifted, I pulled back reflexively. But I still had nowhere to go. He pinched my nose between his thumb and forefinger and gave it a vicious twist. "Get it?"

Hot tears pooled in the corners of my eyes. I quickly blinked them away. I got it, all right. Now it was time for Rick to get his. I brought my knee up quickly. At the same time, I braced both my hands against Rick's chest and gave him a hard shove.

Rick had good reflexes, I had to give him that. But he was so busy dodging the knee, that my push caught him unaware. He went sprawling backward into the bank of stacked crates.

He bounced off a hard metal edge and I heard a satisfying thud as he fell to the ground. Rick landed on his butt. He braced his hands in the grass on either side of his hips and glared up at me murderously.

I stared down at him for a few seconds—long enough to make the point that he didn't scare me—then spun around and strode away.

When I was well beyond Rick's gaze, I reached up and gently checked out my nose. My fingers started at the top of the bridge and slid all the way down to the tip. Thankfully nothing felt broken, but *damn* that had hurt.

I started to shake my head, then quickly

thought better of it. That outcome wasn't even close to how my conversation with Rick was meant to go. Now I had a clearer idea of why people like Jasmine and Tamryn might have been intimidated by him. What I couldn't begin to fathom, however, was why Amanda would have wanted him for a boyfriend.

Back at our setup, Augie was standing up on the table. His collar was on, his topknot was in, his coat had been sprayed up. Davey was using a long pair of curved shears to scissor impossibly small bits of hair from the rounded curves of his front bracelets.

Augie turned his head slightly. His dark eyes followed me as I approached. From his chiseled head to his muscular hindquarter, Augie was every inch a gorgeous Standard Poodle. Even better, he knew it.

Davey already had his jacket and his armband on. Fifteen feet away in the ring, our judge, Darla Denby, was sorting through her Mini Poodle Best of Variety class. I hoped she'd give the win to Crawford. That would give Davey a better chance of success when his turn came.

Terry, Aunt Peg, and Sam were all watching the competition. Davey was tending to Augie. But Kevin jumped up when he saw me coming. I knelt down and gave him a hug.

Kev frowned at me and said, "Your nose looks funny."

Davey glanced over and had a look. "Yeah, it does. It's all red."

"It's nothing." I covered the lower half of my face with my hand. "How's Augie doing?"

"He's ready. He wants to get this over with as much as I do."

"Over with?" I echoed, surprised. "I thought you were having fun showing him."

"I was," Davey said, then quickly amended that. "I mean, I am. But it's time to get this part finished and move on to the next thing."

I could see that.

"What is the next thing?" I asked curiously.

"I don't know." Davey shrugged. "We'll see when the time comes. Maybe obedience. I wouldn't mind teaching Augie to jump over things and retrieve stuff. I think he'd like that."

"I bet you both would," I said.

Crawford came flying back into the setup next door. He had his black Mini special under his arm and a purple-and-gold BOV rosette in his hand. So far, so good.

Terry was ready for him. He took the Mini and plopped it on a tabletop. While Crawford tossed the ribbon in the tack box and grabbed a quick drink of water, Terry swept the handler's Standard puppy dog off his table.

Once on the ground, the puppy gave a good shake. Terry quickly smoothed his hair back into place, then handed the leash to Crawford—who took off toward the ring. As the steward called the Puppy Dog class, Crawford was already filing through the in-gate. The entire exchange had taken less than a minute and was accomplished seamlessly.

I thought Terry would attend to the Mini special, but instead he simply folded up the dog's leash and banded his long ear hair, then came over to stand and wait for the next class with us.

"What?" Terry said, when I glanced over at him. "You think I'm not going to watch this"—his hand gestured eloquently toward Augie—"happen? No way I'd miss it."

"You're supposed to be rooting for Crawford," I said.

"Crawford's puppy can take the points another time. This is Davey's day."

The confidence with which he delivered that pronouncement warmed my heart.

Then Terry turned and stared at me. "What is wrong with your nose?"

"Allergies," I ad-libbed. It was almost time for Augie's class. I didn't want to go into an explanation now.

"They make pills for that," Terry told me. "You really should check it out, because you look *terrible*."

"Thank you," I said curtly. Anything to end the conversation.

"You're welcome, Miss Snappy Pants." Terry's

tone was bland. It took better skills than mine to get a rise out of him.

In the ring, Crawford's puppy had prevailed over one other entry. At today's show, only four Standard Poodle dogs were entered. Just one point was available to be won. But that didn't matter. One point was all Augie needed.

It was never good to be overconfident, however. Mrs. Denby still had to like Augie. And he still had to beat the competition.

Davey hustled Augie into the ring first when the Open Dog class was called. A professional handler with another black Standard followed him. Sam moved to stand beside me.

Without taking his eyes off the ring, he said, "Since when do you have allergies?"

I continued to stare straight ahead too. Davey had Augie stacked just right. He took a piece of bait out of his pocket but the Poodle wasn't watching him. Augie had his eye on the judge.

Mrs. Denby returned the favor.

"Since I came in contact with Rick Fanelli."

"You're allergic to Amanda Burke's boy-friend?" Sam managed not to sound too incredulous. I'd probably told him stranger things.

"Apparently so."

The summer before, Sam had offered to punch someone on my behalf. He'd been kidding about that. At least, I hoped he had. But I had no desire to reawaken my husband's primitive instincts now.

There was something much more important going on right in front of me. And I didn't want to miss a minute of it.

Aunt Peg walked over to stand closer to the ring. As the judge sent the two dogs around for the first time, Aunt Peg was so absorbed in the competition that she probably didn't even realize that she was gaiting in place with them. Aunt Peg's lips were moving too.

She might have been sending up a prayer. Or murmuring an incantation. With Aunt Peg, you can never tell.

"Look." Kevin giggled. "Aunt Peg's dancing."

Terry picked up my son so he could see better. "No celebrating yet," he said. "It ain't over till it's over, kid."

Kev's face scrunched up in an expression of intense concentration as he tried to puzzle out what that meant. Though he knew who Yogi Bear was, I was pretty sure he'd never heard of Yogi Berra.

Augie won the small Open class handily. As the dog who was second exited the ring, Crawford returned with his Puppy Class winner. I wanted Davey to win so badly that I almost wished Crawford would throw the competition.

But as soon as the unworthy thought crossed my mind I knew it wasn't fair. Crawford was our friend, but he was also a professional with a job to do. He had a responsibility to his owners to do the best he could every time he handled their dogs.

If Davey was going to beat Crawford for that last, all-important point, Crawford was going to make sure that he earned it.

The judge sent her two dog class winners around the ring together. Both Standard Poodles were on their game. Both were moving well. The judge's gaze flicked back and forth between them. She'd evaluated the two dogs only minutes earlier, but she was still comparing their merits in her mind.

Sometimes the decision was so clear-cut that the choice was easy. It wasn't going to happen that way today, unfortunately.

As soon as the dogs were back where they'd started, Mrs. Denby came over for a closer look at Augie. She stared at his face, then moved around to his side. She plunged her hands into the Poodle's thick coat to assess the things she couldn't see. Mrs. Denby's fingers measured the angle of Augie's shoulder and traced the length of his solid topline.

That done, she moved back to Crawford's puppy and repeated the same assessment. There were only two dogs in the Winners class. A full five minutes had passed since they entered the ring. The suspense was killing me.

Finally Mrs. Denby was satisfied with what she'd found. She stepped away from the pair and took one last, long look. Davey and Augie were still at the front of the line.

"He's going to do it," Sam said under his breath.

"Don't jinx him!" I shot back.

Oh my God, I thought as the words left my mouth. *I was turning into Aunt Peg.*

I felt as if I was watching in slow motion as Mrs. Denby lifted her hand to indicate the winner. Her index finger was like a slim arrow, capable of conveying joy or doom in a single motion. The judge looked at Augie. She looked at the puppy. Then she looked at Augie again and pointed his way.

After all this time, it was finally done. Davey had a champion Standard Poodle.

Chapter 17

We did it!" Davey whooped.

He jumped in the air. Augie followed. Crawford slapped him on the back, then shook his hand. He was smiling too. The two Standard Poodles danced a jig around their handlers.

The judge had been on the way to mark her book, but now she turned around. "Did what?"

"You made him a champion." Davey's grin was wide enough to light up the whole ring.

"Congratulations, that's wonderful," Mrs. Denby said kindly. "You did a nice job with him and he was a very deserving winner. I hope you'll have his picture taken with me."

"Absolutely."

After that incredible moment, the rest of the judging seemed anticlimactic. In fact, we were so busy congratulating each other and telling Augie what a good dog he was, that we almost missed his return to the ring for the Best of Variety judging. The steward had to call out Davey's number twice, but she was smiling too.

Crawford's Standard special topped that class, but Augie was awarded Best of Winners. Having finished judging all three Poodle varieties, Mrs. Denby took a break for pictures. We waited near the in-gate while the photographer was summoned to the ring.

"I can't believe it finally happened," Davey said. "It seemed like it took forever."

"It did," Sam replied. "But you learned some-thing every step of the way, didn't you?"

"The most important thing I learned is that I should never promise to finish another Standard Poodle," Davey said with a wink.

"Oh pish," Aunt Peg chimed in. "Now that you've got the first one behind you, the second one will be easier."

"Second one?" I sputtered.

We all turned to look at her. We already had a house full of dogs. And each of our Poodles was already a champion.

"I was thinking about Coral," Aunt Peg informed us. "With all the judging I'm doing, it doesn't seem entirely proper for me to be in the show ring too. Now that she's had a few outings for experience, I was thinking it might be time to pass Coral along to another handler."

"Crawford has an opening for a puppy bitch," Terry piped up.

Aunt Peg gazed down her nose at him. "I'll bear that in mind. But I was thinking of someone a little closer to home."

We all knew where she was going with this idea. Dog shows were Aunt Peg's avocation, her recreation, her life's passion. Years earlier, she'd chosen Davey to follow in her footsteps. Things hadn't worked out for her then. Davey had dabbled in Junior Showmanship only briefly before calling it quits. But Aunt Peg had never surrendered the belief that she would eventually succeed in luring him back to the fold.

"Well?" she prompted when Davey remained silent.

He didn't answer right away. I thought he was trying to come up with a way to turn her down. But Davey surprised me.

"I'll think about it," he answered finally.

I'd expected Davey to reject her offer out of hand. It looked like teaching Augie to jump over obstacles and pick up dumbbells might have to wait a little longer.

Even though Augie had probably exited the show ring for the last time, his coat still had to be attended to. The big Poodle was lifted back onto his table and Sam and Davey began the process of brushing out the hairspray, taking down his topknot, and wrapping his ears.

While they were doing that, I took another trip around the showground. The conversation I'd overheard outside the Springer ring, and my subsequent confrontation with Rick Fanelli, had raised more questions than they'd answered. There were still people I needed to talk to, and this dog show was a convenient opportunity for me to find everyone in one place.

The concessions were on the other side of the big, grassy field. I gave Rick's setup—and indeed, the entire other tent—a very wide berth. So the trek around the double row of rings gave me plenty of time to think.

Judging by the timing of Rick's sudden aggression, whatever business he'd been involved in with Jasmine Crane was a sore subject. I wondered what he didn't want me to know.

Up until now, I'd thought of Jasmine as an artist who supported herself by selling paintings and, more recently, beaded leashes and collars. But I couldn't figure out how Rick would have been involved in any of that.

The other connection between Jasmine and Rick—a much more vital link—was Amanda Burke. Several people I'd spoken to had mentioned that Jasmine was instrumental in finding dog-sitting jobs for Amanda and Tamryn. Perhaps she'd been doing the same for others as well.

Those pet sitters were being paid good money for their services. And, judging by Amanda's schedule, they were busy nearly all the time. I wondered if the majority of Tamryn's and Amanda's jobs had been obtained through Jasmine's connections. And whether or not the artist might have been taking a fee for her referrals.

With his small string of dogs and indifferent

handling skills, it didn't seem likely that Rick was supporting himself showing dogs. Abby had characterized her sister's boyfriend as someone on the lookout for an easy source of income. Had Rick tried to muscle in on Jasmine's pet-sitting business? Based on what I'd learned about Jasmine, I could certainly imagine her resisting such a move. Might that have been the source of the altercation that Tamryn had seen? And how would I go about proving any of that?

Luckily, that was when I reached the row of vendors. Otherwise, I would have been gnashing my teeth in frustration. My first stop was at Spenser Pet Supplies.

Lana Spenser was with another customer when I arrived, so I spent a few minutes browsing through her extensive selection of shears. When Lana finished that transaction, she came striding over. Her long braid was bobbing on her shoulder and, as always, she was smiling.

"Great to see you again, Melanie. What can I help you with today?"

"I'm afraid I have a few more questions," I said. "But after that, we can talk scissors. Sam has a birthday coming up."

"Excellent," Lana replied. "I don't think I had any answers for you before, but feel free to try again. Did you manage to locate Amanda?"

"No. Otherwise, I'd have let you know. But her

sister, Abby, got a text from her, so at least that's something."

"I'm glad she's okay." Lana sounded relieved. "So what's your question?"

"Last time we spoke, you said that Jasmine Crane and Alan Crandall were thick as thieves. What did you mean by that?"

"Nothing really. It's just a figure of speech."

"But it must have been prompted by something."

Lana shrugged. "You know what it's like when you go to shows with the same people week after week. We're all on the road a lot. We're stuck in this insular environment. Sometimes things get a little . . . cozy."

"Things?" I asked. "Or people? I gather Jasmine could be quite the flirt."

"That's one way of putting it."

"What's another?"

"Don't get me wrong, Jasmine certainly liked to flirt. She flirted with customers, with fellow vendors, even with the guys who set up the rings. I saw Jasmine flirt with a burger-flipper once." Lana stopped and laughed. "And she scored a free lunch for her efforts."

"Maybe that was the point," I said.

"Oh, I'm sure it was. Because it never seemed like Jasmine was flirting just for fun. Or even to give her sexual appetites a fling. Her vamping had more of a calculated edge. Jasmine liked to use people, to see what she could get from them. All that teasing, and touching, and smiling, was her way of getting her foot in the door."

I'd heard this refrain several times before.

"What did Jasmine want from Alan Crandall?" I asked curiously.

"I have no idea. Maybe nothing. Flirting was Jasmine's default mechanism, you know? She did it with everybody. Alan was probably just another guy in her field of vision. Except that he took her up on it."

"How?"

Lana held up her hands. "Don't ask me for specifics because I don't know how the affair started. But all at once, it was pretty clear that Alan and Jasmine were an item. They weren't even particularly discreet about it."

None of this jibed with what Alan had told me. He'd described his relationship with Jasmine as not particularly friendly. *Or maybe,* I thought, *he'd been speaking with the benefit of hindsight.*

"Was their lack of discretion a problem?" I asked.

"Not for those of us who worked next to them," Lana said. "But Barb Crandall was pissed as hell."

"Alan's wife?" I guessed.

Lana nodded. "She must have figured out that something was up. Before Alan and Jasmine got together, we hardly ever saw Barb at a dog show. Then suddenly she started showing up every weekend. Trying to act casual as she poked around, asking questions. Barb even came over here and had a look at me, trying to figure out if I was the one."

Lana and I shared a grin.

"I assume you managed to convince her of your innocence?"

"It wasn't hard. Especially once I made it clear that I don't even like her husband."

"Did Barb ever figure out that Jasmine was the woman Alan was sleeping with?" I asked.

"It certainly seemed like it. Because Barb and Jasmine had a big blowup at a show one day. Unfortunately I wasn't close enough to hear what they were yelling about, but after that Alan and Jasmine began avoiding each other like the plague. It didn't take a genius to figure out what the problem was."

"How long ago did that happen?"

"The affair probably began before Thanksgiving, and it lasted for a few months. Barb and Jasmine had their showdown maybe six weeks ago?" Lana's eyes twinkled. She was enjoying her competitor's misfortune. "Ever since then, Alan has been hiding in his booth like a whipped dog. I haven't seen him poke his nose out of there in weeks."

"Thanks for telling me," I said.

"No problem. Although if you pass that story

along to anyone else, I'd appreciate it if you keep my name out of it. It wouldn't be good for business if people thought I was gossiping about them behind their backs."

"Sure, I can do that."

"I have to admit, you've made me curious," Lana said. "Is there a particular reason you wanted to know about Alan and Jasmine?"

"Actually, it was the expression you used to describe them."

"What about it?"

"You called them thick as thieves, and it stuck in my mind. Especially since last week I heard about a judge whose house had been robbed while he was away at a show. Then this morning someone mentioned a Chessie exhibitor who'd had the same thing happen. I've been trying to find a link between Jasmine's death and Amanda's disappearance, but when this other stuff came up for the second time, I remembered what you'd said. It seemed like too big a coincidence, so I figured I should check it out."

Lana's eyes had widened while I was speaking. She looked like she'd seen a ghost. "Here's another coincidence for you. I know some guys who were robbed too."

I hadn't expected that. "Who was it?"

"Elliott Bean and his partner, Roger Marx. Do you know them?"

I shook my head.

"They're from somewhere in Westchester. Maybe Rye? They have Scottish Deerhounds. *Big* dogs. Big enough that they thought it would keep them safe from being targeted. But it didn't."

"Was their house broken into while they were away at a show?" I asked.

"Sorry." Lana frowned. "I have no idea about that."

"Do you happen to know if Elliott and Roger ever used a dog-sitter?"

Lana looked surprised by the question. I could see her making the connection. "You mean like Amanda?"

"Precisely. Or maybe her friend, Tamryn."

"I don't know about that either. But I have Elliott's card around here somewhere. I can call him and ask."

"Would you, please?"

"Sure, no problem. I'll let you know as soon as I hear something."

"That would be great," I said. "Now, about those scissors . . ."

"Step right this way." Lana reverted to sales mode as we walked over to the display case. "Are you interested in American made? German? Japanese?"

"Let's start with Japanese."

Lana smiled. "I like a woman with expensive tastes."

We spent ten minutes looking at her selection of

shears. I picked out a pair I was sure Sam would like and put them on layaway. Japanese scissors were an extravagance. Sam would never buy them for himself. But I'd be delighted to surprise him with a pair on his birthday.

My next stop was at Creature Comforts. As I'd expected, the booth was busy. I didn't see Alan Crandall, but a salesman directed me around to the back of the concession where the Creature Comforts truck was parked. Alan was out there unloading a pallet of dog beds.

He saw me coming, set the pallet down on the ground, and straightened. "You've discovered my secret."

Actually I had. But Alan didn't know that yet.

"Which secret is that?" I asked.

"When it comes to this business, I'm a Jack of all trades. I'll do just about anything to keep things running smoothly. What can I do for you, Melanie?"

Usually I try to ease my way into the tough questions. But since Alan had purposely given me the runaround before, I decided to cut to the chase. "Since the last time we spoke, some new information has come to light."

Alan looked politely curious. "Oh? What's that?"

"Why did you lie to me about your relationship with Jasmine Crane?"

"I don't recall that I did."

"You told me that you barely knew Jasmine. Something about proximity and common goals being the only things you had in common. And now I find out that you and she were having an affair."

"Who told you that?"

"It could have been almost anyone," I said. "Apparently you and Jasmine weren't very discreet."

"I'm not going to discuss this with you." Alan turned away. He leaned down to pick up the pallet again.

"Why not? Are you trying to protect your wife?"

Alan spun back up and glared. "Barb has nothing to do with this."

"She was angry about your relationship with Jasmine. She was seen having a public shouting match with her. And a month later, Jasmine was murdered. It sounds like your wife has everything to do with this."

"No, you've got that all wrong. Barb came to a show and talked to Jasmine. She told her what she thought of her. That's all it was."

"All it was . . . *that* time. But maybe she came back again," I said. "Maybe she wasn't finished letting Jasmine know how angry she was."

"You have no idea what you're talking about," Alan snapped.

His hands curled into fists at his sides. I noted

the small movement but refused to retreat. Alan was tall enough to tower over me, but I didn't care. I was done being pushed around.

"Then why don't you tell me the truth," I said.

"Yes, there was an unfortunate blowup between the two of them. But other than that, Barb didn't feel the need to vent her anger on Jasmine. She was too busy taking it out on me."

Chapter 18

W hat do you mean?" I asked. "What did she do?"

"Barb and I are getting divorced. She hired a shark of a lawyer the day after she talked to Jasmine. Barb is suing me for everything I have." Alan made a sweeping gesture with his hand that encompassed everything in his booth. "I'll be lucky if she doesn't cost me my business."

I tried to feel sorry for him and failed utterly. "I guess it never occurred to you that there might be ramifications."

"Barb never came to the dog shows. Ever. As far as she was concerned, they were just my place of business. She had no interest in anything that happened on the show circuit."

That was his excuse?

"And Jasmine . . . she could be magical." Alan was gazing in my direction, but I could tell that his thoughts had turned inward. For a moment, he looked truly smitten. "She had a way of making every rational thought fly right out of my head."

Jasmine was magical all right, I thought. *As long as you were proving useful to her.*

In that same cynical vein, I said aloud, "When Barb left you, I guess that meant you were free to go back to Jasmine."

"She didn't want me back." Abruptly Alan's eyes refocused on me. "Jasmine said all she'd been looking for was a fling. Apparently I was more appealing to her as a happily married man than I was as someone who might have designs on her freedom."

Wow. That had to have been a blow.

"So Jasmine Crane broke up your marriage, possibly cost you your livelihood, and then after all that, she dumped you?"

"That pretty much sums it up." Alan walked around behind the pallet. "Now if you don't mind, I'd like to get back to work."

"Feel free." I could talk while he worked. "What Jasmine did to you must have made you very angry."

"Of course it did. Being treated that way would have made anyone angry." Alan's expression was set in hard lines. "Don't think I can't see what you're getting at. You're wondering if Jasmine made me mad enough to strangle her."

"Did she?"

"Of course not. Don't be ridiculous." He raked a hand through his sparse hair. I'd never seen Alan Crandall look so jumpy. "Sure, I lost my temper. But I'm not a murderer. I got my revenge another way."

"How?"

Alan didn't answer.

I asked again. "What did you do?"

243

"Jasmine was inordinately proud of her art-work. She was convinced that it would make her famous one day. But now that's never going to happen. I took her precious paintings home from the Sedgefield show and got rid of them."

I inhaled sharply, then clamped my lips together to cover the sound of my startled gasp. Alan was supposed to be storing Jasmine's things. Sadie Foster was executor of Jasmine's estate. At some point she was going to come looking for those paintings.

"Got rid of them how?" I asked softly.

"I built a huge bonfire," Alan replied. "And, one-by-one, I burned them all. Jasmine always displayed the paintings she was the most proud of in her booth. And now every single one is gone. There's nothing left but a pile of ashes."

The magnitude of that loss hit me like a blow. Worse still, Alan had the nerve to look pleased with himself.

Alan had finally succeeded in shutting me up. There was absolutely nothing I could say in response to that. I just turned and walked away.

My head was still spinning with everything I'd heard when I got back to the setup. Augie had been undone and was in his crate, resting. His Winners Dog and Best of Winner rosettes were proudly displayed in the open tack box. Aunt Peg had disappeared—I knew she'd wanted to watch several herding breeds she planned to apply for in the near future. Sam and the boys were munching on a late lunch. Next door, Terry and Crawford were prepping their entries for later that afternoon.

Everyone stopped what they were doing and looked at me expectantly. As though they thought I should have news to share. But now wasn't the appropriate time to discuss what I'd been doing.

This was Davey's day. We should be celebrating, not talking about murder.

So I helped myself to a turkey sandwich from the cooler. Then I hopped up and took a seat on the grooming table.

Davey was eating an apple. Between bites, he said, "I'm going to buzz off all of Augie's hair when we get home. We can have a coat-cutting party."

"I like the idea of a party," Sam replied. "But you're not touching that hair until the AKC confirms Augie's championship."

"That's good advice," said Terry. "You wouldn't believe the stories I've heard about people who counted wrong and altered a dog's trim prematurely. Then they had to wait forever for the hair to grow back. Don't let that happen to you."

"It won't." Davey grinned. "Because I can count. It only takes fifteen points."

"Fifteen," Kevin told us seriously. "That's three hands."

"See? Even Kev knows how to do it."

"It's better to be on the safe side," I told him. "It will only take a week or so before you can check the result online."

"I'd wait until you're holding that certificate in your hand," Crawford said.

"Too bad Jasmine's not around anymore." Terry tossed a sidelong glance my way. He was such a noodge. Nobody was allowed to remain reticent around him for long. "Otherwise you could have had Augie's portrait painted while you were waiting."

I refused to take the bait. Instead I tossed the conversational ball back in his court. "Did any of your clients ever have their dogs painted by Jasmine?"

Crawford looked up from the Havanese on his table. "Not while we were showing them. Otherwise we probably would have known about it. Maybe later, after they went home."

"I thought about it once," Sam said. "I spoke to her about a portrait of my foundation bitch, Charm."

"You mentioned that before. You said you decided against it though. How come?"

"I don't know exactly." Sam thought back. "Jasmine was undeniably talented. But there was just something about her that bothered me. She didn't seem entirely trustworthy."

"You have good instincts," I told him.

"Considering what I've learned about Jasmine recently, it's a good thing you steered clear."

"That woman was a whole box of trouble," Crawford said. I glanced at him in surprise. It was rare for the handler to offer a negative opinion about anyone. "Everybody would have done well to steer clear of her."

Crawford gathered up his dog and headed to the ring. Sam took the kids and went to get the SUV from its parking place on the other side of the field. I was left in charge of watching Augie. That was easy. I didn't have to do a thing.

When the two setups had emptied out, Terry sidled my way. "Are you all right?"

"Sure." Reflexively my hand lifted to my nose. "I'm fine."

"Because I'm pretty sure that story about allergies was a crock."

I just shrugged.

"You know, Jasmine Crane is dead."

I stared at him. "I know that."

"And she wasn't even a nice woman when she was alive. So if you decided to stop looking for the person who killed her, nobody would think less of you."

"It's not that," I said quickly.

Then I stopped and considered. What was this compulsion that drove me to solve mysteries, even when my own safety might be at risk? I had no idea where it had come from. All I knew was that I was pretty good at it.

Two weeks earlier, I'd told myself that I was looking for Amanda. But it had quickly become clear that wasn't all I was doing. I was determined to bring Jasmine's murderer to justice too. And suddenly it occurred to me that Terry might be able to help.

"Terry, will you do something for me?" I asked.

"Sure, doll. Anything."

"Remember last week when you were telling us about the judge whose house had been robbed?"

"Marv and Selma Stanberg." Terry nodded.

"Would you ask around and find out if anyone else's home has been burglarized while they were at a dog show?"

"That's an interesting question."

I'd hoped he might feel that way. "And one more thing. If you do run across someone, would you find out if they ever used a dog sitter when they went away?"

Terry's lips quirked in a half-smile. I bet he already knew whom he was going to call first. "Are you going to explain why you're sending me on this fact-finding mission?"

"No," I told him. "Not just yet."

"You're getting close to figuring things out, aren't you?"

"I think so."

"I'll ask around on one condition," Terry said. "Later, I'm going to expect you to tell me everything."

"You got it."

"Don't think I won't hold you to that."

Crawford reappeared behind us. "I always thought you had more sense than that, Melanie. Giving Terry something to hold over you is a dangerous thing."

"Thank you for your concern." I gave the handler a cheeky grin. "But I think I can risk it."

"Just so long as you know what you're getting yourself into," Crawford replied.

I did. Or at least I hoped I did.

When we got home, Bud and the rest of the Poodles were waiting for us. By now, Augie had been told what a good boy he was so many times that he knew he'd accomplished something special. He went prancing into the house like he thought he was Leader of the Pack.

It only took one stern look from Faith to disabuse him of that notion.

The other dogs weren't impressed by Augie's new magnificence either. After all, most of them were already champions themselves. As for Bud, he'd never been anywhere near a dog show. So he didn't know what a champion was.

We stayed up late that night celebrating Davey's achievement. I could still remember the undiluted joy I'd felt when I'd finished Faith's championship. She was the first dog I'd ever handled in the show ring, and the sense of satisfaction had been enormous. Davey was less than half the age I'd been when I'd accomplished that feat. Maybe Aunt Peg was right to think she had a budding Tim Brazier in the family.

Aunt Peg called to summon me to her house the following morning. That was getting to be a habit. Then she surprised me.

"Bring Davey with you," she commanded.

"Davey?" I'd assumed she would want to discuss Jasmine's murder, and all the new things I'd learned recently. "He'll be bored listening to us talk."

"No, he won't. Davey can use the visit to get to know Coral better. I'm thinking I might enter her in a show next month. No time like the present to get their partnership started."

Aunt Peg couldn't see me, but I rolled my eyes anyway. Even her ulterior motives had ulterior motives.

Davey was surprised by the invitation too. But he considered for a moment, then said, "Okay. I'll come."

"You will?"

"Sure, why not? Maybe I'll handle Coral someday and maybe I won't. But I wouldn't mind playing around with her. It beats doing homework. And besides, Aunt Peg always has cake."

Like mother, like son.

Aunt Peg was waiting for us impatiently when we arrived. Let me point out that it was nine-thirty on a rainy Sunday morning. All the other teachers I knew had the day off. They might even still be in bed. But by Aunt Peg's standards, we were already late.

She watched with a sharp eye as Davey knelt down in her front hall and her Standard Poodles gathered around him. He greeted each of them by name. At the end, Davey gave Beau a special hug.

"Coral likes you," Aunt Peg said.

Davey looked up at us. He wasn't fooled by her flattery any more than I was. "Coral likes everybody."

"And isn't that a lovely attribute? I can't imagine who wouldn't want to show a Poodle who enjoys everything about life."

"I haven't made any promises yet," he told her.

"Of course not," Aunt Peg agreed smoothly. "I wouldn't expect you to. For now, the two of you are simply getting to know one another. Maybe when the rain stops, we'll take her outside and you can put her through her paces. You wouldn't mind, would you? You'd be doing me a service. Watching Coral with someone else, I'll be able to see where the holes are in her training."

Davey nodded, but also he snuck me a sly glance.

We were both thinking the same thing. As if any Poodle of Aunt Peg's would have holes in her training. Even one that was six months old. Having spent her entire life under Aunt Peg's tutelage, Coral could probably teach Davey and me a thing or two about being a show dog.

"Now that that's settled, you can take her down to the playroom. Your mother and I are going to chat for a few minutes while you and Coral become better acquainted."

When Aunt Peg and I headed to the kitchen, the entire Standard Poodle pack elected to stay with Davey. They knew who was going to be more fun.

Aunt Peg poured herself a cup of tea. I heated up some water for coffee. There wasn't a pastry in sight. Considering the difficulty I'd had zipping up my pants that morning, I figured that was a good thing.

Within minutes, we were both settled at the table.

"I get the distinct impression that I've been missing out on things," Aunt Peg said sternly. "That won't do at all. I would like to be filled in and you may start with what happened yesterday."

"Yesterday?" It felt like a dozen different things had happened at the dog show the day before.

I had no idea which one she was referring to.

"You disappeared for half an hour, and when you returned you looked like you'd been in a brawl."

Oh. Aunt Peg hadn't said anything at the time. I'd thought she hadn't noticed. I should have known better.

"Rick Fanelli and I had a disagreement."

Her brow arched upward. "About what?"

"Whether or not we should discuss what kind of business he was doing with Jasmine Crane."

"I wasn't aware they'd had any business dealings."

"Nor was I until recently. Tamryn Klein was the one who brought it up."

"That's the other girl who dog-sits?"

I nodded. "She also told me she thought that Sadie Foster was stealing artwork from Jasmine."

"Sadie Foster?" Aunt Peg turned the name over in her mind. "I don't believe we've spoken about her before."

I sidetracked for a few minutes, telling her first about my initial meeting with Sadie, and then that the woman had since been named executor of Jasmine's estate.

"I wonder if she knows what ever happened to my pretty leash," Aunt Peg mused. When I stopped and stared at her, she shook her head and directed me to continue.

"Sadie denied everything Tamryn said. In fact,

she accused Tamryn of being the thief. She said that Jasmine had recently confronted Tamryn, and the two of them had had a major fight about it."

"That doesn't sound good."

"No, it doesn't," I agreed.

"So you were given two differing accounts of the same story. Between Sadie and Tamryn, which one seems more credible?"

I frowned. "This probably doesn't help, but my answer is neither one. I also asked Sadie about Jasmine's association with Rick, and she refused to comment."

Aunt Peg put down her mug and peered at me across the table. "Maybe she thought it was none of your business."

"Or maybe she has something to hide," I replied. "And speaking of hiding things . . . Alan Crandall."

"What about him?"

"He was having an affair with Jasmine."

"Alan? Really?" She sat in silence for a minute. I knew she was picturing the tall, studious-looking man who ran the concession that had been a dog show mainstay for years. "He always seems so straight-laced."

"He probably didn't initiate it," I said. "Apparently Jasmine was quite the seductress."

Now Aunt Peg looked amused. "There were others?"

"Other men that Jasmine appears to have conned things out of, yes. I believe that Alan was the only one she was sleeping with. It didn't end well."

"I should hope not." Aunt Peg snorted. "Alan Crandall is a married man, isn't he?"

"He was. His wife is divorcing him."

"Oh my. Over Jasmine? That's a shame. What could that man have been thinking?"

"Apparently that he wouldn't get caught," I said. "Like every other man who ever cheated on his wife. Barb has hired a lawyer and she's suing Alan. There's a chance he may lose his business."

"How very distressing for him."

"Don't waste your sympathies. You won't feel sorry for Alan when you hear what happened next."

Aunt Peg sighed. She hated it when people she knew had been caught behaving badly. "You may as well tell me everything."

"After Barb found out about the affair, Jasmine dumped Alan. And in retaliation, he destroyed her paintings."

"You're not serious." Aunt Peg looked appalled.

"Unfortunately, I am. At the end of the day that Jasmine was killed, the Sedgefield show committee needed to clear the park. Alan had his big truck there and he volunteered to have his crew dismantle Jasmine's booth. He told Gwen

255

Kimble that he would store Jasmine's things in his warehouse until it was determined where they should go. But sometime between then and now Alan built a giant bonfire and burned everything."

Chapter 19

I don't believe it," Aunt Peg said.

"Alan told me so himself. He actually seemed proud of himself."

"Then he's a fool," she replied sharply. "And perhaps worse. What you're describing sounds like the behavior of an out-of-control, and perhaps dangerous, man. Who's to say that he stopped there?"

"Alan told me that he had nothing to do with Jasmine's death."

"Of course he *told* you that. It doesn't mean it's true. Maybe he confessed to the other thing to throw you off the track. In his place, that's what I would have done."

I loved watching Aunt Peg's devious mind at work. She also made a good point.

She frowned and said, "Does Gwen know about that?"

"I don't know. I doubt it."

"She's going to be livid when she finds out. Gwen trusted Alan to keep those paintings safe. And since she's the one who put them in his care, there may be liability issues for her kennel club as well."

"I'm sure Alan never considered any of that," I said. "I think he just got mad and wanted revenge."

"A man with a temper is a perilous thing."

It felt like we'd come full circle.

"That brings us back to Rick Fanelli," I said. "Another man with a temper."

"Yes, let's talk about him." She didn't say "finally," but the thought was strongly implied.

"First I have to backtrack again—"

Aunt Peg stifled a small groan.

I ignored that and continued. "Remember last week when Terry was telling us about a judge whose house was robbed while he and his wife were at a dog show?"

"Of course. The Stanbergs and their Norfolk Terriers. What a nasty business that must have been."

"It turns out they're not the only ones."

"Who have Norfolks? Certainly not."

Trust Aunt Peg to consider the dog connection first.

"No," I said. "The Stanbergs aren't the only members of the dog community to be robbed while they were away at a show."

Aunt Peg shoulders lifted. Her head came up. I had her attention now. "Who else?"

"Raina Gentry, for one. She has Chesapeake Bay Retrievers. Also Elliott Bean and Roger Marx. And the fact that they were at dog shows when their houses were broken into isn't the only connection."

"Oh?"

"In at least two of those cases, the thieves knew there would be dogs in the homes when they arrived. And they brought marrow bones with them to distract the dogs while they worked."

"Marrow bones?" Aunt Peg repeated.

I nodded.

"Both times?"

My head dipped again.

"How very interesting."

"I thought so," I said. "And here's another interesting thing. I'm pretty sure that all the people who were targeted had previously had pet-sitters come to their houses when they were out of town."

"Pet-sitters?" Aunt Peg's eyes narrowed. "Like Amanda?"

"Yes. Tamryn too. And they may not have been the only ones involved. And do you know who was helping them find jobs?"

Aunt Peg wasn't slow on the uptake. "Jasmine Crane," she said.

"Yup. Now think back to what else Terry said last week. It wasn't only that the thieves knew about the dogs ahead of time. They also knew that there were valuables in the homes that were well worth stealing. Things like Marv Stanberg's coin collection or Raina Gentry's vintage jewelry."

"Almost as if one of them had already been inside the house and had a good long look around," Aunt Peg said slowly. "Someone who might have been there by herself overnight, taking care of a few dogs."

"Bingo," I said.

Almost immediately Aunt Peg shook her head. "I can't believe Amanda would have been involved in a scheme like that."

"Unless she wasn't entirely aware of what was going on." I tossed out a possible scenario. "Amanda and Jasmine were friends. They saw each other all the time. Maybe Jasmine would casually inquire about the houses Amanda had been to and what she'd seen. Amanda might have been giving up information without even realizing it."

Aunt Peg pounced on my explanation with evident relief. "And when she did figure things out, that's when Amanda decided to disappear."

I wasn't as convinced of Amanda's innocence as Aunt Peg was. But I was happy to let that point slide for now.

"Rick must have been part of it too," I said. "Either that or he wanted to be, and Jasmine was keeping him at arm's length. Maybe Amanda let slip what was going on—"

Aunt Peg frowned ferociously. She was still determined to think the best of the young woman to whom she'd entrusted the care of her beloved Poodles.

"Or maybe he found out from Jasmine. It doesn't really matter how he got involved. But

I'm betting that's what Tamryn was talking about when she said that Rick and Jasmine were in business together. What else could it have been?"

"That's the question that got you punched," Aunt Peg said roundly.

Tweaked was more like it, but I let her misconception stand. It made me sound like more of a bad-ass.

"Tamryn also heard Rick threaten Jasmine."

"Rick appears to be quite proficient at bullying people." Aunt Peg was not amused. "Why on earth would Amanda want that lout for a boyfriend?"

"Maybe she was afraid to break up with him. Don't forget what Abby told us. And Amanda wasn't the only one who was scared of Rick. It seems like nobody wants to make that guy mad, and then have to suffer the consequences."

"Except perhaps for Jasmine Crane," Aunt Peg pointed out. "Because we know that she stood up to him at least once."

My coffee was cooling on the table in front of me. I didn't even want to pause long enough to take a drink. "But that makes sense when you consider that Jasmine manipulated everyone around her. Of course she'd fight back when Rick tried to do the same to her."

"And it could have been exactly that response that got her killed."

We both pondered that.

"We know that Rick was at the dog show when Jasmine died," I said thoughtfully. "And so was Amanda. Maybe *that's* why she disappeared. Maybe when she heard that Jasmine had been killed, she was afraid she knew too much and that Rick might turn on her next."

"So now what do we do?" Aunt Peg wanted to know. "That all sounds plausible to me, but how do we go about proving it?"

"Let's start with a phone call," I proposed. "Can you talk to Raina Gentry and see if she ever used a dog sitter?"

"Of course. I'll do it right now."

While Aunt Peg was on the phone to Raina, I checked in with Terry.

"It hasn't even been a whole day since you told me to ask around," he grumbled.

"Nobody works faster than you, Terry. I bet you already have something for me, don't you?"

"Lucky for you, you're right," he cooed.

Terry had indeed located another pair of victims. Chris and Susie Bradshaw lived in Pound Ridge and showed French Bulldogs. Their house had been burglarized three months earlier. Previously they'd used a pet-sitter, but after the home invasion, the couple felt more secure with a house that was locked down and guarded by a comprehensive alarm system.

"Don't forget you owe me one," Terry said at the end.

"Never," I replied with a laugh. "Especially since I'm sure you'll enjoy collecting."

When Aunt Peg and I were both off the phone, we shared what we'd learned. Raina Gentry had only used a dog-sitter once—a girl named Meg, who'd been recommended to her by Jasmine Crane. But that one time had apparently been enough to make her a target.

"That's the third girl we know of," I said. "And maybe there were more. Jasmine must have had quite the operation."

"Apparently she was more talented than any of us realized," Aunt Peg agreed unhappily. "We don't have all the answers yet, but we have quite a few. It's time for you to take this information to the police."

It wasn't as if I hadn't thought of that myself.

"Your suggestion would be an excellent idea except for one thing," I said. "Which police should I talk to? Jasmine was killed in eastern Connecticut. Amanda disappeared from Weston. The robberies that we know of happened in Rye, Pound Ridge, Trumbull, and wherever Raina lives—"

"Hamden," Aunt Peg supplied.

Which was no help at all. "That's exactly what I mean. The events took place all over the map. The only thing they all have in common is the connection to the dog show circuit."

"If you had told me that you were going to talk

for this long, I'd have stayed home and done my homework," Davey complained as he appeared in the doorway.

Four black Poodles eddied around his legs. The remaining dog, Beau, walked past him and entered the kitchen. He walked over to the water bowl and had a long drink. Then he flopped down on a nearby bed.

"See?" said Davey. "Even Beau is bored."

Aunt Peg and I had talked ourselves straight into a dead end. We were both ready to do something else.

"You're quite right. It's time for us to take a break." Aunt Peg hopped to her feet. "And look, the clouds have even parted for us. Let's go outside and have a handling lesson."

She shouldn't have called it a lesson, I thought. Davey had already endured enough handling lessons from Aunt Peg. He would balk at that.

She must have been reading my mind because she quickly amended her invitation. "Mind you, the lesson is for Coral. Not you, Davey. I'm sure you'll do a fine job."

My son smiled at that. When Aunt Peg handed him a chain collar on a narrow lead he happily slipped the loop over Coral's head. Jasmine Crane wasn't the only one who knew how to bend boys and men to her will.

We took Coral outside to Aunt Peg's spacious backyard. The rest of the Poodle group tagged along. Even Beau, who'd seen everything, decided that this was going to be something worth watching.

"Set her up over there." Aunt Peg indicated a level, sunny spot. "Pretend I'm your judge."

As if anyone ever would have assumed otherwise.

Davey walked Coral into an almost correct stance. As he reached out to reset her hind feet, Zeke, Hope, and Willow swarmed around them. Immediately Coral began to wiggle in place. If the other Poodles were going to play, the puppy wanted to join them.

Augie's basic show ring education had taken place two years earlier. So it had been a long time since Davey'd had to deal with a Poodle who didn't already have her training down cold. Which was probably the lesson that Aunt Peg intended to teach him.

Davey reset Coral's feet a second time. Then a third. Hope and Willow moved on. Now they were sniffing around the edge of the lawn. Coral looked after them longingly. Davey repositioned the puppy's feet again, but by now he'd totally lost her attention.

The puppy bounced up in the air like a spring. Davey grimaced. He looked over at Aunt Peg in frustration.

"That's not fair," he said.

"What's not fair?" she asked innocently.

"Them." Davey indicated the wandering Poodles. Beau, sitting in the grass no more than five feet away, gave him a doggy grin. "Coral won't listen to me while they're here. They're too much of a distraction."

"Oh? So there aren't any distractions at dog shows? Is that what you're telling me?"

"No. But—"

"Perhaps you'd rather choose your own distractions then? Maybe a flock of geese or a marching band?" Aunt Peg paused and pretended to think. "Although where I might procure either one on short notice is a bit problematic."

Davey smiled reluctantly. He reached down and gave Coral a pat. Even Zeke had moved on by now. He was examining a nearby tree. The puppy was finally beginning to settle.

"And that's why I provided you with a few home-grown distractions instead," Aunt Peg finished.

"But these guys are her best friends. Of course she wants to play with them."

"Dogs she sees every day are much less enticing than ones she's never met before," Aunt Peg pointed out. "Which includes virtually every other Poodle Coral is going to show against."

"That's different," Davey blurted out.

"Is it? How?"

Smart boy, Davey didn't even try to defend that indefensible position. Instead he turned his attention back to Coral. And, more importantly, he got her attention back on him. He walked her forward several steps, spun her back in a small circle, then set her up again.

This time, the puppy was listening. With only one small bobble, he quickly managed a very creditable stack. Aunt Peg stared at the pair critically for a long minute.

She was waiting for handler and puppy to break their concentration. To Davey's credit neither one did.

Aunt Peg approached Coral from the front. She held out her hand for the puppy to sniff. Coral wagged her tail madly in reply. *Hi, Mom!* When she started to wiggle again, Davey deftly smoothed her back into place.

That was well done.

For this first attempt, Aunt Peg made short work of her physical examination. Then she got Davey and Coral moving. The two of them were great at that. Davey's loose-limbed energy was a great compliment to the puppy's long, elegant stride.

Even Aunt Peg couldn't find anything to criticize.

Five minutes later, the lesson was over. Davey removed Coral's collar and leash, and released the puppy to play with her friends.

Watching her race across the yard, Aunt Peg said, "That was a bit of all right. Of course, the two of you will still need some work before you become a proper team. But I definitely see potential there. I believe you passed the audition."

I snorted under my breath. Davey's head whipped around.

When he spoke, his voice sounded huffy. "You asked me to show Coral for you. You didn't tell me there was going to be an audition."

"As I recall, you didn't ask."

"Well, luckily for you," he replied, "you passed the audition too."

Aunt Peg's eyes narrowed. She stared down her nose at him. In another few years, he would be as tall as she was, but for now the gesture was still effective. "What's that supposed to mean?"

Davey crossed the small space between them and held out his hand. "Partners?"

She hesitated. Then I saw the moment that Aunt Peg's surprise at the gesture turned to grudging respect. She extended her hand too.

"Partners," she agreed.

I'd never gotten Aunt Peg to acknowledge me in that way, I realized. Then again, maybe I'd never demanded it. It occurred to me that I'd raised a pretty savvy kid.

Davey had agreed to show Coral, but Aunt Peg wasn't going to be allowed to pressure him, or push him around, as she'd done previously. Good for him for setting the ground rules for their alliance right up front.

"I have a brilliant idea," Aunt Peg said as we were all walking back into the house. "I'm going to get in touch with Amanda."

I looked at her in surprise. "How?"

"By text, of course. That seems to be her preferred mode of communication."

"Amanda isn't answering Abby's texts. What makes you think she might respond to yours?"

"Because I'm going to tell her that we've figured out what's going on."

I paused to pull open the door, cocked my head to one side, and said, "Have we?"

"Well, obviously not all of it. But Amanda doesn't have to know that. When she comes back, she can fill us in on the rest. It will all work out rather neatly."

If it happened, I thought. Although when Aunt Peg took charge, unexpected things often came to pass. Why should this time be any different?

Even so, I shook my head. "Amanda clearly thinks she has a good reason for staying away. How do you intend to change her mind?"

"I'll let her know we're aware that she left because she was afraid of Rick. *And* I'll promise to protect her from him."

"How are you going to do that?"

"I'll think of something," Aunt Peg said blithely. "I always do."

The last of the Poodles scampered through the

doorway and I closed the door behind us. "Like what?"

"Perhaps Amanda would like to move in with me for a few days, just until we get things sorted out."

"In here?" I couldn't imagine any vivacious twenty-something girl wanting Aunt Peg for a roommate. Even for a few days.

"Why not? She's stayed here on numerous occasions when she was dog-sitting for me. This will be just the same."

"Except that *you'll* be here."

Aunt Peg rolled her eyes. "Of course I'll be here. That's the whole point. Otherwise how can I keep an eye on her and make sure she stays safe?"

"Of course," I echoed faintly. I was fresh out of objections. If Aunt Peg could make that plan work, more power to her. "While you're working on bringing Amanda back, I think I'm going to go talk to Detective Young."

"He works for the Greenwich police. And as far as we know, Greenwich is one of the few towns in the state where Jasmine wasn't hatching some nefarious scheme. How will he be able to help?"

"I don't know yet," I admitted. "But at least he and I have a relationship of sorts."

The detective and I had first crossed paths when he was seeking the man who'd killed a Santa Claus impersonator. And then again when a millionaire philanthropist had been murdered in his own home. Both times I'd been on the spot—or near enough—when the deed happened. Even so, the detective hadn't taken kindly to my involvement in his investigation.

But beggars couldn't be choosers, I reminded myself. Besides, all I intended to do was ask him to point me in the direction of the right person to contact.

Davey was sitting on the floor, playing with the Poodles. Now he stood up and frowned. "You people are still boring."

"I can fix that," Aunt Peg replied cheerfully. "Who's ready for cake?"

Chapter 20

It was Sunday, so I had to wait until the following afternoon to see Detective Young. In the meantime, I went to work. I started the school day in Russell Hanover's office.

On Friday after speaking with Francesca, I'd attempted to make an appointment with the headmaster. His secretary, Harriet, guarded access to the Big Man with all the fervor of a miser dispensing gold coins. She had—over my objections—penciled me in for early May.

That wouldn't do at all.

When Harriet arrived at seven-thirty on Monday morning, I was already sitting in a chair right next to Mr. Hanover's office door. The secretary's small frown was the only sign of her disapproval. Then she ignored me and went on with her morning routine.

By the time the headmaster rolled in twenty minutes later, I had scooted the chair even closer. Now I was blocking the heavy oak door to Mr. Hanover's domain. He had no choice but to stop and talk to me.

Russell Hanover II was a man well aware of his position at the top of our pecking order. He was tall, austere, and always impeccably dressed. Every bit as intelligent and sophisticated as the parents who placed their children in his care, the headmaster cultivated a stern, almost frosty, demeanor. Supposedly it was intended to inspire those around him to never give anything but their best.

I know it scared the crap out of me.

"Good morning, Ms. Travis," Mr. Hanover said. "You're here early."

Not the best way to begin. I'd hoped he hadn't noticed those times Faith and I had come sliding in just before second bell.

He looked at me appraisingly. "To what do I owe the honor?"

I stood up and said, "I need to talk to you."

"So it appears." As always, he remained totally unruffled. It would take more than a teacher's ill-timed intrusion to put Mr. Hanover off his game. He turned to Harriet. "Does Ms. Travis have an appointment?"

"Yes, she does." She lifted her calendar and showed it to him. "It's on May fifth. Let me further point out that today's roster is full. Your appointments are scheduled back to back."

His head swiveled back in my direction. "Is this urgent?"

Mr. Hanover and I had needed to attend to urgent business on several previous occasions. I was thankful this situation didn't involve anything as dire as those incidents.

"Umm . . . school-on-fire urgent, no. But otherwise, yes."

Back to Harriet once again. "What time is my first appointment?"

She looked down to consult her book, though I was sure she already knew what it said. "Eight-fifteen."

The headmaster gave a clipped nod. "Ms. Travis, you have ten minutes. I'd advise you not to waste a second of it. Move that chair out of the way and let's get on, shall we?"

Howard Academy's main building was the former residence of early twentieth century robber baron Joshua A. Howard. The great stone mansion sat high on a promontory above downtown. Over the years, it had been updated to meet current standards, but otherwise left mostly intact.

The school's reception area had once been a soaring, two-story entrance hall. Mr. Hanover's office was originally the formal parlor. Its wide windows looked out over the spacious grounds. An antique mahogany desk, imposing enough to impress even the most jaded parent, held pride of place in front of them. The room had been decorated to convey an aura of achievement, stability, and good taste—clearly a reflection of the headmaster's own sensibilities.

This morning I didn't have time to appreciate any of that. I had just ten minutes to tell Mr. Hanover everything he needed to know about Francesca Della Cimino's rocky transition to his student body. Hopefully we'd be able to use most of that time to agree on a solution.

Mr. Hanover sat behind his desk and listened somberly to what I had to say. Now that I had the floor, he gave me his full attention. As I'd expected, he didn't like what he was hearing. Never one to equivocate when a direct course of action presented itself, the headmaster acceded to my suggestion that I first attempt to deal with Francesca's tormentors myself. If that didn't work, we would call in the big guns.

"I want you to continue to monitor this situation closely," Mr. Hanover said as he walked me to the door. "And I expect to receive frequent updates on your progress."

"Yes, of course," I replied.

Mr. Hanover pulled open the door and I walked through. Harriet was sitting at her desk just outside the office. She hadn't looked up from her work, but I knew she was listening to every word that was being said.

"Should I leave messages for you with Harriet?" I asked.

"No, talk to me directly. I'm sure Harriet will be able to fit you in, if you need time." He turned to his secretary. "Isn't that so?"

"Certainly, Mr. Hanover."

"Then it's settled. I'll expect you to get right to work on that."

"I will," I told him. "I'll meet with the girls today."

The headmaster was still frowning. Clearly I hadn't gotten his morning off to a good start.

"We have zero tolerance for that kind of behavior at Howard Academy," he said firmly. "It will be made to stop. Any student who continues to cause a problem will be removed. Is that clear?"

"Yes, sir."

"Good. Off you go, then. Harriet, who's next?"

I'd been dismissed. *Thank God.* I respected Mr. Hanover enormously. I had worked for the man for years. But I still breathed a sigh of relief every time I survived a meeting with him with both my job and my wits still intact.

With the full weight of the headmaster's support behind me, I sent notes to Taylor's, Brittany's and Alicia's teachers, clearing their schedules for a meeting with me, in my classroom, right after lunch. Howard Academy was a small enough school that I had at least a nodding acquaintance with every student. I was equally certain they all knew who I was. But none of these girls had ever needed tutoring. None had ever visited my room before.

They arrived together in a boisterous group. Obviously good friends, the three girls were chatting and giggling as they came through the door.

Two blonds and a brunette, the preteen girls were all fashioned from the same enviable mold. Each had sleek hair, clear skin, and bright teeth.

Even the dowdy school uniform—navy plaid wool skirt, white button-down shirt, and knee socks—couldn't dim their luster.

Although they'd been given no reason for the unusual summons, this trio of golden girls was sure they couldn't possibly have anything to fear. I was about to change their minds about that.

"Please take a seat." As I closed the door, I indicated the round table in the middle of the room. "Alicia? Ditch the gum."

She blinked her big, blue eyes, certain she must have misheard. "But I always chew gum after I eat. It's almost as good as brushing your teeth."

I didn't know if that was true and I didn't care. In my classroom, we followed the rules. I pointed toward the waste basket.

As Alicia grudgingly complied, Taylor muttered under her breath, "It's not like this is a real class."

I ignored the comment, and the snicker from Brittany that followed. By the time I was finished these girls were going to wish they'd been sent to a real class. I waited until each of the three had found a seat. Then I walked over to the table and stood above them.

Brittany glanced toward the empty dog bed in the corner. Even students I didn't see regularly knew my big black Poodle. "Where's Faith?"

"She couldn't come with me today," I said. To Faith's annoyance, I'd left her home because I knew I'd be running around all day. As soon as I was finished at school, I'd be heading downtown to talk to Detective Young.

"Who cares about the dog?" Taylor said with a smirk. "Why are we here, Ms. Travis? I'm supposed to be in French class now."

"You're here because your behavior has been causing problems," I said bluntly. "I'm sure you've all read the Howard Academy code of ethics that you agreed to abide by when you became students here. Would one of you like to define bullying for me?"

"Bullying?" Alicia managed to sound surprised. "I don't know why you would think that has anything to do with us." She gazed around the table for support. And she got it. All three girls shrugged innocently.

"How about name calling?" I asked. "Does that sound familiar?"

Francesca might not have been this trio's only victim, so I didn't want to get specific. It turned out I didn't have to. Comprehension dawned. These girls knew what I was talking about. Brittany and Alicia shared a troubled glance.

"My parents taught me to always tell the truth," Taylor announced. "I don't see why that's a bad thing."

"Even if it means insulting another girl to her face?" I asked.

"I guess that would depend on what the girl

looks like, wouldn't it?" She smiled at her own cleverness, then glanced at her friends for approval. It wasn't forthcoming. Alicia and Brittany were beginning to look nervous.

Taylor shook her head, dismissing them. She was still defiant. "I don't know why any of this is *my* problem."

I'd hoped we could discuss the problem amicably. Apparently not. As a teacher, I was never supposed to lose my temper. But Taylor's arrogance was driving me perilously close to that edge.

"Taylor, I gave you more credit than that. But since this is hard for you to understand, maybe I need to be more specific. Would you consider it your problem if your so-called honesty caused you to be suspended from school? How about if your recommendation to Exeter was revoked? Would that get my point across?"

Judging by the startled, and then angry, expressions that chased across the girl's face, it would. Finally I'd struck a nerve. It was about damn time.

Taylor had been slouching in her seat. Now she bolted upright and straightened her shoulders. "You can't talk to me that way. Do you know who my father is?"

Of course I knew who Taylor's father was. John Simon was a founding partner of an enormously successful hedge fund. In the girl's twelve years, I suspected that few people, if indeed any, had ever told Taylor Simon that she couldn't have whatever she wanted. Or do whatever she wanted.

I crossed my arms over my chest. "Actually, I can talk to you that way. While you're here, in my classroom, you are under my authority."

"Your authority?" Taylor scoffed. "You must be joking. You're not even a teacher. You're just a tutor."

Alicia's brow rose at that. She edged her chair slightly away, deliberately distancing herself from Taylor and what she had said. Brittany had her hands clasped tightly together in her lap. Her lips were pressed in a thin line. She looked as though she might cry.

"Yes, you're right," I agreed mildly. "I'm *just* a tutor. But I spoke with Mr. Hanover this morning about the way you three have been behaving yourselves. Would you like me to ask him to join us here so he can clarify the hierarchy? Maybe you'd like to discuss your concerns with him. Considering that he's already well versed on the topic, I know he'd be happy to talk to you about it."

I paused and let my gaze rest on each of the girls in turn. "If you three don't think I'm important enough to handle this, I'd be happy to escalate the matter. Would you prefer that I hand it over to a higher authority?"

"That won't be necessary, Ms. Travis," Alicia said quickly.

Brittany's head bobbed up and down in agreement. "I'm sorry," she mumbled. "We never should have said those things to Francesca."

"Why did you?" I asked.

"We only told her what she would see for herself if she looked in the mirror," Taylor snapped.

"That she looks like Porky Pig?"

"It's just a silly cartoon," Alicia told me. "Francesca took things way too seriously. She should have laughed it off. She's new here. She doesn't know how things work. So it was just as much her fault as ours."

"You must be joking," I retorted. "Please tell me that you don't really believe that."

Alicia's cheeks reddened. Her mouth clamped shut. I supposed that was as close to an admission of guilt as I was going to get.

I yanked out a chair and sat down. Now we were all eye to eye.

"Let me tell you something," I said sternly. "I don't care whose fault it is. I only care that it stops. *Immediately.* Look at me."

I waited until the three girls had done so. "You girls are better than that. You know you are. And from now on, I'm going to expect you to act like it."

Taylor was clearly the leader of the group. She

looked like she wanted to slap me. But I was pretty sure that Brittany and Alicia were coming around.

I glared at them some more. "And if I'm wrong about you three, and you're actually not better than that? Then I'm going to expect you to pretend to be. Now I'm setting the bar pretty low here. So if that's too hard for you—if you don't think you can manage to be civil to your fellow students— then Howard Academy probably isn't the right school for you. Do we understand each other?"

Two heads nodded right away. Taylor waited a beat, then followed suit reluctantly.

"Can we go now?" she asked.

"Yes, you're dismissed." I stood up, walked over to the door, and opened it. "But don't forget what I said or you'll find yourselves right back here. I mean that."

Alicia shoved back her chair and raced from the room like her skirt was on fire. Taylor followed at a more sedate pace, the arrogant tilt to her head meant to illustrate that I hadn't succeeded in scaring *her*.

Well, we'd see about that. Taylor thought she was tough, but I intended to keep repeating myself until I got my point across. And if I needed to up the stakes, I was ready to exercise that option too.

Brittany hung back until the other two girls were gone.

"Do you need something?" I asked.

She dropped her head guiltily. "I knew it was wrong," she admitted. "We shouldn't have behaved like that. I didn't mean it. But Taylor, she's . . ."

"Impossible?" I said when Brittany didn't finish her thought.

The girl managed a very small smile. "I was just trying to fit in."

"You know what? Francesca is just trying to fit in too. It's hard to be the new kid. To go someplace in the middle of the school year where you don't know anyone, and everything, even the language, is different. Things are difficult enough for Francesca without you girls making it worse."

"I know," Brittany said. "I'm sorry."

"I'm not the one you should apologize to. Why don't you deliver that apology to the person who needs to hear it?"

"Maybe I will," Brittany said uncertainly.

"Think about it," I told her, and she nodded.

It wasn't a promise, but it was a start.

Chapter 21

When I finished with the three girls, my school day was over. Then it was on to my next assignment.

The Greenwich police station was just off Greenwich Avenue, an easy drive from Howard Academy. I was lucky to find a place to park on Mason Street, which meant that I was a few minutes early for my appointment.

I hadn't seen Detective Raymond Young since the previous summer. From my point of view—and his as well, I'm sure—that was a good thing. The less time I spent on any police detective's radar, the happier I was. But I had a story to tell. I needed to talk to somebody in law enforcement. And Detective Young was the nearest thing I had to a connection.

I knew better than to hope that he'd be happy to see me.

I signed in at the reception desk and was told to take a seat. Detective Young didn't keep me waiting long. A black man with broad shoulders and close cropped hair, Young moved with surprising grace. I stood up as he approached, but when he stopped in front of me, I was still dwarfed by his size.

"It's nice to see you again, Ms. Travis," he said.

I might have been able to fault the honesty of the detective's sentiment, but his manners were flawless. When we shook hands, his grip was firm enough to convey strength and inspire confidence. Maybe I had come to the right place after all.

I looked up at him and smiled. "Is there somewhere we could talk for a few minutes?"

"If you don't mind my asking, what is this about?"

"It's kind of a long story. But it started with a murder."

His brow lifted. "Recent?"

"Two weeks ago. In eastern Connecticut."

"And you think I can help with that?"

"I hope so," I replied fervently. "Because I don't know where else to turn."

Detective Young pondered that for a moment, then nodded. "In that case, let's go to my office. You can tell me everything you think I need to know."

I followed Detective Young through a rabbit warren of connecting corridors. His office turned out to be small and sparsely furnished. But at least it had a window. And a door that closed. Not that he shut it behind us. I wondered whether he'd left the door open for his protection or mine.

Young waved me to a straight-backed chair. I expected him to sit down behind his metal desk. Instead he remained standing in front of it. Maybe that was his way of telling me that I wouldn't be there long?

The detective leaned back against the edge of the desk and waited for me to speak. Finally he said, "Well?"

"I'm gathering my thoughts."

I had a lot to tell him. It was hard to know where to begin.

As if he could read my mind, Young said, "Start with the murder."

Or maybe that was what policemen always said in circumstances like these. Detective Young made it sound so simple. When in truth it was anything but.

I did what he requested—sort of. I started with Jasmine Crane. And the dog show. And Aunt Peg's custom-made leash. In my mind, it was all part of the same explanation. But then no one has ever accused me of brevity.

I went from there to Amanda's disappearance. And Amanda's boyfriend. He was definitely key. I told Detective Young that Alan Crandall had taken possession of Jasmine's paintings and subsequently burned them. And that Jasmine—a woman always on the lookout for an easy score—had been finding dog-sitting jobs for at least three girls that I knew of.

About that time, Detective Young began to look bored, so I spiced things up by telling him about the robberies. The Stanbergs in Trumbull, Raina

Gentry in Hamden, Elliott Bean and Roger Marx in Rye, and the most recent addition to my list, the Bradshaws in Pound Ridge. All dog show people, and all of them away at shows when the crimes occurred.

I'd hoped that the detective would start to see the same patterns emerging that I had. Instead he appeared flummoxed by the sheer amount of information I'd thrown at him. I needed to get down to specifics.

"Marrow bones," I said.

"What about them?"

"The thieves knew ahead of time that there would be dogs in the homes they robbed. They brought marrow bones with them to use as a distraction."

"That could have been a coincidence," Detective Young pointed out. "Or maybe they'd had the houses under surveillance. They might have seen the dogs and known to come prepared."

I'd suspected that he would object to that assertion. The detective had never found my theories involving canines to be compelling. Someday I was definitely going to have to educate that man about dogs.

"That's not all," I said. "The thieves also targeted people with things like rare coins, art collections, and valuable jewelry. They weren't just picking random houses and grabbing cash and electronics."

Young walked around behind his desk and sat down. "So they were smart thieves. Not much use in robbing a house that doesn't have valuables, is there?"

I refused to give up. "What about this? Each of the couples who were robbed had recently used the services of a pet-sitter who was recommended to them by Jasmine Crane."

"Now you've got my attention," Detective Young said.

Finally.

He didn't even give me a minute to bask in what I'd accomplished. Now that the detective was engaged in the conversation, he had questions of his own.

"Suppose you're right. Suppose Jasmine Crane was the brains behind this rash of robberies. How did she end up dead?"

That query brought me back around to Amanda—Aunt Peg's dog-sitter and Jasmine's disciple. I posited that she was the one who'd introduced her boyfriend to this crooked crew. The boyfriend, Rick Fanelli, who appeared to have a larcenous streak of his own. Making that connection must have seemed quite fortuitous to him.

Next thing everyone knew, Rick was in business with Jasmine. But whatever kind of business that was, nobody wanted to talk about it. In fact, they didn't want to talk about Rick at all. Probably because he had a bad temper and a tendency to lose it. I told Detective Young that Amanda had gone missing on the day that Jasmine was killed.

"Still missing?" he asked curiously.

"Yes and no."

That required yet another explanation. But thankfully Detective Young was no longer bored. Now he was with me every step of the way.

"The way the robberies were set up was ingenious," I said at the end. "As long as Jasmine continued to pick houses that were spread out all over the place, each burglary looked like a one-time job. She was probably counting on no one ever making the dog-sitter/dog show connection and putting it all together. But Rick must have. I think he tried to muscle in on her business and when she resisted, he killed her."

"Your idea may have merit." Young steepled his fingers in front of his face thoughtfully. "But I'm not sure what you expect me to do about it. We're in Greenwich, and none of the things we're talking about happened here."

"Not yet," I told him. Suddenly it occurred to me that Amanda had dog sat for Aunt Peg too. Perhaps her house had been another intended target?

"Still . . . I guess I find myself wondering why you're telling me all this."

Good question. The only thing I could do was opt for honesty. "Because I had to give this information to someone who would know what to do with it. And I know you."

"It's true that we're acquainted," Detective Young conceded. "But you don't like me."

I'd always been aware that the man sitting across from me was too perceptive for my own good.

"You don't like me either," I pointed out.

He shook his head. "What I don't enjoy is your tendency to get involved in things that are better left to the authorities whose job it is to deal with them."

"It just happens," I said. It wasn't much of an excuse.

"Trouble follows you around?"

"You might say that. I'm kind of like a bad luck charm."

Detective Young's lips quirked. "I probably shouldn't admit this, but I'm impressed by the way you put all those different pieces together."

"Thank you."

"Will you agree with me that it's now up to law enforcement to proceed with the investigation?"

"Absolutely." Especially since he hadn't made me promise to discontinue my own poking around.

"In that case, I'm sure I can find a way to make sure this information gets put in the proper channels." Detective Young opened a drawer. He pulled out a small recorder. "I'd like you to tell me your story again. I want to make sure we get every detail right. Start at the beginning."

When I got home late that afternoon, Sam was outside cleaning the grill. Every fall, he lovingly covered his oversize barbecue with a plastic tarp, then stored it in the garage for the winter. As soon as the weather started to get warm again, he couldn't wait to get the thing back out.

The first robin was supposed to herald the coming of spring. But at our house, the first sign was the return of that big, shiny barbeque. Sam liked his SUV, but he didn't treat it with nearly as much tender care as he lavished on his grill. There had to be something about cooking meat outdoors that fueled testosterone—and made men feel like they'd returned to their primitive roots.

"I see we're grilling tonight," I said.

"Steaks," Sam told me. *Manly food.* His voice had even dropped to a lower register. The grill had that effect on him. "How did things go with Detective Young?"

"Just like I'd hoped."

Along with the grill, Sam and the boys had also brought the deck furniture outside. I sat down on a nearby chaise longue.

Davey and Kevin were out in the middle of the yard. Davey was helping Kev climb the ladder that led to the tree house. Now that both boys were older, they were allowed to visit their hangout without adult supervision. Five Standard Poodles were milling around the base of the tree watching the activity. One small, spotted dog was suspiciously missing.

"Bud?" I said.

Busy scraping the cooking grid clean with a stiff brush, Sam glanced at me over his shoulder. "In the kitchen. He watched me unpack the rib eyes. Now I'm pretty sure he's parked in front of the refrigerator hoping those steaks find a way to jump out and land in his mouth."

I swiveled to one side, pulled my feet up, and lay down on the plump cushion. I rolled my shoulders and closed my eyes. This was bliss.

"He hasn't figured out a way to open the refrigerator door yet, has he?" I asked amiably.

"Not that I'm aware of. That's Faith's trick. If she decides to teach it to the boys we're all in trouble. Don't think I didn't notice that you changed the subject. Detective Young?"

"Right," I said, eyes still closed. "Nice man."

I heard Sam chuckle. "I take it that means he agreed with you?"

"For the most part. We talked about Jasmine and Amanda, and pet-sitters. And of course Rick Fanelli. I told him about the dog show participants whose houses were being robbed while they were away at shows. He did point out that all those things seemed to be happening everywhere but in his jurisdiction."

"But he agreed to work on getting the police involved anyway?"

"Yup. Mission accomplished. Detective Young also praised my powers of deduction."

I raised my head slightly and slitted one eye to see how that went over.

Sam had one brow cocked sardonically. "No wonder you think he's a nice man."

"You know me," I said with a happy sigh. "I'm easy."

"Kudos always cheers you up," he agreed. "Food works too."

Especially food I didn't have to cook. "Are you making dinner tonight?"

"Of course." Sam gestured toward the grill, indicating the absurdity of my question. How could there be any doubt?

"Perfect," I said.

Well, of course I knew that wouldn't last. But I had expected to be able to coast along on a tide of well-being for more than a couple of hours. That was how long it took Aunt Peg to call.

She wanted an update about my visit with Detective Young. But even more than that, she wanted to deliver news of her own. Aunt Peg was nearly crowing with satisfaction.

"You'll never guess what happened," she said.

No, I probably wouldn't. In Aunt Peg's world that could mean anything from a new judging assignment to a rebel uprising she'd instigated in some small third world nation.

Aunt Peg probably realized that herself. She didn't even wait for me to guess.

"I texted Amanda and she answered back right away. Apparently she was growing quite tired of not seeing or talking to anybody. When I extended an invitation for her to come in out of the cold"—Aunt Peg tossed out her espionage analogy with relish—"she accepted gratefully."

"Good work. Is she going to come and stay with you until everything gets sorted out?"

"Even better," Aunt Peg replied. "She's already here."

"Now?"

"Yes, of course now. What else would I mean?"

"You might have started with that news." Yes, I sounded huffy.

"First I wanted to hear whether you'd managed to move things along with the police. And luckily you have. But now you need to come here."

"Now?" I said again.

"What's the matter with that? It's barely eight o'clock."

"I was about to put Kevin to bed."

"Sam can do that." Aunt Peg brushed off my excuse. "He's good at it."

Yes he was, but that wasn't the point.

"Amanda's unpacking a bag in my guest room and she appears to be in a talkative mood," Aunt

Peg told me. "I know you have questions and so do I. I would hate for you to miss anything."

Put like that, how could I resist?

"I'll be there in half an hour," I said. "Don't start without me."

"I wouldn't dream of it," Aunt Peg replied. "As long as you hurry."

Chapter 22

Aunt Peg had her front door open before I'd even turned off my car. Her canine early warning system must have alerted her to my arrival. Either that or she'd been staring out the window since we'd hung up.

Usually I stopped to greet the Poodle welcoming committee. Not tonight. Aunt Peg rushed me inside the house as if she was afraid Amanda would disappear if she left her alone for too long.

"Where is she?" I asked. I was whispering. I had no idea why.

"In the kitchen. We're having dessert."

Of course they were.

"Amanda arrived an hour ago and I haven't asked a single question. I figured she would be more comfortable, and perhaps more forthcoming, if she only had to tell her story once."

No wonder Aunt Peg had been in such a hurry for me to arrive. The suspense must have been killing her.

Amanda stood up when I entered the room. If Abby hadn't told me they were twins, I never would have guessed. Abby had fair hair and blue eyes. Amanda had a honey-colored complexion and brown hair that curled around her ears. There were dark circles under her eyes, and her smile was shaky.

"I'm glad you could join us," she said politely. "Peg is making me eat cake."

"She does that," I replied, taking a seat. The empty cake plate in the center of the table indicated that I'd arrived a few minutes too late to take part.

The five Poodles had followed us into the kitchen. As they chose their spots and lay down on the hardwood floor, it was obvious that the dogs were every bit as comfortable with Amanda as they were with Aunt Peg and me. Right off the bat, that earned Amanda some bonus points.

"I'm happy to see you're well," I said when everyone was settled. "Your sister has been very worried about you."

Amanda sighed. "Abby's like a mother hen. You'd think she was three years older than me rather than three minutes. She worries about everything."

"In this case, it sounds as though she had good reason to be concerned," Aunt Peg said. "You've been missing for two weeks."

"That's Abby's version of events. I've always known where I was. Just because I wanted to get away for a few days didn't mean I was missing."

"Where were you?" I asked.

"Staying with a friend in the city. Sleeping on a roll-up futon on the floor in a studio apartment."

She wrinkled her nose. "An apartment with cockroaches. Yuck."

"That doesn't sound like much of a treat," Aunt Peg said. "And surely you can understand how the timing of your abrupt departure was bound to raise questions."

"We know that Jasmine was involved in some shady dealings," I told her. "And that you and Rick were at the dog show together on the day that she died. But we'd like to hear your story. Why don't you tell us what happened?"

"I really don't know much of anything," Amanda replied.

Aunt Peg and I shared a look. Nobody in the room believed that lie. Even the Poodles looked skeptical.

"I can't protect you if I don't know what I'm protecting you from," Aunt Peg said firmly. "Now start at the beginning, and tell us what you do know. It was the day of the dog show. You were there helping Rick. . . ."

Amanda didn't pick up the thread of the story right away. Aunt Peg and I both waited. Neither of us said a word. Finally Amanda spoke.

"I was there helping Rick," she repeated quietly. "He'd asked me to go to the show with him. He said he had too many dogs to manage on his own. We left together from his place that morning. On the way, I found out that he only had five dogs entered."

Amanda frowned. "*Five dogs*. That's nothing. My parents would have had that many in the ring by nine a.m. on a show day. Even Abby could have managed easily. But not Rick. He's always too lazy to buckle down and do the work."

I was happy to hear Amanda speak about her boyfriend with a notable lack of affection in her tone. It would make things much easier if we were all on the same page where Rick Fanelli was concerned.

"As you can probably imagine, I've had a lot of time to think recently," she said. "When I met Rick, he pursued me like I was the most interesting girl in the world. He told me I was special and I believed him. At the time, he was trying to get his handling business off the ground. Looking back now, I wonder if he didn't hook up with me because he thought my knowledge and connections could be useful to him."

"Not that you don't have many other wonderful qualities," Aunt Peg said. "But I wouldn't be surprised."

"Rick Fanelli is not a good person," I added firmly.

"I guess I know that now." She sighed. "I just wish I'd realized it sooner."

"Tell us about the show," Aunt Peg prodded.

"For me it was just another boring dog show day. I was at Rick's setup the whole time, grooming his dogs and prepping them for the ring. Rick was in and out of the tent all day. When he wasn't in the ring, he'd be off schmoozing potential clients. Stuff like that made him feel important."

Amanda stopped and grimaced. "Meanwhile he was treating me like the hired help."

"I'd have been pissed at that," I said.

"I know, right?"

Aunt Peg got us back on topic. "So even though you went with Rick, you were unaware of where he was, or what he was doing, for much of the day?"

"That's right. At shows, he was always running around like that, so it wasn't anything unusual. It never crossed my mind that there would be a reason to keep tabs on him that day."

I didn't know if the police had narrowed down the time of Jasmine's death. But even if they had, it sounded as though Rick probably didn't have an alibi.

"When did you find out that Jasmine had been killed?" Aunt Peg asked.

She and I had been among the first to know. But I was sure the news must have traveled around the showground like wildfire shortly thereafter.

"Not until midafternoon," Amanda replied. "At first, all I knew was that there was a definite buzz in the tent. People were talking about *something*. But I was busy, you know? Rick was slacking off, and that made me feel like I should work harder. I felt a responsibility to try to do right by his clients."

Another point in Amanda's favor.

"Then what happened?" I asked.

"When I finally heard the news, I didn't believe it." Her voice wavered. "I mean . . . it just seemed impossible. Jasmine wasn't just my landlady. She was my friend too."

A friend who'd been using her, I thought. *Just like Rick.*

"I put the dogs in their crates and went to see for myself," she said softly. "The police were there. I couldn't even get near Jasmine's booth. But I managed to see enough to know that the rumors were true."

"You must have been in shock," Aunt Peg said.

"I guess I was. I just stood there for a long time. It was like I couldn't figure out what to do next. Or even where to go. Nothing seemed real to me. Not the police. Not the dog show. And certainly not the fact that I would never see Jasmine again. It was all unimaginable." A tear slid down Amanda's face. She sniffled loudly. "I didn't know what to think."

I knew what *I* thought. Amanda was protesting entirely too much.

"You were that surprised," I said. "Even though you were aware of Jasmine's illegal activities?"

Amanda's shoulders stiffened. She lifted a hand

and swiped it across her cheek. "I don't know what you're talking about."

"I think you do," I replied. "And you'll only make things worse for yourself if you lie to us. I've been in touch with the authorities and they're going to be looking into all the circumstances surrounding Jasmine's death. You'll save everybody a lot of time and trouble if you just tell us what you know."

"I don't know anything," Amanda protested.

There was no way this girl was as stupid as she wanted us to believe. Even Aunt Peg, who was on Amanda's side, was beginning to look annoyed.

"Do you want my help?" she asked.

Amanda hesitated briefly, then nodded.

"Then let me tell you how this is going to work. Melanie and I will begin by telling you what we've already learned. Then I'm sure you will find yourself motivated to fill in any gaps in our knowledge. Is that understood?"

You had to hand it to Aunt Peg. Nobody did a wake-up call better.

I didn't wait for Amanda to agree. Instead, I said, "We know about the robberies."

"You do?" The girl looked shocked. She gazed back and forth between us. "How did you find out?"

"We put two and two together," Aunt Peg snapped. She'd probably picked up her interrogation technique by watching old reruns of *Dragnet*.

"We know that Jasmine was getting pet-sitting jobs for several girls, including you," I said. "And that while you were taking care of people's dogs, you were also checking out their houses to see if they had anything worth stealing."

"That's not how it happened," Amanda said quickly. "I mean, not really."

"Explain it to us," said Aunt Peg.

"In the beginning, I didn't know anything. I didn't even suspect." Amanda was the picture of wide-eyed innocence. "I just wanted to have a job where I worked for myself. Jasmine suggested pet-sitting and it seemed like a great idea. She said she could help me get started with a few referrals. I was so grateful to her for that. It meant that I didn't have to keep working in the mall."

"Go on," Aunt Peg encouraged.

"It started out perfectly. I loved pet-sitting. And I was good at it." She glanced Aunt Peg's way.

"Yes, you were. The Poodles loved you and you took wonderful care of them. It's a shame that wasn't all you were doing."

Amanda's face went still. She looked ashamed. For a moment, I almost felt sorry for her.

"When I would return to my apartment after a couple of days away, Jasmine would come and welcome me home," she continued. "She always asked about the houses I'd been to and the things I'd seen. We laughed about bad decor and ugly artwork. I thought she was just curious, maybe even a little nosey. But it never occurred to me that her interest was anything more than that."

"But eventually you found out," I said gently. "Didn't you?"

Amanda nodded. "One of the families I had worked for was robbed. They told me about it when I went to sit for them again. The husband and wife were devastated. They'd lost some things that were irreplaceable. Things that Jasmine and I had talked about. But even then, I didn't put it together. I thought it was just a terrible coincidence."

Amanda paused and bit her lip. "Until it happened a second time."

"But that didn't prevent you from continuing," Aunt Peg said drily.

"No, I couldn't stop. I had clients who depended on me. And besides, I needed the money. If I'd stopped I would have had to find another job. No way I was going back to the mall. That would have been awful." Amanda had forgotten she was supposed to be feeling guilty about the part she'd played. She still seemed to think she could make us understand.

"Clients who depended on you?" Aunt Peg's voice rose. "People like me, you mean?"

"Yes," Amanda whispered.

"I suppose I should count myself lucky that my things weren't considered valuable enough to steal?"

The girl said something under her breath.

"What's that?" Aunt Peg demanded.

"Your house was on the list."

Aunt Peg scowled. That hadn't improved her mood at all.

"It's a terrible thing not to feel safe in your own home," she said. "Jasmine's victims didn't just lose their valuables, they also lost their peace of mind. I will never again make the mistake of thinking I don't need an alarm system because I have a houseful of dogs."

"The alarms didn't make any difference," Amanda told us. "People who had them gave us the codes, so we could get in to take care of their pets. You'd think they would have reset the codes when they got home, but most of them never did. Every time I went back, it would be the same numbers. Now whose fault was that?"

I seriously hoped Amanda didn't expect me to answer that question. Because I was quite certain she wouldn't enjoy hearing what I had to say.

"So you and the other pet-sitters were assessing your clients' homes," I said. "Who committed the burglaries? Was that you too?"

Amanda's head came up. She appeared surprised by the question. "No, of course not. The only time I was in anyone's house was when

I was taking care of their pets. The rest of it was all Jasmine's doing. I didn't know anything about that end of things, and I didn't want to know."

"Did it ever occur to you to go to the police?" I asked.

"How could I do that? They would have thought I was just as guilty as Jasmine. Maybe more. It would have been my word against hers."

"And besides," Aunt Peg said sharply, "you needed the money." Her tone left no doubt what she thought of that excuse.

"How did Rick become involved?" I asked.

"That was my mistake," Amanda admitted. "Back when I was starting to figure out what Jasmine was up to, I talked to him about it. I thought maybe he could help me make sense of things. I thought I could trust him."

"I thought I could trust you," Aunt Peg informed her. "Apparently it's easier to get that wrong than you might think."

I sent Aunt Peg a quelling look and drew Amanda's attention back to me. "Go on."

"Rick doesn't like to work hard. He's always looking for jobs that don't take up much of his free time. What he calls easy money."

He and Jasmine sounded like a great pair, I thought.

"He sounds like a real loser," Aunt Peg snorted.

"I know that now," Amanda said defensively. "But back then, I had no idea. I barely talked to him about Jasmine at all, but somehow Rick must have figured out what she was doing even before I did. He went to Jasmine and told her he wanted a piece of the business."

"How did Jasmine respond to that?" Aunt Peg asked.

I already knew the answer. I wasn't surprised when Amanda said, "She told him to get lost. They had a big fight about it. Maybe more than one. Rick thought Jasmine had a sweet deal. He was determined to get in on it."

"Melanie heard that Rick and Jasmine were in business together," Aunt Peg said. "Does that mean that Jasmine eventually gave in?"

Amanda shook her head. "No, she didn't. Not until Rick changed tactics."

"What do you mean?" I asked.

"Rick realized he didn't need to be Jasmine's partner. He could still get money from her anyway. Rick threatened to expose what Jasmine was doing. He told her he knew enough about her business to go to the police. And then he started blackmailing her."

Chapter 23

*B**lackmail?* I gulped. That put a new spin on things. No wonder Rick had been so touchy about his business dealings with Jasmine Crane.

"Are you sure?" I said to Amanda.

"Of course I'm sure. Rick even bragged about it. He was proud of how he'd worked things out."

"Jasmine must have been livid," Aunt Peg said.

I was thinking the same thing. Under the circumstances, it was surprising that Rick was still alive and Jasmine was the one who was dead.

"She actually agreed to pay him money to keep quiet?" I asked.

Amanda was annoyed at my repeated query. "It's not as if she had a choice. She not only agreed, she *did* pay him. It had been going on for several months."

"And then Jasmine was killed, and you disappeared. Why?"

She stared at me. "What would you have done if the woman you worked for was suddenly dead and you were afraid your boyfriend had something to do with it?"

"I'd have confronted him," Aunt Peg said immediately.

At the same time, I answered, "I'd have taken

some time to think about what my next move should be."

Amanda nodded in my direction. "And there you have it. I chose option B." Her voice lowered as if she was confiding a secret. "Rick has a temper. And when he gets mad, everybody better watch out."

I reached up and touched the side of my nose. *You think?*

"Jasmine had a temper too," Aunt Peg pointed out. "It's not hard to see how that arrangement could have blown up in both their faces."

"And ended in violence," I said.

We all pondered that for a minute.

"Have you been in touch with Rick since you left?" Aunt Peg asked Amanda.

"No, of course not. That was the whole point. I didn't want him to know where I was. Or what I was doing." She tossed her hair. "In fact, I didn't want Rick to think about me at all."

I wondered if she'd be comforted to know that he hadn't been doing so. For some reason, I suspected not.

"But I'm no fool," Amanda added with satisfaction. "Even though I wasn't around, I was still keeping tabs."

"Keeping tabs?" said Aunt Peg. "What does that mean?"

"I was keeping an eye on things. *On Rick.* Who—by the way—has been in my apartment since I left." She was clearly angered by the thought. "That's what I get for trusting him enough to give him a key."

Aunt Peg looked just as startled by that admission as I was.

"How do you know what Rick's been up to?" I asked.

"There's this woman who's been by the house a few times. Sadie. She was Jasmine's friend. She tells me stuff."

Sadie? I was so focused on Rick Fanelli that it took me a moment to even place the name. Then I thought, Oh God, *Sadie*. The executor of Jasmine's estate. I was going to have to tell her about the paintings that Alan Crandall had incinerated. I definitely wasn't looking forward to that.

"She ran into Rick a couple of times. He was in and out of my apartment like he thought he owned the place. Going behind my back, pawing through my stuff. Bastard was probably looking for something he could steal." Amanda frowned crossly. "I'm done with him now. That's the last straw."

I glanced over at Aunt Peg. I knew we were both thinking the same thing. There was a good chance that Amanda's boyfriend was guilty of murder, *but going through her things was the last straw?*

"A few minutes ago I asked you why you left,"

I said to Amanda. "You stayed away for two weeks. Why did you come back?"

"It was just time. You know? That futon was frickin' uncomfortable. New York was okay, but it wasn't home. And I finally realized that what I really needed to do was look Rick Fanelli in the eye and tell him to take a hike. Peg and I talked about it. She was very convincing when we talked about what I ought to do next."

"She was?"

That came as a surprise. Not the convincing part. Aunt Peg was a master of persuasion. She could wheedle a squirrel out of his supply of winter nuts. But I'd thought Aunt Peg had brought Amanda home by promising to protect her from Rick—and not by proposing to act as the girl's second when she took him on.

Aunt Peg looked pleased. "I merely offered Amanda some advice, based on the wisdom one accrues with age."

Amanda grinned. "She also offered to hold Rick for me if I wanted to punch him in the gut."

I absolutely hoped that came to pass. And that I was watching when it did.

"You have to talk to the police," I said to Amanda. "I'll go with you to see Detective Young. You need to tell him everything you've told us."

"I know." Amanda's shoulders lifted and fell as she sighed.

I couldn't blame her for not looking forward to the task. But nevertheless it had to be done.

"I will do that," she said. "But my first priority is dealing with Rick. I have to get that settled. I want my key back and I want that guy out of my life for good."

"We'll attend to it first thing tomorrow," Aunt Peg told her.

Amanda nodded in agreement. "I'll call him and tell him to meet me at my apartment."

"Not tomorrow morning," I said. "That won't work. I have school."

Aunt Peg tipped her head in my direction. "Are you coming?"

"Of course, I'm coming. I can't believe you even have to ask. This is like all those horror movies where the stupid blond girl goes into the dark cellar by herself—and you just know the ax murderer is down there waiting for her. I'm not letting you do that by yourselves."

"It's not the same thing at all." Aunt Peg frowned. "Amanda isn't even blond."

"And I'm not stupid," she said, sounding affronted.

They didn't get it.

"Amanda is going to break up with her boyfriend," I said. "But the two of you will also be confronting a man who we know is capable of violence, and who could be a murderer. There's safety in numbers. We'll all go together."

Plus, I thought, *I had a few choice things to say to Rick Fanelli myself.*

When I was a student, school days often seemed to drag. Now that I'm the one who sets the schedule and decides on the lesson plan, I usually enjoy every minute of my time at Howard Academy. Tuesday morning, however, I watched the clock like a sixth-grader. I couldn't wait to get out of there.

Faith and I drove straight home at one o'clock. I barely had time to leave the Standard Poodle in the house with Sam and Kevin before Aunt Peg's minivan was pulling in the driveway. Amanda was sitting in the passenger seat. I slid open the door and hopped in back. We were on our way.

"You spoke with Rick?" I asked Amanda as I fastened my seat belt. Aunt Peg drove like a fiend. When she was behind the wheel, body armor wasn't a bad idea either.

"Yes. He likes to sleep late, so I waited until midmorning to call. Rick was delighted to hear from me." Amanda turned in her seat to look at me. The skepticism was clear on her face. "He told me how much he missed me."

"Did he ask where you'd been?"

"No. He didn't ask any questions at all. Rick's the kind of guy who thinks he already has all the answers."

He was about to learn differently, I thought.

A battered looking panel van was sitting in the driveway next to Amanda's car when we arrived at Jasmine's house.

"That's Rick's van," Amanda told us. She hopped out of Aunt Peg's minivan, peeked inside the other vehicle's window, then turned back to us with a frown. "He must have gone inside my apartment to wait. Typical."

Before Aunt Peg and I had even disembarked, Amanda was already racing up the steps on the side of the garage. A curtain flicked in the window above. Rick must have watched us pull in.

I wondered if he imagined that love—or perhaps lust—was compelling Amanda to run up those stairs toward him.

Then, as Aunt Peg and I started toward the stairway ourselves, I suddenly wondered if maybe we were the ones who were wrong about where Amanda's sympathies lay. She'd already admitted to helping Jasmine check out her victims' homes, so she was hardly blameless. Maybe the girl wasn't angry at Rick. Maybe the two of them had been partners all along.

In that case, Aunt Peg and I could be walking into a trap.

"Are you sure we're doing the right thing?" I asked her.

"No." She gripped the rail and began climbing. That was hardly reassuring.

"What if Amanda was lying to us?" I asked.

"This is a fine time to worry about that. Thank goodness I had the sense to consider it earlier and come prepared." Aunt Peg paused on an upper step, opened up her purse, and held it out toward me.

I couldn't imagine what she had in there to show me. I knew Aunt Peg didn't own a gun. At least I hoped she didn't. Then I saw a glint of steel.

"That's a Swiss Army knife," I said. "If we need a corkscrew or a toothpick, we'll be all set."

Aunt Peg snapped her bag shut and continued climbing. In her haste, Amanda had left the door to the apartment open behind her. What we saw when we reached the landing at the top of the steps wasn't reassuring.

Rick and Amanda were standing in the middle of the small living room. Their arms were wrapped around each other. His face was buried in her hair. Their bodies were pressed together from shoulder to thigh. From our vantage point, Amanda certainly appeared to be a willing participant in the embrace.

Then, as I glanced back down the steep stairway and contemplated the wisdom of a hasty retreat, Amanda stepped away from Rick, looked up at him with a sneer on her face and said, "You can consider that my good-bye."

"What?" He looked dumbfounded. "Wait? *What?*"

"You're a jerk and an ass and I never want to see you again," Amanda said. Silently I cheered her on. "I only came here to tell you that face to face. And to reclaim my apartment." She held out her hand. "I want my key back. Right now."

"Wait," Rick said again. It was a pleasure to see him so flustered. "You don't know what you're saying. Let's sit down and talk about this. Whatever's wrong, we can fix it."

Aunt Peg moved forward into the room. For the first time, Rick appeared to notice that he and Amanda weren't alone. His face screwed up into a scowl. He turned my way angrily.

"This is your fault. What have you been telling her?"

"I didn't have to tell Amanda anything," I replied. "She already knew the truth about you."

"What truth?" Rick demanded.

"That you're a jerk and an ass," Aunt Peg said. "To quote someone who knows you better than I do. And maybe a murderer as well."

"Lady, I don't even know who you are, but you must be crazy." Rick shook his head vehemently. He spun back to Amanda. "That's not true. You know it isn't. I have no idea what they're talking about."

"Jasmine," she said softly.

Rick began to back away. His hands flew upward. He held them out, palms facing us, in a protest of innocence. "I had nothing to do with that. Nothing, do you hear me? You can't pin that on me."

"You were blackmailing Jasmine," I said.

Rick didn't even try to deny it. "Yeah. So?"

"Maybe she decided to stop paying you," Aunt Peg declared. "We know you have a temper."

"No." He shook his head again. "That's not what happened."

"What did happen?" I asked.

"Nothing. Just like I said a minute ago." His gaze found Amanda's and held it. He looked at her beseechingly. "You have to believe me, 'Manda."

I hoped she wouldn't melt. Thankfully, Amanda was made of sterner stuff than that. She looked mad enough to spit. "Why should I believe anything you say?"

Rick's voice softened into a caress. "Because you love me. You do, don't you, babe? I know you do."

"I thought I did. But that was before I realized that you were only using me to get the things you wanted."

"The things we *both* wanted," Rick corrected her. I noted that he didn't deny her accusation. "We make a great team, don't we?"

The look in Amanda's eyes was steely. I thought I heard her growl under her breath. "We were never a team. Not even when I was dumb enough to believe that we were. You were always the boss. You treated me like I was a flunky you could order around."

"But it worked for us, didn't it?" Rick wheedled. "We're a great couple. I supply the brains and you're great at doing what you're told."

Holy crap, I thought. *That* was his declaration of love and partnership? Couldn't this creep hear how offensive he sounded?

Apparently not, because Rick was still looking at Amanda hopefully. As if he was sure he could convince her to give him another chance. When she spoke again, however, she quashed that notion emphatically.

"I might have thought we were in love," she said. "But I was a fool to ever believe that. And now I know you for who you really are."

"No, you don't." Rick held out his hand, willing her to take it. "I'll change if I have to. We'll work on it together. Let's just talk—"

"I'm done with you." Amanda glanced at his outstretched fingers, then looked pointedly away. "And I'm going with Melanie to talk to the police."

Abruptly Rick went still. "What are you going to tell them?"

"That I made mistakes. And that I'm sorry for letting people down." Amanda edged back until she was standing between Aunt Peg and me. When I nodded in support, she added, "I'm also going to tell them that for the last two weeks before Jasmine died, you and she were at each other's throats."

"Hell no!" Rick roared. "You can't say that."

"I can. And I will."

"That will give them the wrong idea."

"Or the right one," Aunt Peg said.

"You don't get it." Rick looked pained. "You're wrong. All of you. Yes, Jasmine and I were fighting. We were always fighting. But I'm not stupid. Jasmine Crane was my cash cow. Why would I have wanted to kill her when she was worth so much more to me alive than dead?"

Chapter 24

I hated that Rick sounded so convincing. It killed me to realize that I almost believed him. But I couldn't, could I? Because if he was telling the truth, I was sunk. After all this, I would still have no idea who killed Jasmine Crane.

No, I decided. Rick had lied before, and now he was lying again. The man would probably say anything to save his own skin.

So I stood there and didn't say a thing. Neither did Aunt Peg.

Amanda just shook her head. I didn't know if she believed Rick or not. She was just ready to be *done*.

His statement having not achieved the reaction he was hoping for, Rick opted not to stick around to see what we might do next. He pushed past us and ran out the door. I heard the clatter of his feet as Rick dashed down the wooden steps. A few seconds later a door slammed, then an engine started.

I moved over to the front window and watched the panel van back rapidly out of the driveway. I wondered where Rick thought he was running to. If the authorities needed to find him, they would.

Amanda didn't move to follow me. Instead she

just stood in place with her arms hanging limply at her sides. The poor girl looked shell-shocked.

"I didn't get my key back," she said in a small voice.

"Change your locks," Aunt Peg snapped. "You would have had to do it anyway. You of all people should realize that."

Indeed.

"I can't believe that just happened," she said.

I turned back to face the room. "Wasn't that what you came here to do?"

"Yes, but . . ." She chewed on her lip. "I thought I would feel better than this afterward. I don't know. Empowered, or something."

"How do you feel?" Aunt Peg's voice was gentle.

"Empty." Amanda shook her head sadly. "I really thought I loved Rick. I thought he loved me."

"Rick doesn't seem like the kind of man who's capable of loving anyone but himself," I told her.

"I guess you're right." Her voice caught on a sob. "How could I have been so stupid?"

Aunt Peg put her arms around Amanda. She pulled the girl close and held on tight. "Because you're young and you haven't learned everything yet. We all make mistakes."

"Not like this," Amanda sniffled.

"The important thing is that you learn from your mistakes," Aunt Peg told her. "And you have. You've put Rick behind you, and now you're going to talk to the police and make things as right as you can. That's all anybody can ask."

Except maybe for Marv Stanberg, I thought. He might have wanted his coin collection back. With Aunt Peg in touchy-feely mode, I decided it was better not to voice that thought aloud.

Instead I let my gaze wander around the small apartment. It looked pretty much the same as it had when I'd visited two weeks earlier. Maybe the place was a little messier, but who could really tell?

Once again, I found my eyes lingering on the oil painting above the couch. A pair of Foxhound puppies were romping on a lush, green lawn. The tumbling, tricolor pups looked so lifelike I felt as though I should be able to reach out and touch their warm, chubby bodies.

"That's a lovely painting," I said to Amanda. "It's too bad Jasmine didn't sign it for you." Especially in light of the fact that she would never be able to do so now.

The girl straightened out of Aunt Peg's embrace. The hug had done its job. Amanda appeared to be feeling a bit better. "That's because Jasmine didn't paint it. Sadie did."

Sadie?

She nodded at my surprised expression. "Sadie's an artist too. Didn't you know? That's how she and Jasmine met. It was years ago when they were in an art class together."

Aunt Peg came over to take a closer look. Her first reaction to the painting was the same as mine had been. It made her smile.

"That's rather amazing," she said. "It looks like Jasmine's work."

Amanda tipped her head to one side. She studied the painting too. "I guess it does. I just like it because of the cute puppies. This apartment is pretty bleak. It cheers the place up."

"You'll have to move now, won't you?" I asked.

"Why would I do that?"

"Sadie's the executor of Jasmine's estate. She said she was going to be putting the house on the market. The property will probably be easier to sell without a tenant in place."

"Damn," Amanda swore under her breath. "Sadie never mentioned that to me. I guess I'd better talk to her about it."

"Before you do that, take a look at your lease," said Aunt Peg. "Depending on what it says, I don't think Sadie can toss you out just to make her life easier. You might want to consult a lawyer to find out your rights."

Mention of the house being offered for sale reminded me of the day Sadie and I had walked around the small home together. At the time I'd wondered where Jasmine had kept her art supplies. Now my thoughts went one step further. It occurred to me that the house hadn't contained a studio either. Surely an artist as prolific as Jasmine would have needed a dedicated space in which to work?

Unless . . . ?

No, I thought firmly. Then my eyes strayed back to the oil painting. Unsigned. Painted by Sadie. Jasmine's best friend and another artist. And a woman who'd been seen on numerous occasions moving paintings into and out of Jasmine's house.

Was it possible that Sadie had been the true talent behind Jasmine's creative facade? Maybe. Considering what I'd learned about Jasmine so far, I wouldn't put anything past her. It certainly wouldn't hurt to do some digging in that direction.

I turned to Amanda. "You spent a lot of time with Jasmine, didn't you?"

"Um . . . I suppose."

"Where did she do her painting?"

"I don't know. I guess I never thought about it. I never saw Jasmine at work."

"Never?" I asked incredulously.

Amanda shrugged. "She would only show me a finished product. She said that the process of creating art was intensely personal. There were lots of things in her life that Jasmine liked to keep private."

"I can understand that," Aunt Peg said. "I wouldn't want someone staring over my shoulder all the time either."

"I want to talk to someone who commissioned a pet portrait from Jasmine," I said. "I'd like to hear more about how she created her paintings."

Aunt Peg gave me an odd look. "It's a little late to worry about that now, isn't it?" She turned and headed for the door. Having disposed of Rick Fanelli, Aunt Peg was ready to move on. "It's time to go," she said. "Are you two coming?"

Amanda and I both nodded.

"If it's all right, I'd feel more comfortable staying with you for another day or two until I have a chance to change my locks," Amanda said to Aunt Peg.

"And time to talk to Detective Young," I added. It would be easier to ensure the girl's compliance if we were keeping an eye on her.

"And to call your sister," Aunt Peg said. "That's long overdue. But yes, come along. It's fine."

Amanda drove her own car back to Greenwich. Aunt Peg dropped me off at my house. Davey was still at school and Sam and Kev were out somewhere, but the Poodle posse rallied around me like I was a long lost friend. I had been so busy that I'd been neglecting them recently.

"I could use some exercise," I told them. "Who wants to go for a run?"

By run, I actually meant *jog*. With maybe some

325

walking thrown in. But the Poodles didn't care how fit I was. They were up for anything that got us all out of the house and doing something together.

My area of North Stamford is strictly residential. There's very little traffic. We don't have sidewalks, but we do have a wide, grassy verge that serves as a buffer between lawns and pavement. Joggers and cyclists abound in my neighborhood. And my neighbors are used to seeing me go rolling by, accompanied by a rambunctious group of big black dogs.

I put on my running shoes and grabbed Bud's leash from the hook beside the back door. The Poodles could be trusted to stay with me and to pay attention when the occasional car went past. But Bud was a law unto himself.

Once outside the confines of the house or the fenced yard, the spotted dog was like a kid in a candy store. He wanted to see and do everything at once. And the more exciting things Bud found to explore, the more selective his hearing became.

I snapped the leash onto his collar before opening the door. As the Poodles raced past him out to the driveway, Bud gave me a dirty look.

"Really?" I said. "Whose fault is this?"

He wagged his tail innocently. *Not me! Not me!*

I pulled the door shut behind us. "Who chased a rabbit across the road, up the Newcombs'

326

driveway, and under their porch just last week?"

Bud sniffed the ground at the base of a nearby bush. He pretended not to hear the question. That was just as well, because we all knew the answer.

The rabbit had barely escaped with its life. Jan Newcomb had been startled to discover me kneeling in her flower bed, yelling obscenities under her porch. And when Bud had finally emerged from the crawl space, he'd been covered in mud from head to tail. He'd also had the nerve to look pleased with himself.

It wasn't an episode I wanted to repeat anytime soon.

"We feed you plenty," I told the little dog sternly as we followed the Poodles across the lawn. "You don't have to catch your own food."

Bud was already panting in anticipation. His long, pink, tongue was flopping out of the side of his mouth. *It's the chase! I love the chase!*

"And that's why you're on a leash," I said.

Tar circled back to Bud. He wanted his friend to come and play with him. The Poodle stared pointedly at the slim strip of leather connecting Bud to me. The pair began to wag their tails in unison.

"You're not supposed to gang up on me," I grumbled.

But a plea that cute was hard to resist.

"If I let him loose, will you watch him?" I asked Tar.

Thank goodness Faith was too far ahead to hear *that* question. She'd have died laughing. Tar was hardly a paragon of good behavior himself. Nevertheless he woofed at me softly.

That male Poodle would promise you the world. Delivering was another matter. Especially since Tar was never able to figure out what he'd done wrong. He was so kindhearted, it was impossible to stay mad at him.

"This is all on you," I told Tar as I unsnapped the lead.

Freedom beckoned. The two dogs immediately went dashing away together. They didn't spare me so much as a backward glance. *Boys.*

An hour later, after a mostly mishap-free run, we were all back in the house. I hoped my neighbor at the end of the street wouldn't miss the rubber ball Bud had picked up at the edge of his property and promptly dropped down a storm drain. I thought I should probably leave a note in his mailbox on the way to school the next morning, offering to replace it.

The dogs went straight to their water bowl. I grabbed a bottle of green tea out of the refrigerator. Sam and Kevin still hadn't returned home and Davey's bus wasn't due for half an hour. So I got out my phone and called Gwen Kimble.

"Well, hello Melanie." She sounded pleased to hear from me. "I was just thinking about you."

"You were?"

"I was wondering if you ever found that girl you were looking for. Abby Burke's sister?"

"Happily, I did," I said. "What made you think of that?"

"There was a mention in the morning newspaper about the investigation into Jasmine's death, and that reminded me of your search."

"What did the article say?"

"Just that new information had come to light and that the police were going to be checking into additional leads."

I hoped that was Detective Young's doing. The police could be tracking Rick down right now. I was sure that with their resources and expertise, they'd have more luck getting the truth out of him than I had.

What a relief to know that was now in the hands of the professionals.

I turned back to my conversation with Gwen. "I was curious about something with regard to Jasmine. I heard that you once commissioned a pet portrait from her?"

"Yes." Her reply was clipped. "I did."

"I gather you weren't pleased with the result?"

"No, I was not. Nobody would have been. Jasmine took three months to complete the painting. And when she delivered it to me, it was atrocious."

"What was wrong with it?"

"It would be easier to tell you what was right. Which was basically that the portrait was of a Whippet. But Lotus was a very special bitch. I made sure that Jasmine met Lotus and got to know her, so she could capture her personality on the canvas. But what I ended up with was a flat rendering of a gray and white Whippet that could have been anyone's dog. Worse still, the Whippet in the portrait was lacking in under jaw. And her eye was too light, which completely destroyed her expression."

"Did you talk to Jasmine about possibly making some changes?"

"There would have been no point. Especially since she was insisting that the painting was perfect as is. To tell you the truth, I think she did it on purpose. Jasmine and I were always butting heads—and this was how she got her revenge. Giving me a generic portrait that looked as though it had been painted by someone who'd never even seen the bitch. I'm sure Jasmine thought she would have the last laugh. She was sneaky like that, always trying to get the better of people."

Little did Gwen know, I thought.

"But she didn't have the last laugh," I said, "because you refused to pay her."

"Which was precisely what she deserved. Nobody would have accepted that painting."

"It interests me that Jasmine came to see Lotus in person."

"She didn't want to," said Gwen. "She told me she always worked from photographs. But I insisted. For all the good it did me."

"Did Jasmine make any sketches of Lotus while she was there?"

"No, not one. She did snap a few pictures of Lotus running around the backyard. And I supplied her with several others. Lotus was getting on in years. I wanted Jasmine to portray the bitch as she'd been in her prime. So I gave her win pictures from the show ring."

"No close-ups though?"

Gwen growled in exasperation. "Why would Jasmine need close-ups when she'd met Lotus in person? Everything she needed to know was right there in front of her."

Not if she hadn't been planning to paint the Whippet herself, I thought. Maybe Jasmine's on-site snaps hadn't been good enough. And those small details like eye color and under jaw couldn't be seen in Gwen's pictures that had been taken from a distance. Jasmine had all the information she needed to create a portrait of Lotus for her discriminating owner—but Sadie didn't.

"One last question," I said. "Did you ever meet a friend of Jasmine's named Sadie Foster?"

"No." Gwen didn't even have to stop and think. "Aside from the one time she came here, I only ever saw Jasmine at shows. She and I never socialized. Jasmine was bad enough on her own. I wouldn't have had any desire to meet her friends."

I thanked Gwen for her time and hung up.

Obviously the next person I needed to talk to was Sadie herself. The last two weeks had shown me that Jasmine wasn't the only one who'd been keeping secrets. Nearly everyone connected to her had also had something to hide. I couldn't help but wonder if Sadie's secret might turn out to be the most explosive one yet.

Chapter 25

The next morning, I took a quick break between tutoring sessions to get in touch with Sadie. I had no intention of asking anything of a sensitive nature over the phone where it would be too easy for her to dodge my questions. Instead I told her that I had news for her about the possessions Jasmine had taken to the Sedgefield dog show. Sadie agreed to meet with me that afternoon.

The address she gave me was in Darien, the town that bordered Stamford to the east. From Greenwich, it was just a quick hop up the Connecticut Turnpike.

Sadie had asked about Faith when we'd met previously, so this time the Standard Poodle and I made the trip together straight from school. Sadie wasn't the first person who'd preferred my dog to me—and considering the questions I was hoping she'd answer, I was willing to try anything to make our meeting proceed smoothly.

Sadie lived in a wood-shingled cottage on a small plot of land not far from the Ox Ridge Hunt Club. A crumbling stone wall bordered the road in front of her heavily wooded property. There wasn't room for both our vehicles in the driveway, so I parked the Volvo on the other side of the narrow road.

As Faith and I crossed the front yard, I could hear birds singing all around us. A pair of robins swooped down across the driveway, heading for the rear of the house. I was betting there was a bird feeder back there. Possibly more than one.

I had to knock twice before Sadie opened the door.

Even though I had a smile on my face and Faith standing politely beside me, Sadie didn't look happy to see us. Her gray hair was gathered in a messy bun on the top of her head and she was wearing a paint-smeared smock over blue jeans and a long sleeved T-shirt. A pair of reading glasses was perched on the end of her nose. They did nothing to hide the remnants of her nearly healed black eye.

I frowned when I saw the slight discoloration still visible high on Sadie's cheek. Somehow I'd forgotten about that.

"I suppose you'd better come in," she said.

I hesitated on the step and Faith took her cue from me. Along with the bruise, I'd also forgotten about the reason for it—Jasmine's two dogs whom Sadie had brought home with her on the day that Jasmine died.

"Well?" Sadie prompted.

"I can leave Faith in the car if that's easier," I said.

"Why would that be any easier?" She reached down and gave Faith a pat.

The Poodle wagged her tail obligingly. Making friends and winning hearts, that was Faith's goal in life.

"Jasmine's dogs . . . you have them here, don't you?"

"Oh yeah, Toby and Hazel. They were here for a few days. But those two dogs were wild. Jasmine hadn't taught them much and they were driving me crazy, barking and running around the place. So I found them another home."

"Already?" It was difficult enough to rehome mature dogs, much less poorly behaved ones. And two at once made it harder still. Accomplishing that so quickly was a neat trick—if indeed Sadie had managed it.

"Sure. They were nice dogs. It was a piece of cake. Faith isn't going to bark and go racing around, is she?"

"No, of course not," I said.

"Then unless you want to hold this conversation standing on the stoop, you'd better get in here."

We walked straight into a small living room whose most notable feature was a large picture window in the rear wall. Through the glass I could see three cylindrical bird feeders hanging from a tree branch outside. Each feeder was filled with seed. Though it was early in the year and I hadn't yet seen many birds at my house, all three feeders were doing a brisk business.

Several robins and sparrows were perched on the trays, along with a striking male cardinal.

"What a beautiful view you have," I said.

For the first time, Sadie smiled. "It's great, isn't it? I love my birds. They nest in the trees around the house. Some even stay with me all winter long. They know they can depend on me to take good care of them."

She waved me toward a lumpy-looking couch that was covered in a dark green polyester fabric. I took a seat. Once I was settled, Faith lay down at my feet.

"You said you had news for me. You might as well spit it out."

"I'm afraid it's bad news," I told her. "Did you ever meet a man Jasmine knew named Alan Crandall?"

"The name doesn't sound familiar." Sadie removed her reading glasses and set them on a nearby table. "Who's he?"

"Alan owns a business called Creature Comforts. He was one of Jasmine's fellow concessionaires at the dog shows. When Jasmine died, her booth and the rest of her belongings needed to be cleared from the showground. Alan offered to help out. He took her things and stored them in his warehouse."

"That was nice of him."

"Well, not entirely, as things turned out."

"Oh?" she asked with interest.

"The reason I thought you might know him is because you and Jasmine were close, and she and Alan had recently had an affair."

"So? It sounds to me like they were both consenting adults."

"The problem was, there was also a non-consenting party. Alan's wife. Apparently she took great exception to their behavior."

Sadie sighed like she was hoping I'd move things along. "What does that have to do with me?"

"Jasmine broke up Alan's marriage. And possibly cost him his business. Then she dumped him. So when he volunteered to take her things home from the dog show, his motives weren't entirely altruistic."

"Don't tell me he thinks he can hold those paintings for ransom," Sadie said sharply.

It was interesting the way her mind worked.

"I'm afraid it's worse than that. He destroyed them."

"Destroyed them?" she echoed faintly. "All of them?"

"I believe so."

"Totally destroyed?"

"He built a bonfire."

"Hellfire and damnation," Sadie swore. "That sounds like true love all right."

"True love?" I almost laughed. It sounded like the opposite to me.

"Jasmine had a way of inspiring devotion in people. Sometimes more than she deserved."

"So I've discovered," I said. "Are you aware that Jasmine was behind a series of recent home robberies?"

Sadie's gaze lifted. "You're kidding, right?"

"I'm afraid not."

"I knew Jasmine had a head for funny business, but I had no idea it extended that far."

"What kind of funny business do you know about?" I asked casually.

Sadie's eyes narrowed. She wasn't fooled by the offhand nature of my question. "There's no need to get into that now that Jasmine's gone. I'm not one to speak ill of the dead."

"Did it have anything to do with Rick Fanelli?"

"Rick who?"

I ignored the evasion. Sadie knew who I was talking about. "Amanda's boyfriend. He was around here a lot. I'm sure you must have known him."

"Oh, that guy," she said dismissively. "I guess I saw him once or twice."

Faith nudged the side of my leg with her shoulder. She was probably telling me to get to the point. So I did.

"I'm sorry about what happened to Jasmine's artwork," I told her. "But I'm sure you won't have trouble replenishing your stock."

"I don't know what you're talking about. Those paintings were a huge loss."

"But you're an artist too." I looked pointedly at her smock.

"This old thing? I just wear it to do housework," Sadie said with a shrug. "It keeps my clothes clean. As for painting, I dabble a bit. But I don't have anything like Jasmine's talent."

"That's not true," I replied. "I saw the painting you did for Amanda. The one that's hanging in her apartment? It's wonderful."

"The little hounds? That one was a favorite of mine." Sadie's expression softened. "I wanted it to go somewhere it would be appreciated."

"I can understand why you're proud of that painting," I said. "Which is why I'm surprised you didn't sign it."

"I didn't?"

"No," I said mildly. "You didn't."

"Oh well. I guess I must have forgotten."

I gave us both a minute to ponder that implausible lapse. Sadie had begun to fidget in her seat. I liked the fact that I was making her nervous.

Finally I said, "I know what was going on, Sadie. All those paintings you were moving back and forth between your house and Jasmine's, those were yours as well, weren't they?"

"No way." She swiftly denied the allegation. "Where would you get a crazy idea like that?"

"Mostly from the fact that in the last few weeks, I've talked to many of Jasmine's friends and acquaintances. All of whom said that she was good at manipulating people. And that she wasn't above using larceny to supplement her income. Once Amanda told me you were the one who'd painted the puppies, I realized that you were just another con that Jasmine had been running."

The words were insulting on purpose. I wanted to get a rise out of Sadie. Angry, she would be more likely to be indiscreet about what she knew.

Just as I'd hoped, she scowled ferociously. "Now you listen here. I was never *just another* anything. Not to Jasmine. Not to anybody."

"No. You're a very talented artist who let Jasmine take credit for your work. What I don't understand is what was in it for you?"

"Money, of course," Sadie snapped. "What do you think?"

To clarify, I said, "So all those beautiful paintings that Jasmine took to the shows, the artwork she was promoting and selling as her own, had actually been created by you?"

Sadie nodded. Then sighed. Maybe it was a relief to finally have her contribution recognized.

"Your artwork is gorgeous," I said. "You must realize that. So why not claim it as your own? Why hide behind Jasmine?"

"You don't get it," Sadie replied. "I wasn't

hiding anything. If that's what you think, you're missing the point. Look out there."

She gestured toward the picture window. We both gazed through the glass at the busy feeders. The cardinal had left. Now a blue jay had joined the group. It was busy asserting its right to eat first.

"That's my passion," Sadie said. "Birds. All kinds, all colors. To me, they're the most beautiful creatures on God's green earth. If I could, I'd never paint anything else. But you know who wants to buy paintings of birds?"

I hoped that was a rhetorical question. There were few subjects I knew less about than the market for avian art.

"Nobody," Sadie told me. "Leastwise nobody I know. But you slap a Cocker Spaniel on a canvas and people line up to pay good money for it. Especially if it's their own dog. People just about go crazy for portraits of their pets."

I glanced down at Faith, who wagged her tail in acknowledgment. We couldn't argue with that.

"Jasmine was a middling artist but she had marketing down cold. Particularly when it came to selling herself. Take it from someone who knew, Jasmine was her own best product. Once she got the idea to set up a canine art booth at dog shows, there was no stopping her. Next thing I knew, she had a web site and a brochure. That woman could sell sand to a Bedouin."

Sadie looked over at me to make sure I was paying attention. "When Jasmine started taking commissions, she had more orders than she could fill. All I did was offer to help out. Then everything just kind of snowballed." She stopped and grimaced. "Soon Jasmine was just a pretty face making sales in her booth. And I was behind the scenes doing all the work. Nobody cared where the paintings had come from as long as they were good."

"They're more than just good," I said. "They're wonderful. Wasn't it hard for you to watch someone else take credit?"

"Of course it was hard. It was even worse to watch her smile and sign her name to a painting that I'd slaved over for days to get just right. As if she deserved that recognition for doing nothing more than bringing in a check. Sometimes I wanted to slap that stupid smile right off her face."

I should have seen that black eye as a red flag sooner, I realized. I should have been paying more attention. But now wasn't the time for second-guessing. Sadie had finally started talking and I was all ears. The only thing I wanted her to do was keep going.

"Once you saw how popular your portraits had become, why didn't you end your arrangement with Jasmine?"

"Because I'm an idiot, that's why," Sadie

retorted. "Before the business took off, Jasmine had me sign a contract. It spelled out our responsibilities, and what each of us would make in return. We agreed to split the proceeds fifty-fifty. Later, when it became clear to me that my contribution to our success far outweighed hers, I told her I wanted to renegotiate the terms."

Jasmine Crane was one of the most avaricious people I'd ever met. I couldn't imagine that would have gone over well. Sadie's next words confirmed my suspicions.

"She just laughed," Sadie told me. "I guess I should have had a lawyer read the contract before I signed it. But Jasmine and I were friends and I trusted her. Do you know what a non-compete clause is?"

"Yes."

"Well, this contract had one. It turned out I'd signed away the rights to my own name and to any paintings I created during the term of our agreement. In addition, I'd agreed not to start any artistic venture of my own that would compete with what Jasmine was doing."

The conversation was suddenly starting to sound a whole lot like a motive for murder. Abruptly I decided that I'd be more comfortable on my feet. Faith stood up too.

Sadie gazed up at me and grinned. "No need to get your knickers in a twist. I can guess what you're thinking, and believe me, when things came to a head, I was mad enough to contemplate mayhem. But that was over and done two years ago. Jasmine and I got things sorted out and found a way to make the partnership work."

"How?"

My senses were still tingling, but my more rational side insisted that Sadie Foster made an unlikely threat. The woman was at least a decade older than I was and she looked significantly out of shape. Her clothing didn't have any pockets, so unless she had a weapon hiding in the cushion of her chair—and it was hard to imagine why that would be the case—there didn't seem to be a way she could pose a problem. And besides, I still wanted to hear what she had to say.

"I told Jasmine I was through painting for unfair compensation so she could take her contract and shove it," Sadie said with satisfaction. "And then I went on strike. There were eight commissions waiting at the time. Knowing Jasmine, she'd probably already collected that money and spent it. When I put my foot down, she had no choice but to listen to me."

"And did she?" I asked.

"Eventually. It took a month for us to come to terms. Jasmine spent the entire time trying to placate disgruntled customers. She got more and more desperate for me to go back to work. It was great. I knew she'd have to cave in. In the end, we agreed to change the split to seventy-thirty in my favor."

"That was quite clever of you."

"I thought so." Sadie rose to her feet opposite me. "I'm sorry to hear the news about what happened to those paintings. Losing that much hard work feels like a damn shame. Especially since—according to the terms of Jasmine's will—most of them would have been returned to me. But I suppose it can't be helped."

She strode across the small living room, heading in a direction away from the door. When I didn't follow, Sadie stopped and looked back. "Are you coming?"

"Where?"

"Now that someone's finally discovered my secret, I'd love to show off some of my stuff. I bet you have just as many connections in the dog show world as Jasmine did. And if I'm going to rebuild my business from the ground up, I'd sure like to have someone out there telling everyone how much they like my work."

Sadie began walking again. This time she didn't bother waiting for me.

I hesitated, then started after her. I walked slowly and lagged a few steps behind, making sure to leave some space between us.

"That big Poodle of yours is very pretty. Have you ever thought of having her portrait painted? I could give you a great deal on the price. You know, in exchange for you giving me some good PR at the shows?"

Sadie opened the door to a small, sun-filled room and walked inside. Through the doorway I glimpsed an easel holding a partially finished canvas standing near a large window. A nearby table was littered with brushes and tubes of paint. "We could snap some photos of her while the two of you are here today. If you're interested, I could get started on it right away."

I'd been keeping a careful eye on Sadie, but now I briefly looked away. When she mentioned Faith, I turned to make sure that the Poodle was still with us. It took me several seconds to register that Faith had remained in the middle of the living room. And that she was staring at me uneasily.

Something was wrong.

The shock when I was suddenly drenched with something cold and wet was both visceral and immediate. My nose wrinkled at the harsh chemical smell. My eyes squinted shut, then began to water.

What the hell? I jumped back but it was already too late.

The liquid was on my clothes and in my hair. Rivulets streamed down my shoulders and dripped onto the floor at my feet. My senses were overwhelmed by a corrosive stench.

It took me a few seconds to identify the smell. When I did, I nearly gagged. *Turpentine.*

It was a good thing I'd turned away just before Sadie threw the caustic liquid. Otherwise she would have hit me in the face. Which must have been her intent.

A burst of anger shot through me. I whirled around to face her.

Sadie cackled happily. "I took you for smarter than that. But luckily for me, you're not."

Unfortunately I was in no position to dispute that opinion. And Sadie was already advancing on me.

A scant five feet separated us. Quickly I began to back away. Another fifteen feet would get me to the door. I hoped Faith was moving too, but I couldn't afford to take my eyes off Sadie to check.

One hand dove into my pocket, reaching for my phone. It wasn't there. I'd stashed it in my purse, still sitting on the couch.

"It's not too late to fix this," I blurted.

"I think you're wrong about that."

Watching me as intently as I was watching her, Sadie sidled over to a nearby table. She swept a small object into her hand, then twirled it between her fingers.

I still had no idea what she'd picked up when I heard a lid flip open. Sadie's thumb snapped downward and there was a sharp hiss. My stomach plummeted as a bright orange flame appeared.

"Now it's time to end things," she said.

Chapter 26

My next move was pure reflex. Both my hands shot upward. I held them in front of me defensively.

I didn't dare turn my back on Sadie as I began to scramble backward. Faith knew something bad was happening. She had the good sense to get out of the way.

Sadie was coming toward me as quickly as I retreated. I couldn't seem to widen the distance between us.

"Let's talk about this," I said. "You're making a huge mistake."

"It doesn't look to me like we have anything else to say."

Stalling for time, I began to pepper Sadie with questions. Anything to keep her talking. Anything to distract her thoughts from the lighter that was still flaming brightly in her hand.

"You told me that you and Jasmine settled things. Your disagreement was dealt with years ago. So how did she end up dead now?"

"Maybe I wasn't entirely truthful with you," Sadie admitted. "You see, I did know about Jasmine's side business with the robberies. That woman never saw a money-making idea that she didn't want to grab with both hands. She was smart like a fox."

Sadie paused as if waiting for me to agree. I didn't bother. Clearly she was only humoring me because she felt she had nothing to lose. The realization roiled in my gut like acid.

"Anyways," she continued, "everything was swell until Amanda's boyfriend started hanging around."

"Rick Fanelli," I said. The person she'd claimed to barely know.

"Yeah, Rick. He got this notion in his head that he should be part of what was going on. Not the work end," she clarified unnecessarily. "But the money part. And when Jasmine said no, he got an even better idea."

"He was blackmailing her."

Sadie grinned. "I take back what I said earlier. Maybe you're not as dumb as you look."

Under the circumstances, that was debatable. Right then, standing there covered in turpentine, I was feeling very stupid indeed.

"I didn't really care about that," she said. "I figured it was Jasmine's problem. But then that sorry bastard made it my problem too. When that happened, I had to do something about it."

The fumes must have been making me light-headed, because I didn't get it. "How did Rick make it your problem?"

"That guy was always snooping into things

that were none of his business. And somehow— probably Jasmine let it slip, although she denied it—he realized she wasn't the one making all those paintings she was selling. After that, it didn't take him long to put two and two together. That's when Rick came up with the bright idea that if Jasmine would pay good money for him to keep quiet about her secret, I ought to be willing to do the same."

"Rick was blackmailing you too?" I blurted. I hadn't seen that coming.

"Well, he was trying to. Except that I didn't have as much disposable income as Jasmine, and I wasn't about to pay. First thing I did was tell Jasmine what Rick was up to. Then I let her know that it was time for the two of us to come clean. Our customers might be surprised at first, but eventually they'd get over it. Nothing about our business model would change except the signature on the bottom of the paintings."

"Jasmine didn't like that idea, did she?"

"She hated it," Sadie replied. "She turned me down flat and we had a huge fight. I pointed out that if I didn't give Rick the money he wanted, he was going to reveal the truth anyway. So we might as well beat him to the punch. But logic was never Jasmine's strong suit. All she ever cared about was what *she* wanted. Everything else was just background noise to her."

"How long ago was that?" I asked.

"Around the beginning of the month."

"So Jasmine was happy with the status quo and you were deciding what to do about Rick. Then what happened?"

"The Sedgefield dog show."

The flame in Sadie's hand sputtered, then went out. Quickly she relit it. I hoped that holding on to that lighter was causing her fingers to cramp.

Then to my dismay, Sadie came up with a solution. Still standing near the doorway to her studio, she reached inside the room and picked up a paint-smeared rag. She dipped the tip in the same noxious liquid she'd poured on me, then lit it. Immediately the rag flared like a small torch.

"I thought you didn't go to the shows," I said, averting my gaze from the potentially lethal weapon in her hand. "Wasn't that Jasmine's job?"

"It was just a fluke that day. Soon as she got to the show that morning, Jasmine called me. She'd forgotten some custom orders at home. You know those beaded leashes she was making?"

I nodded. Aunt Peg's lead had probably been among them.

"Jasmine wanted me to go pick them up at her house and deliver them to her. As if I had nothing better to do on a Saturday. I was the backbone of the whole business, but Jasmine had the nerve to act like I was just her errand girl."

"But you did what she asked," I pointed out.

"Yeah, I did." Sadie didn't look happy about

that. "I got to the show and the first thing Jasmine did was ask me what took so long. Not even a thank-you for going so far out of my way. She just grabbed the box out of my hands and turned her back on me. She was still mad about the fight we'd had. But so was I."

Sadie drew in a deep, angry breath. "When Jasmine ignored me like that, I just saw red, you know what I mean? I was over it. So I gave her a good shove. And it felt great."

The hand holding up the flame began to wobble. Sadie's arm must have been growing tired. But she continued to tell her story with relish.

"Jasmine lost her balance and dropped the box of leashes. All those little geegaws she'd made went spilling out all over the grass. Man, Jasmine was pissed. She whirled around, pointed to the ground, and told me to pick everything up. Like that was going to happen. I told her what she could do with her stupid leashes—and she hauled off and socked me."

Sadie winced at the memory. Her free hand rose to touch the tender skin beneath her eye. "So there you have it. Everything that happened after that was her fault."

It seemed like a stretch to blame Jasmine for her own death. I stopped just short of shaking my head.

"It was all her fault that I fell down and landed on those stupid beads. Which hurt like hell, by the way. And it was her fault that when I got up I had a leash in my hand. Meanwhile Jasmine had turned her back on me again. She was going to walk back into her booth. She just assumed I'd do what she said. I don't even know how it happened, but that fancy leash got wrapped around Jasmine's neck. And when she struggled, it pulled tight."

Sadie's eyes sought mine. She wanted me to believe in her innocence. "I was angry, but I didn't mean to kill her. All I wanted to do was teach her a lesson."

"And you succeeded," I said softly. "Jasmine will never have an opportunity to make you angry again."

"Damn straight," Sadie agreed. She punctuated the comment with a sharp flick of her wrist.

I jumped back reflexively and barked my shin on a table. That was going to leave a bruise. I hoped I lived long enough to care.

"Jasmine hit you first," I said. "So you acted in self-defense. Anyone can see that. You should hire a lawyer to explain your side to the police."

Sadie wasn't buying it. "Don't think you can fool me by spinning a pretty story. That's not how this is going to work. It'll be much cleaner if we end things here and now."

We. As if I was a willing partner in the process. I didn't think so. And I was done trying to placate her.

"So what's your plan then? Are you going to use that rag to set me on fire?"

"That's the idea." Sadie sounded entirely too calm for my peace of mind. "With you covered in turpentine like that, I don't see how I can miss."

I'd slid sideways when I hit the table. Now there was an upholstered chair behind me. I was stuck. I didn't dare turn around to chart a better course.

"If you throw that rag at me, you'll burn your house down too."

"That's okay. I've got insurance. Besides, it's probably time I made a fresh start somewhere else anyway."

I was barely listening to what she said. My entire worldview had narrowed to a six inch flame that danced in the air in front of me. The only thing I cared about right then was keeping that lit rag as far away from my hair as possible.

I could hear Faith whining under her breath from somewhere behind me. I couldn't take my eyes off Sadie to reassure her—not that I had any reassurances to offer. Faith was a smart dog. Hopefully she would figure out a way to save herself if things went from bad to worse.

The upholstered chair was pressed against the back of my legs. It was still blocking my path. I knew it matched the couch I'd been sitting on earlier. I pictured its size and shape, debating whether to go over or around if I had to move fast. And with that thought, inspiration suddenly struck.

The couch had a big, plump cushion on its seat. The chair had a smaller version. I desperately hoped those padded pillows weren't attached to the furniture. Because I was only going to have one shot to try to make this work.

I darted a quick look back for Faith. She was on the other side of the room. She'd walked as far as the door, probably hoping that I would follow. The Poodle was trying to help in the only way she knew how: by showing me the way out.

Good girl, I thought. *Get ready.*

"I think a fresh start is a great idea," I said brightly. "Where would you go?"

Sadie actually appeared to pause and think about that. That brief moment of distraction gave me the opening I needed. I whipped around, grabbed the cushion off the seat of the chair, and launched it at Sadie like a big, fat Frisbee.

By the time she saw the projectile coming, it was too late to react. The cushion slammed into her outstretched arm and sent her staggering backward. I'd been hoping that the blow would cause Sadie to drop the rag. Or that it would hit the flame and smother it.

Instead, as soon as the fire came in contact with the cushion, its polyester cover sizzled, then flared. I felt a shocking burst of heat. Suddenly the open flame between us was exponentially larger than it had been only seconds earlier.

For the space of an instant, Sadie and I locked eyes in mutual horror. Then I spun around and ran. I swept my purse up off the couch without breaking stride and was through the front door with Faith before there was even time to draw another breath.

I assumed Sadie was right behind me but I didn't stop to look. Racing side by side, Faith and I ran from the house like the devil was chasing us. We didn't slow down until we were both on the opposite side of the quiet road. Even there, I wasn't sure I felt safe.

Gasping for air, I yanked my purse open, pulled out my phone, and called nine-one-one. When the dispatcher had assured me that police and fire trucks were on the way, I finally had a moment to take stock of my surroundings. That was when I realized that Sadie was nowhere to be seen.

Abruptly my stomach plummeted. Already I could see tall flames licking up the walls and shooting out the door I'd left open behind me. Sadie couldn't still be inside the house, could she? Surely she'd have made a hasty escape just as I had. Hopefully the house had a back door.

Faith and I moved behind the parked Volvo, putting even more space between us and the burning building. The Poodle was still uneasy. Her lips quivered as she continued to whine softly.

I started to crouch down. I want to give her a hug. But as I drew near, Faith reared away from my touch. I was still coated in turpentine. Her nose wrinkled at the foul stench. I settled for giving her a pat, but both of us wanted more. Unfortunately that would have to wait.

The first of the emergency vehicles arrived within minutes. The police cruiser was quickly followed by two fire trucks. I informed the first officer on the scene that there might still be a woman in the house, then Faith and I withdrew once more.

Soon we were joined on the side of the road by some of Sadie's neighbors. Faith drew several curious glances. Everyone gave me a wide berth. I couldn't blame them for that. It took the firemen an hour to contain the blaze. The cottage hadn't been completely consumed, but I suspected that it would be a total loss anyway.

When there was a lull in the activity, the officer I'd spoken to previously came to find me. He introduced himself as Officer Magner, then said, "What can you tell me about what happened here?"

Before I had a chance to reply, he frowned and took a step back. "What's that smell?"

"Turpentine. The woman who lives in that

house threw it on me. She also threatened to set me on fire."

"Why would she do something like that?"

"Because she had just confessed to murdering her business partner."

Magner's eyes narrowed. He looked like he wasn't sure whether or not to believe me. "You'd better come down to the station with me," he said.

"I will. But not until I've had a chance to take Faith home and have a shower."

"Who's Faith?"

At the sound of her name, the Poodle looked up eagerly and wagged her tail. *Nice to meet you,* she told him.

Magner didn't get it. Even when I nodded in her direction. He spared Faith a quick glance, then asked me where I lived.

"In Stamford." I got out my driver's license and showed it to him. "But if you contact Detective Raymond Young of the Greenwich police department, he'll vouch for me."

At least I hoped he would. I waited while Officer Magner wrote the name down. "He can also tell you about Jasmine Crane, the woman who was killed two weeks ago."

"So it happened in Greenwich, then?"

"No, in eastern Connecticut. It's kind of complicated."

The adrenaline that had been coursing through

me must have been wearing off. Suddenly I felt totally drained. I gestured across the street. "Did the firemen find anyone inside the house?"

"No, it was empty. You're sure someone was supposed to be in there?" Magner still sounded skeptical.

"Sadie Foster is the person who started the fire," I told him. "This is her home. She was still inside when I came running out."

"According to the fire chief, there's no one in there now."

I didn't know whether to be relieved by that news or not. I was glad Sadie hadn't died in the blaze, but I was sorry she'd succeeded in eluding the authorities. I had figured out who'd murdered Jasmine Crane, only to allow her killer to slip through my fingers.

It looked as though Sadie was going to get her fresh start after all.

Chapter 27

Officer Magner verified my ID, then told me I was free to go.

Later that afternoon, I returned to Darien and told my story to a sergeant in the police department there. He had been in touch with Detective Young and had plenty of questions. I was happy to have answers for most of them.

Two days had passed since Detective Young and I had spoken, and he'd been busy in the meantime. Now that the authorities in numerous jurisdictions were comparing notes, a cohesive story was beginning to emerge. Everyone whose name I'd supplied to the detective was being interviewed, beginning with major player Rick Fanelli. With so much new information coming in, the police were also able to start rounding up the members of Jasmine's band of thieves.

Detective Young and I had a long conversation a few days later. He even thanked me for my input. That was new and different. I hoped it might bode well for our relationship going forward.

Aunt Peg made sure that Amanda Burke was accompanied by a lawyer when she told her story to the authorities. "One mistake shouldn't be allowed to ruin a young person's entire life," she told me firmly.

Though she'd played only a peripheral role in the crimes that were committed, Amanda was deeply ashamed of the poor decisions she'd made. In exchange for a complete accounting of everything she knew about Jasmine's illegal activities, Amanda was sentenced to a year's probation and two hundred hours of community service.

Aunt Peg had her own idea of how the girl might make restitution for her actions. It took her nearly a week, but she'd finally managed to track down Hazel and Toby. Sadie had dumped Jasmine's dogs in a pound in West Haven. Aunt Peg reclaimed the pair and delivered them to Amanda, who promised to care for them for the rest of their lives.

As for Sadie Foster, she was still missing.

Though I was the only witness to her confession, there was enough circumstantial evidence for the police to be convinced of her culpability in Jasmine Crane's murder. The fact that Sadie had disappeared after her house burned down didn't help her case either. Amanda probably could have told her that.

Now the authorities were hot on Sadie's trail. Detective Young seemed to think it was only a matter of time before they would have her in custody.

A few weeks later, Augie's official championship certificate arrived in the mail from the American Kennel Club. Sam fired up the grill, Davey oiled his blades, and we held a coat-cutting party. The shocked expression on the Standard Poodle's face when—for the first time in his life—the clipper ran all the way up the middle of his back, and a huge hunk of hair fell to the floor, was almost laughable.

After years spent "in hair" some Poodles are embarrassed by how naked they feel when they're cut down. Augie adjusted to the change right away. He couldn't wait to get down off the grooming table and race around the yard with the rest of the gang.

The other Poodles had seen it all before, but Bud was confused by Augie's new look. He kept staring at the big male Poodle as if he wasn't sure who he was. The little dog even offered a halfhearted growl, which Augie was kind enough to ignore. Luckily it only took a few minutes for canine equanimity to be restored. Too bad people weren't that easy.

Friday morning I had a tutoring session with Francesca. I knew it was unrealistic to expect the situation to have been resolved in less than a week. But I'd received encouraging reports from two of her teachers, so I was hopeful that my conversation with the other girls had started things moving in the right direction.

What I really wanted was to hear from Francesca herself about whether or not *she* felt the quality of her experience at Howard Academy was improving. If not, I still had more work to do.

"I guess I'm okay." Francesca was sitting on the floor of my classroom with Faith draped over her crossed legs. "Taylor and Alicia mostly just ignore me now." She gave me a faint smile. "I don't really mind. It's better than how they used to act. Brittany talks to me sometimes. You know, like I'm a real person. That's nice."

Nice. I snorted under my breath. But Francesca looked relieved, so I took that as a positive sign.

"You have to learn not to care about what people like Taylor and Alicia say and do," I told her. "Their opinions shouldn't be important to you. You know those girls were never really your friends, right?"

"I guess." She sighed. "Except in the beginning, it felt like they were. They said that they liked me. And that they would show me how to fit in at Howard Academy. I thought they meant it."

"But now you know better," I said firmly. "And you're starting to make other friends, aren't you?"

"Yes." Her voice was quiet.

"Real friends who like you for who you are?"

Francesca nodded.

"I know it's hard to cope when your whole life gets turned upside down overnight. And it's especially hard when you're twelve years old—not quite a child and not yet an adult—and you can't figure out where you belong." I reached down and placed my finger under the girl's chin, raising it so that she was looking at me. "But better times are coming. You're going to grow up and be wonderful."

"That's what my mother says too."

"Well, she should know. After all, look how wonderful she is. And you're going to be just like her."

"Maybe." Her lips quirked. "Except I can't sing."

"That won't matter in the slightest. You're going to find some terrific talent of your own that makes you just as happy as your mother's singing makes her."

Francesca looked as though she wanted to believe me but couldn't quite bring herself to. "Are you sure?"

"I'm positive. But even then, things won't be perfect. Even when you're all grown up and living your fabulous life, you're still going to meet people who will try to treat you badly or take advantage of you."

I thought of Amanda, who'd allowed herself to be used by both Jasmine and Rick to further their own ends. "I know a young woman who was manipulated into doing bad things by people she thought were her friends. She should have known better but she got taken in anyway. And she was a lot older than you."

"Really?"

"Really and truly."

Francesca brightened. "I guess maybe I don't feel so dumb then."

"Dumb? You? I don't think so. And Faith agrees with me. She has very high standards. She wouldn't be sitting in your lap unless she thought you were pretty special."

Francesca ran her hand down the length of the Poodle's back, her fingers threading their way through the dense hair. Faith arched into the caress and swished her tail from side to side happily.

"I think she's pretty special too," Francesca said.

"Perfect. It looks like we've found something we can all agree on."

The girl giggled. "Faith too?"

"Of course, Faith too." I laughed with her. "She communicates with us all the time. You just have to know how to listen."

Francesca gazed down at the Poodle. Faith looked up. Their eyes met.

"I think she's telling me she wants a peanut butter biscuit."

"Really?" I lifted a brow. "I think she's telling

you it's time to open your books and get to work."

"Maybe we can do both." Francesca lifted Faith gently off her legs. Then she stood up and reached for her backpack.

"I think that's a perfect idea," I said.

Books are produced in the United States using U.S.-based materials

Books are printed using a revolutionary new process called THINKtech™ that lowers energy usage by 70% and increases overall quality

Books are durable and flexible because of Smyth-sewing

Paper is sourced using environmentally responsible foresting methods and the paper is acid-free

Center Point Large Print
600 Brooks Road / PO Box 1
Thorndike, ME 04986-0001 USA

(207) 568-3717

US & Canada:
1 800 929-9108
www.centerpointlargeprint.com